LAURA GRIFFIN

HIDDEN

BERKLEY
New York

BERKLEY

An imprint of Penguin Random House LLC

penguinrandomhouse.com

Copyright © 2020 by Laura Griffin

Excerpt from *Flight* copyright © 2020 by Laura Griffin

Penguin Random House supports copyright. Copyright fuels creativity, encourages
diverse voices, promotes free speech, and creates a vibrant culture. Thank you for buying
an authorized edition of this book and for complying with copyright laws by not
reproducing, scanning, or distributing any part of it in any form without permission.
You are supporting writers and allowing Penguin Random House to continue to
publish books for every reader.

BERKLEY and the BERKLEY & B colophon are registered
trademarks of Penguin Random House LLC.

ISBN: 9780593197325

First Edition: August 2020

Printed in the United States of America

1   3   5   7   9   10   8   6   4   2

Cover design by Rita Frangie

Book design by George Towne

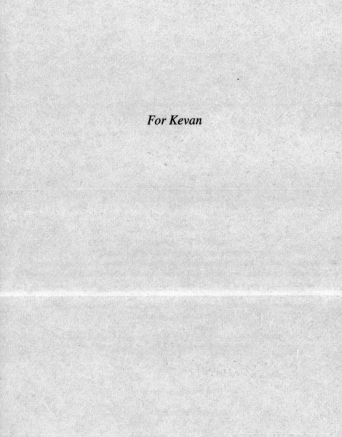

For Kevan

CHAPTER

ONE

DANA WAS IN love with a complete stranger. She could admit it. Or she could have admitted it, if she'd had anyone to admit it to.

She eyed him in the parking lot as she leaned against the lamppost and stretched her quads. Tall, wide shoulders, strong runner's legs. He had shaggy brown hair that Dana would have once considered sloppy but now seemed sexy beyond belief. She imagined combing her fingers through it, imagined it would feel thick and silky.

The main attraction wasn't his looks, though. It was his commitment. He was here every day at six a.m. sharp. You could set a watch by it.

He closed the door of his dusty black Jeep—one of the old ones that clearly had lots of miles on it. Not a fancy car, and he probably didn't have a fancy job, either, but Dana didn't care about that. She'd dated men with money before. They'd burned her life beyond recognition, and she'd made a vow to herself: never again.

It was one of the many vows she'd made over the last year.

He set off on the hike-and-bike trail, and Dana waited a moment to give him a head start. She zipped her phone into the pouch clipped around her waist and then stepped onto the path, taking a deep breath as the soles of her shoes hit gravel. Setting a brisk pace, she felt her muscles start to loosen and warm.

She looked ahead at Blue. That was the name she'd given him the day he glanced up from the drinking fountain and his turquoise eyes hit her like a sucker punch. She'd been so mesmerized she'd hardly noticed the water's rusty taste as she gulped down a sip and watched him walk away.

Blue was way ahead of her now, and he would stay way ahead of her for the entire six-mile loop. If she was lucky, she'd pass him beside the fountains, and they'd trade nods before she set off on the rest of her morning.

Or maybe not. Maybe this would be the day she summoned the courage to strike up a conversation.

The morning air was already thick with humidity as the sky went from indigo to lavender over the treetops. The trail was almost empty, which was how she liked it. Just the die-hard runners and some power walkers. Dana settled into her rhythm as she passed the boat docks where long red kayaks still were racked and chained. She smelled fresh dew on the reeds by the lake, along with the faint scent of rotting vegetation, which would grow more pungent as the sun climbed higher in the sky. It would hit triple digits today. Again. Dana still wasn't accustomed to the Texas heat or the way the weather here could turn on a dime.

"On your left," a voice growled.

Dana's heart lurched as a cyclist whisked past her. She muttered a curse at him. The guy swerved, barely missing a jogging stroller coming around the bend, pushed by a flush-cheeked woman in yoga pants.

Of everyone on the trail, the manic stroller moms bugged Dana the most, especially at this hour. She couldn't imagine rousting a child from sleep and driving to the lakefront, then shoving a sippy cup into pudgy little hands to serve as a distraction while Mom squeezed in a workout. Passing the stroller, Dana caught a glimpse of a cherubic toddler with brown curls, not much older than Jillian.

Just thinking of Jillian made Dana's heart swell. It was something she'd never expected when she'd first taken the nanny job. How could you truly love someone else's kid? But it turned out you could. Dana would have jumped in front of a bus for that child. Maybe it was human instinct. Protect the innocent. Or maybe it was something else, some deep-rooted impulse that hinted at future motherhood. When Dana had first identified the feeling, she'd felt relieved. It told her she was okay. Mostly. It told her that despite the ugly things she'd seen and done, her moral compass was still intact.

The trail narrowed and wended through the cypress trees. Most people hung a left onto the pedestrian bridge at this point, but not Blue. He did the full loop and crossed the lake at the dam, predictable as clockwork. At first when Dana began shadowing him it had been a struggle, and she'd ended each workout feeling dizzy and depleted. But now she was stronger. Her thighs still ached, and her lungs still burned, but she pushed through, and the heady rush at the end of each run was her reward.

The trail narrowed again, and the woods became thicker. Dana heard the faint crunch of gravel. Her senses perked up, and she glanced over her shoulder.

Her blood chilled.

A man jogged behind her, maybe twenty yards back, and she'd seen him before. Dana focused on the path ahead, listening to the rhythm of his footsteps. Her pulse started to thrum. Where had she seen him? Her brain kicked into gear, retracing her steps over the past twenty-four hours. She'd been to work, the grocery store, home. She tried to recall the faces in the checkout line, or anyone she'd passed in the lobby of her apartment building. She pictured the man without looking back: tall, buzz cut, heavy eyebrows. Where had she seen him before?

You're being paranoid.
You're being paranoid.
You're being paranoid.

The words echoed through her mind as she pounded down the trail. She peered ahead, searching for Blue on the path, but she couldn't see him anymore, couldn't see anyone. This section was practically deserted.

The footfalls came faster, and panic spurted through her. Why had he changed his pace?

Dana changed hers, too, trying to catch up to Blue—or anyone, at this point. The slap of shoes behind her sounded closer now.

Sweat streamed down her back. She visualized where she was on the trail. About a quarter mile ahead was a nature center. To her right, through a patch of trees and bushes, was a parking lot. Would someone be there now? It wasn't even six thirty.

Dana's breath grew ragged. Her skin prickled, and her blood turned icy. With every footfall she knew that the years and the miles and the lies had finally caught up to her. There would be no more running.

And there would be no mercy.

With a trembling hand, she unzipped her pouch and took out her phone. She thumbed in the passcode. Should she really do this? Maybe she was overreacting.

But no. She wasn't.

She darted another glance over her shoulder.

Eye contact. And Dana *knew*.

She bolted into the woods, plowing through bushes and darting around trees. Behind her, she heard the distant but unmistakable *swish-swish* of her pursuer moving through the brush. Dana's heart thundered as she pressed the contact number. Every *swish-swish* ratcheted up her terror. Finally, the call connected.

"Tabby, it's me. It's happening!" Just saying the words made her stomach clench. *"It's happening!"*

Dana hurled the phone into the bushes and cast a frantic glance behind her. She couldn't see him anymore, but she knew he was back there, felt it in her core. Every nerve ending burned with the certainty of being *chased*.

Where was the damn parking lot? Through the trees, she glimpsed a patch of asphalt and the red hood of a car. She ran faster, swiping at the branches. Thorns snagged her clothes and sliced her arms, but she clawed through the bushes as fast as she could, sprinting for the red.

A tall figure stepped into her path. Dana gave a squeak and stopped short.

The man moved closer. His eyes bored into hers, and she knew she'd been right. Not paranoid at all, but *right*.

He took another step forward, and Dana's gaze landed on the knife in his hand. A silent weapon. Of course.

Terror pierced her heart as he stepped nearer. Tears stung her eyes.

"Please," she rasped. "I'll do anything."

Another step, and she could smell the sweat on his skin now. He was that close. Her heart jackhammered and she knew this was it. Fight-or-flight time.

"Please."

She let the tears leak out. Let him think he'd won.

"Please . . ."

The man smiled slightly.

Dana turned and ran.

CHAPTER

TWO

BAILEY RHOADS WATCHED the parking lot through the veil of rain. It poured off the overhang, splashing the sidewalk in front of her and soaking the cuffs of her jeans. She pressed her phone to her ear as a police car pulled into the lot and slid into the handicapped space beside the door.

"Metro desk."

"Hey, it's me," Bailey said as the officer got out. Skip Shepherd. That figured. He pretended not to see her as he ducked through the sheet of water and jerked open the door to the convenience store, letting out a waft of cold air.

"Tell me something good, Rhoads."

"Sorry, can't do it."

"Crap."

"This is a bust," she said. "A couple teens boosted some beer from the stock room, ran out the back. Clerk chased them and a patrol car pulled up."

Her editor muttered something either to himself or someone else in the newsroom.

"I'll write up a brief, but I'd give it two grafs, max," she said.

"They minors?"

"Yeah."

"Then don't bother. Listen, where are you?"

"In my car," Bailey said, pulling the hood of her sweat-shirt over her head before ducking through the water. She jogged across the lot to her white Toyota that had been in desperate need of a bath until this afternoon. "Why? What's up?"

"I don't know."

But something in Max's voice made her pulse quicken. She slid into her car, dripping water all over the seats as she kicked off her flip-flops.

"Some chatter on the scanner," Max said. "Lance heard something about a code thirty-seven."

"What's Lance doing in on a Saturday?"

"Some drama with one of the councilmen. Long story. Listen, you know what a thirty-seven is?"

"A shooting," she said, starting up her car. "Where is this?"

"The lake, I think."

"Lady Bird Lake?"

"Yeah. But this could be nothing. Scanner's been quiet since."

"I'll check it out."

"Text me if it's anything," Max said. "And do it soon. I'm trying to get out of here."

"Got it."

She dropped her phone onto the seat beside her, along with the damp spiral notebook where she'd jotted the details of the convenience store holdup that wasn't. Would this be another dud? Probably, given her pattern lately. For the last three weeks she'd been chasing down court filings and scanner chatter and only netted a few short briefs.

Saturday traffic was light, but the afternoon downpour had thrown everyone for a loop, and she passed two fender-benders before reaching Barton Springs Road, which took her straight into Austin's biggest park. On a typical sunny weekend, the place was busy. Several weeks a year it wasn't just busy, but packed, with traffic choking the streets and the soccer fields crammed with festivalgoers. Today, the fields were empty except for a few clusters of people sheltering from the drizzle under sprawling oak trees. Bailey parked in the lot near the pedestrian bridge, noting the conspicuous lack of police vehicles. This was probably another non-event.

It was time for Bailey to get creative. It had been a slow month, and rumor had it the newsroom was in for another round of layoffs. She should spend her Sunday brainstorming feature ideas. Something about local law enforcement that wouldn't be interchangeable with a story pulled off the wire. Maybe an innovative new forensic technique. Or budget overruns. Or official corruption. She had to dig up something. For months she'd been hanging on to this job by her fingernails. Her industry was shrinking, and she was in a constant battle to prove her worth relative to more seasoned reporters who fed at a bottomless trough of news tips.

Bailey shed her wet hoodie and grabbed a blue zip-up jacket from the back seat. She stuffed her notebook into the pocket and looked around. It was unusually empty for a Saturday evening—just a few wet dog walkers and a guy strapping a paddleboard to the roof of his Volkswagen. She zipped her jacket and ran her fingers through her wet brown curls. With this weather, she probably looked like Medusa, but it was pointless to fight her hair. It did what it wanted.

Bailey hurried across the parking lot, hopscotching around potholes as she made her way to the pedestrian bridge. The six-lane highway overhead provided cover, along with a roar of traffic noise as she crossed the lake, which was narrow here.

She reached the trail marker on the opposite side and glanced around. Normally, this area was bustling with cyclists and pedestrians, but this evening it was empty except for a pair of shirtless runners in burnt-orange shorts. UT track and field, if she had to guess. They didn't spare her a glance as they blew past her.

Looking up the trail, Bailey noticed the orange barricade positioned in the center of the path, along with a sign: *CLOSED FOR MAINTENANCE*. Bailey had been here three mornings this week and that sign was new. She walked up the path, skirting around the barrier. The trail curved into some leafy trees, and Bailey's pulse picked up as she noticed the swag of yellow crime scene tape.

"Area's closed, ma'am."

She turned around to see a bulky young cop striding toward her. He had ruddy cheeks and acne, and Bailey didn't recognize him.

"What's going on?" she asked.

"Trail's closed off." He stopped beside her and wiped his brow with the back of his arm. His dark uniform was soaked from what looked like a combination of rain and sweat.

"I'm with the *Herald*." She unzipped her jacket and held up the press pass on a lanyard around her neck. "We got word about a possible shooting here?"

He frowned and shook his head. "I'm going to have to ask you to leave."

"Leave?"

He gestured toward the sign. "This is a restricted area. You're going to have to step back."

"But—"

"Step back, ma'am."

"Okay, but do you know what this is about?" She took her time moving toward the barricade.

"No, ma'am."

What a liar. "Can you confirm it was a shooting?" she asked.

"You'll need to talk to our public information officer."

He corralled her toward the barrier. She sidestepped it and turned around, and the cop was watching her suspiciously, as though she might sprint right past him if he turned his back.

At last, he did. He proceeded up the trail, tapping the radio attached to his shoulder and murmuring something as he went. Probably giving people a heads-up that the media had arrived on the scene—whatever the scene was.

The cop reached the yellow swag of tape blocking the path. He walked around a tree and darted a look of warning at her before disappearing into the woods.

Bailey dialed her editor. Max picked up on the first ring.

"I'm here at the hike-and-bike trail," she told him. "Something's definitely up."

"Who's there?"

"I've only seen one cop, but they've got the trail barricaded, and there's a scene taped off."

"*One* cop?" Max sounded skeptical.

"So far, yeah." Bailey walked away from the barrier, looking for any other sign of law enforcement. The nearest parking lot on this side of the lake would be behind the juice bar. Maybe the cops had parked there.

"What about a crime scene unit?" Max asked. "Or the ME's van?"

"Haven't seen either," she said, scanning the area as

she walked. She spied several cars parked along the street, but no police vehicles.

"Keep asking around," Max said. "The scanner's been quiet, so maybe this isn't out yet."

Bailey would definitely ask around, but she didn't see anyone to ask.

"Where are you exactly?"

"The trailhead near the nature center," she said, "but it's pretty deserted."

The rain started again. It streamed down her neck and into her shirt, and Bailey moved faster. Up the street that paralleled the lake was Jay's Juice Bar. She spotted a patrol car in the parking lot. *Bingo.*

As she hurried closer, she saw not just one but *four* police cars in the lot behind the place, along with an unmarked unit with a spotlight mounted on the windshield—probably a detective's car. How had this stayed off the scanner? Someone must be trying to keep a lid on the story.

Bailey surveyed the juice bar. Typically, Jay's had a line of sweaty customers at the window waiting to order smoothies. But today the window was closed. A guy in a green apron stood beside the door, talking to a tall man with a badge clipped to his belt.

"Rhoads? You there?"

"I see a detective," she told Max. "Let me go talk to him."

"Who is it?"

"I don't know. I'll call you back."

"Do it soon. I need to know if this is going to blow up the front page."

Bailey tucked her phone into her pocket and watched the detective interview the juice bar guy, who clearly was agitated. He kept wiping his brow with his hand and gesturing toward the trail. Was the man a witness? Had he heard the gunshot? The detective towered over him, watching intently as the man talked and shook his head.

Bailey started to pull out her notebook, but then thought better of it. The detective dug a business card from his pocket and handed it to the man. Perfect timing. They were wrapping up the interview.

Bailey crossed the street, and the detective glanced at her. His gaze narrowed when he spotted the press pass around her neck. Bailey felt his guard go up as she strode toward him. She took a deep breath and squared her shoulders.

She was about to get stonewalled.

JACOB WATCHED HER coming up the sidewalk. Bailey Rhoads. *Austin Herald*, metro desk. The reporter wore faded jeans and a soaked blue rain jacket that swallowed her. She stepped under the overhang to get out of the drizzle.

"I'm Bailey Rhoads with the *Herald*." She swiped a dark curl out of her eyes. "And you're Detective . . . ?"

He didn't answer, and she pretended not to notice as she pulled a notebook from her pocket. Jacob glanced at her feet. The cuffs of her jeans were wet, and she wore purple flip-flops.

"We understand there was a possible shooting at this location," she said. "Can you tell me what happened?"

"No."

Her eyebrows arched. "No?"

"We have no official comment at this time."

"What about unofficial?"

"No."

She huffed out a breath and glanced behind him, and

Jacob was relieved to see that the witness he'd been interviewing had disappeared into his shop. He'd cautioned the man about talking to the media, but Jacob didn't want to take any chances, so he moved away from the door and led the reporter around the side of the building, where he stepped under another overhang.

The woman looked up at him, clearly annoyed. Her skin was wet, and her makeup was smudged. She had dark corkscrew curls, and her eyes were the same pale gray color as the T-shirt under her jacket.

"Detective . . . ?"

"Merritt."

"Could you brief me on what happened, Detective Merritt?"

"You can talk to our public information officer."

She tipped her head to the side. "Seriously?"

"Seriously."

"Can't you give me a break here? We'll find out anyway. If you could just sketch out the basics."

"Sorry."

Jacob wasn't ready to tell a reporter what was going on. He didn't even know himself. It was an odd crime scene, which made him antsy. And more guarded than usual.

The reporter blew out a sigh. "Look, Detective . . ." She trailed off and checked her watch. "I'm on deadline here, and I've got to get *something* to my editor in the next half hour."

"That's not my problem."

She gave him a strained smile. "You're right, it's not. But could you help me, anyway? Please?"

It was the *please* that did it. And the pleading look in those cool gray eyes. He got the feeling she didn't usually plead for things. He glanced at her feet again, noting her blue nail polish and silver toe ring.

Jacob shifted his attention across the parking lot to the line of trees. The scene had already been cordoned off, and now they were just waiting for the ME's team. And she was right. News would get out. He wasn't sure how she'd gotten wind of this, but it was only a matter of time before the rest of the media picked up the scent.

"Was it a shooting?" she persisted.

"No."

She looked surprised by his answer and took out a pen.

"About five fifty, one of our units responded to a call about an unresponsive female near the hike-and-bike trail," Jacob said. "The officers—"

"Wait, 'unresponsive'?" She glanced up from her pad.

"The officers confirmed that the woman was dead."

"Does it look like she was shot, or—"

"That's all I have at this time."

"Okay." She kept scribbling. "And when did *you* get the call?"

"About six twenty." Thunder rumbled overhead, and Jacob looked up. "You know, we're losing daylight and the sky's about to unleash again."

"Just one more question. Does it appear to be a homicide?"

"You need to direct your queries to our public information officer."

Jacob sounded like a prick, and he knew it, but he really didn't want to get into it with a reporter right now—especially one with a reputation for being sneaky and pushy as hell.

A white van pulled into the parking lot and slid into a space beside Jacob's unmarked unit. A pair of ME's assistants got out, and Bailey glanced over her shoulder to watch.

"I need to get to work," he said.

"But—"

"Contact our press office."

"Wait. Here." She flipped over her notebook and tugged a business card from a stack she had clipped there. "Call me if there's anything else you can share tonight."

Jacob took the card, even though he knew he wouldn't use it.

"I'll be up," she said. "Even if it's late."

THREE

B AILEY RAN THE yellow light and slowed down as she neared the police station.

"Did you get it?" she asked Max.

"Yeah, and it reads thin."

A man on a scooter sailed into the intersection, and Bailey slammed on the brakes.

"There's a lot missing here," Max complained.

"They barely released anything. The whole press conference lasted maybe fifteen minutes. Including questions."

Bailey waited as another scooter buzzed through the intersection, probably on the way to Sixth Street, Austin's hub for nightlife. A hatchback pulled out of a metered parking space ahead, and Bailey put on her blinker to claim the spot.

"Max?" she asked, passing the space and then zipping backward into it.

"Yeah, I'm still reading. I mean, I get that it's early in the investigation, et cetera, et cetera, but they hardly told us anything. What about her ID?"

"Caucasian female, that's it."

Bailey flipped down the mirror. Her makeup was practically gone now, and her hair was all over the place. She twisted it into a bun and tucked her curls behind her ears.

"What about age? We've got sixty thousand college kids in this town, half of them female, and half of those probably use the lake trail. Was this a sexual assault?"

"They wouldn't say."

"Is it related to the string of muggings last month? Maybe a robbery that got out of hand?"

"I asked that, but they said it's too soon to tell. I put the quote there in the second-to-last paragraph."

"And she was recovered from the water, right?"

"Correct."

Bailey grabbed her purse and got out of the car. The rain had let up, and people who had been holed up inside all day looked to be out in full force now.

"Well, was she drowned? Dumped? Thrown off a bridge?" Max sounded frustrated. "Is it a suicide?"

"I don't know, but I plan to find out."

She waited for a break in traffic and jogged across the street. A block ahead was the police station. All the metered spaces in front were taken. She passed several cars and spotted a black Chevy Silverado just up the street. According to Bailey's source in dispatch, Detective Merritt drove a black Chevy pickup.

"We need a follow-up," Max said, "and it needs to have a lot more in it than what you've got here."

"I'm working on it."

"I've got you budgeted for A-1, but we need some meat on the bone. And get some better quotes. This PR flack is terrible."

"I will."

"Check in tomorrow and let me know how it's going."

Bailey tucked her phone away as she neared the entrance to the station. A pair of cops emerged and headed to a patrol unit parked along the curb. Bailey watched the double doors as people streamed in and out—civilians, uniforms, plainclothes detectives. By the volume of people, it looked like they were having a shift change. Bailey found a concrete bench near the black pickup and sat down to wait.

Her stomach rumbled. She hadn't been home since Max had sent her out on the gas station story, and she hadn't eaten in twelve hours. She dug through her purse and came up with a pack of cherry Life Savers. She popped two into her mouth and swished them around.

Jacob Merritt stepped through the door, and Bailey's senses went on alert. She didn't move—just watched him from afar. He was tall, with broad shoulders and excellent posture. He moved with the smooth confidence of an athlete, and she wondered what sport he might have played once upon a time. She could see him on a pitcher's mound, staring down a batter. Or maybe reaching up to pluck a football from the air before sprinting to the end zone.

She stood and walked toward him, catching his notice as he reached the truck. She saw a flicker of surprise in his expression, but then it turned wary.

"Hey," she said with a smile. "You headed out?"

He tipped his head to the side and regarded her with curiosity. Maybe he wasn't used to being accosted by disheveled reporters after work.

"Why?" he asked.

"I'm guessing you've had a long day. Thought I'd see if I could buy you a beer?"

"I'm not thirsty."

Ouch.

She tried not to react as he gazed down at her.

"I wouldn't mind something to eat, though." He looked over her shoulder. "Ever been to Paco's?" He nodded at the food truck parked down the street.

"Sounds good."

He opened his locks with a *chirp* and tossed a backpack into the back seat of the pickup, watching her as he did it. He had deep brown eyes. Trustworthy eyes. He shut the door and turned to face her, and she felt a flutter of nerves.

"How did you know my car?" he asked.

"I've got sources."

His gaze narrowed, and she thought he might make an issue of it. But instead he locked up and slid the keys into the pocket of his leather jacket. He started walking toward the taco truck, and she fell into step beside him, noticing the bulge under his jacket. She couldn't imagine carrying a gun all the time.

"You always work this late?" he asked.

"I'm on weekends this month."

"They do it by month?"

"Sort of. Also has to do with seniority. I'm low in the pecking order, so I work a lot of Saturdays and holidays."

They neared Paco's, which occupied the corner of a parking lot. The air smelled of grilling onions, and beside the truck was a picnic area festooned with Christmas lights. It looked like Paco's business was based on the steady flow of people coming and going from the bar district. A cluster of college-age guys in T-shirts and baseball caps read the menu board and placed a semicoherent order.

When Bailey and Jacob reached the window, he gestured for her to go first.

"Chips and salsa and a Coke," she told the attendant.

Jacob frowned. "That's it?"

"Yeah."

He ordered a beef-and-cheese taco basket and a water. He took out his wallet, and Bailey held out some cash, but he waved her off.

She claimed an empty picnic table beneath a swag of rainbow lights, and Jacob scanned the area with a sharp look before sitting down across from her.

"What's wrong?" she asked.

"Nothing."

Jacob's gaze settled on her as she sipped her soda. It was cold and syrupy, and she didn't realize how thirsty she'd been.

He was watching her with a look she couldn't read. He had strong cheekbones and thick stubble along his jaw, which was exactly her thing, and she wished they were on their way to a bar together tonight instead of working.

He took a sip of water, then set the bottle on the table and looked at her expectantly. "Well?"

"Well, what?" she asked, picking up a chip.

"I'm waiting for the questions."

"Relax. I already filed my story."

He lifted an eyebrow skeptically and unwrapped his food.

"I will say your PR guy was pretty tight-lipped."

"Yep." He chomped into his taco, and she watched the muscles of his jaw as he chewed.

"So . . . does it look like a homicide?"

"The autopsy's tomorrow. We'll have something official then."

"What about unofficial?"

He just looked at her, and Bailey tamped down her frustration.

"How about ID?" she asked.

"None."

"You mean she didn't have one with her? Or you didn't find her prints in the system?"

"Both."

Bailey tipped her head to the side. He'd just told her a lot, and she wondered if he realized it. The fact that they could even get prints from the victim meant she couldn't have been in the water that long.

"So . . . it's possible her ID was stolen during the incident?"

He sighed and looked at her. "Anyone ever tell you you're very stubborn?"

She smiled. "Yes. But not usually in those words."

He crumpled his foil wrapper and dropped it into the carboard tray. "She had no ID on her," he said. "No phone, no money, no keys."

Finally, she was getting somewhere. "And does it look like she was jogging on the trail when it happened?"

"Possibly."

"A lot of people don't take valuables with them when they exercise. Still . . . you'd expect her to at least have a key with her, right? To a car or an apartment, if she lived close."

He didn't comment.

"You think this is related to the muggings from last month?" she asked. "Maybe the assailant is escalating?"

He shook his head. "Don't know yet."

"Or maybe someone took her keys and stole her car?"

"Don't know yet."

"What about timing?" she asked.

"What about it?"

"Well, the trail is a high-traffic area."

"Not today it isn't."

"Yeah, that's my point. Maybe it happened last night or this morning, before all the rain, and that's why no one found her until this evening?"

Again, no comment.

"The juice bar is open seven to seven," she said. "But Alvaro said he didn't hear any gunshots."

"You interviewed Alvaro?" He sounded ticked off.

"He also didn't see any unusual cars parked behind the shop today. When the other lots get full, people sometimes park there and use the cut-through to the trail."

Jacob finished off his taco and didn't offer to support or refute anything she'd said.

"So, you still haven't nailed down the time frame?" she asked.

"The ME should be able to help with that."

Bailey itched to get out her notepad and write all this down, but she sensed he'd clam up on her. She was lucky to have him here at all. She munched on her chips and decided to change the subject for a while.

"Can I ask you something?"

"Does it matter if I say no?" He smiled slightly, and she got a warm flutter in the pit of her stomach.

"I've been covering the crime beat for almost a year. How come I haven't crossed paths with you?"

He shook his head. "Don't know."

But something told her he *did* know. He seemed like the type who avoided reporters at all costs. Some cops liked to talk to the media, and they got all puffed up when they were interviewed—especially by a woman. Others said nothing and directed questions to the PR people.

A *whoop* went up across the street, and Bailey turned to see a pair of young-looking guys laughing and shoving back and forth. They seemed to be vying for the attention of two blond girls climbing into a pedicab.

Bailey turned around, and Jacob was watching the scene. She tried to guess what he was thinking. Was he wondering whether each of those people was going to make it safely home tonight? After years as a cop, was he able to see people out having fun without thinking of all the ways things could go wrong in a heartbeat?

There was no way he could do his job without becoming at least a little jaded. Her job was like that, too, and she felt an odd connection with him.

"It was weird being there today," she said.

"Being where?"

"The lake." She cleared her throat. "I'm down there almost every day. Seeing the ME's van pull up . . ." She shook her head, and Jacob's brow furrowed with concern.

His phone buzzed, and he pulled it from his pocket, glancing at the screen before answering. "Hey, what's up?" he said, turning so she couldn't eavesdrop.

Bailey watched him, and she had the distinct impression he was talking to a woman. She didn't know why, or why it would matter one way or another.

"Okay." He glanced at Bailey, his expression grim. "I'll be there." He ended the call and stood up. "I need to go. Where are you parked?"

"Go ahead. I'm fine."

"Where are you parked?"

She sighed. "Just down the block."

They pitched their trash and headed back without talking, and Bailey stopped beside her car.

He pulled a business card from his wallet and handed it over, surprising her. Maybe she'd made some progress after all.

"My cell's on the back," he said. "And if you go to the lake, be careful."

"Always am."

"I mean it."

His sharp tone startled her, and she tried to read the look in his eyes.

"It's really bad, isn't it? What happened to her? That's what you're telling me," she said.

"I'm not telling you anything."

"Yes, you are."

He looked at her for a long moment, then gave a slight nod. "Just be careful."

J ACOB DROVE WITH his windows down, letting in the humid air and the street noise. The bars were closing soon, and people lined the sidewalks, flagging down taxis and Ubers and heading to parking lots to retrieve cars. He made his way through downtown and turned onto Cesar Chavez Street, which paralleled the lake. The storms had cleared, and through the trees he saw moonlight glittering off the water. It looked pretty. Peaceful, even. And most people didn't know that just hours ago a woman's brutalized body had been recovered from this same lake.

The sign for Jay's Juice Bar came into view. The parking lot was empty, as he'd expected, and he swung into the lot. His headlights swept over the wooden shack and the dumpster beside it. He cut the engine and sat for a moment, looking and listening as the smell of garbage drifted over.

Jacob ran through his fact base. No ID, no wallet, no phone. No keys of any kind. No witnesses, either, and thanks to a combination of rain and lake water, they had shit in terms of trace evidence. Any footprints or drag marks they might have found had washed away.

The main evidence was the body itself, and Jacob was counting on the medical examiner to make sense of it. Normally he dreaded the ME's office, but he was so desperate for answers right now, he was actually looking forward to tomorrow's autopsy—which showed how fucked up his perspective had gotten.

He grabbed the Maglite from the console and got out, closing his door with a soft *click*. He turned the beam to high and swept it over the corners of the parking lot.

People sometimes park there and use the cut-through.

Bailey's words came back to him, and he pictured her at that picnic table, slurping on her Coke. He should have known she'd go back and talk to the juice bar attendant. This case was shaping up to be a mess, and now he had Bailey Rhoads to deal with, with her plump mouth and her silver toe ring and her razor-sharp questions. He never should have given her an interview. Not that he'd revealed much, but still. She'd penetrated his defenses once, and he had no doubt she'd try to do it again.

Jacob aimed his flashlight at the sign posted on the chain-link fence: *RESTAURANT PARKING ONLY. VIO-LATORS WILL BE TOWED.*

Had the victim parked here and used the shortcut? Maybe someone had followed her, killed her, and then stolen her keys and her car?

But this didn't feel like a car theft. After twelve years on the job and five as a detective, he had a gut instinct for these things. Based on the clothing and the victim's condition, it seemed more like a sexual assault. It was also possible the murder hadn't happened here at all. Maybe the victim had been killed by her boyfriend or husband, and he brought her out here and dumped her in the lake.

Jacob walked around the fence and squeezed past a wall of overgrown brush. Lo and behold, there was a trail here, just as Bailey had told him. Jacob followed it slowly, careful not to trample any potential evidence in case this was a secondary crime scene. Not likely, given that CSIs and cops had spent hours combing this entire area. But Jacob erred on the side of caution, always, when it came to his work.

The brush thinned out, and he stepped around a puddle. Whatever footprints might have been here this morning or yesterday had long since disappeared.

Snick.

Jacob paused to listen, turning off his flashlight. The air smelled of rain and decaying plants. A warm breeze moved through the trees, making the shadows shift.

Snick.

Jacob stepped off the path. He moved through the brush, pushing leaves and branches aside.

Scritch-scratch.

He pivoted and switched on the beam, lighting up an armadillo rooting around a rotten log. The armadillo scratched and burrowed, unbothered by the spotlight. Jacob watched him for a moment, then turned and swept his beam back toward the path. Everything was wet and dank, and mud sucked at his shoes as he picked his way through the brush.

Something shiny glinted up at him. Jacob stepped closer, homing in with his flashlight on an object at the base of a mesquite tree. Pushing aside a leafy branch, he crouched down.

Damn. How had they missed this? A team of cops and crime scene techs had been out here for hours.

Jacob dug a latex glove from his jacket pocket. He took out his phone and snapped a photo. Then another. And another.

His heartbeat quickened as he studied the object partially buried in the muck. It was a cell phone. People lost them all the time. It might have nothing whatsoever to do with his case.

But Jacob's gut told him it did.

CHAPTER

FOUR

BAILEY PULLED UP to her sister's bungalow and was relieved to see Hannah's silver Honda. Bailey eyed the car as she walked up the driveway. A layer of morning dew covered her brother-in-law's pickup, but not the Honda, which meant her sister had probably just come off the graveyard shift.

Bailey passed the kitchen window, and Hannah glanced up from the sink and waved. Bailey let herself in the back door to the utility room. The dryer was going, and the cramped little space smelled of fabric softener.

"Morning," Hannah said as Bailey stepped into the kitchen. Her oldest sister wore black Nikes and blue scrubs, and Bailey noticed the blood spatter on the cuffs.

"Hey." Bailey gave her a hug. "You just get home?"

"Ten minutes ago. How about some coffee? I've got pecan praline."

"Yum."

"Sit down."

The kitchen table was blanketed with stacks of neatly folded T-shirts and dish towels, so Bailey perched on a stool beside the back door.

Hannah took down a bag of coffee from the cabinet and measured out scoops, moving with the brisk efficiency of an ER nurse. She and Bailey had the same petite build, and they'd traded clothes growing up. Hannah got the good hair gene, though. Unlike Bailey and her middle sister, Miranda, Hannah's dark brown hair was gorgeously thick and manageable, but instead of flaunting it, she always wore it in a loose bun secured with a scrunchie.

"You headed to the lake?" Hannah asked.

"Not today. I've got to work."

Hannah smiled, but her tense expression didn't fade as she filled the carafe with water and poured it into the machine.

"Long night?" Bailey asked.

"Traffic fatality. Point-two-two blood alcohol." She shook her head. "Kid was twenty-three." She switched on the coffeepot and leaned back against the counter with a sigh. "How are *you*?" She nodded at a newspaper on the counter. "I saw your story. Nice job."

"Thanks."

"You want some oatmeal?"

"I'm good. Hey, you happen to know an APD detective named Jacob Merritt?" Hannah frequently crossed paths with detectives, who were in and out of the emergency department to interview crime victims or suspects.

The microwave dinged. Hannah took out a glass measuring cup and poured hot water over a bowl of cereal.

"Homicide detective?" she asked.

"Yeah."

She took a spoon from a drawer. "Tall, good cheekbones?"

"Yeah."

Hannah nodded. "He's been in some. Last time was . . . I don't know, two or three months ago?"

"You remember the case?" Bailey asked.

"GSW." She leaned back against the counter and stirred her oatmeal. "I remember the kid was a bleeder."

"Kid?"

"Oh, you know. Nineteen or twenty. Something like that. We saved him, but he lost a kidney." She scooped up a bite, giving Bailey a suspicious look. "So, what's the deal? Please don't tell me you're dating another cop."

"He's the lead on this case I'm writing about."

"The murder from the hike-and-bike trail?"

"It's not confirmed as a homicide yet, but yeah."

"Was it a sexual assault?"

"Don't know yet. The detective's dodging me." Bailey pictured him standing beside her car last night as he'd handed her his business card. Whatever rapport she'd managed to build seemed to have evaporated overnight. She'd texted him this morning to ask about the autopsy timing, but he hadn't responded.

The coffeepot beeped, and Bailey stepped over to the cabinet to get down a pair of mugs.

"That's for you," Hannah said. "I'm not having any."

"You sure?"

"Yeah, I'm tapped. I'm going to get a shower and crash."

Bailey poured coffee for herself and dumped several scoops of sugar into it. She perched on the stool and watched her sister over the rim as she took a sip.

"So, what do you hear about him?" Bailey asked.

"Not a lot." Hannah took another bite and squinted as though she was trying to remember something. "Seems like I heard talk about him a while back, though. I think he or someone he works with got caught up in something."

Bailey's ears perked up. "Something bad?"

"I don't think it was *bad*. I just can't remember it."

"When was this?"

"Had to be a year ago, at least. Maybe longer." She shook her head. "I don't remember what it was, though. He's not exactly talkative. His partner's the chatty one."

"Really? Maybe I'll try him."

"Her." Hannah turned and put her bowl in the sink. "Kendra Porter. Long blond hair, big boobs, thin. You can't miss her."

So, Jacob's partner looked like a Barbie doll. Interesting. Bailey filed that away, along with the "something" Jacob had maybe gotten caught up in.

Hannah was watching her suspiciously, probably knowing she had more than a professional interest in Jacob Merritt. Bailey had sworn off cops after her relationship with Skip Shepherd had ended badly.

Actually, the *ending* part had been okay. It was your typical this-isn't-working-maybe-we-should-see-other-people conversation. But then Bailey started covering the crime beat and did a big exposé on a couple of bad cops, and Skip caught heat from people who assumed he'd been her main source. Skip had shown up at her apartment and demanded that she tell him where she'd gotten her inside information, so he could get himself off the hook with his friends, and Bailey had refused. She wouldn't out her sources, period. So Skip had called her a bunch of names and left, and she was pretty sure he'd gone on to spread a lot of crap about her with his friends in the department.

After that it had taken Bailey months to build up some decent rapport with people outside Skip's circle so that she could do her job effectively.

"So, you're *not* interested in this guy?" Hannah asked.

"Of course I'm interested. He's a source for my story."

Hannah lifted an eyebrow at her as her husband entered the kitchen in sweatpants and a faded T-shirt, with Bailey's one-year-old nephew in his arms. Drew started squirming and reaching for his mother.

"Ma-ma!"

Her face lit up as she crossed the room. "*There's* my boy. I missed you!"

Matt kissed his wife as he handed over the baby. "When do *I* get to be your boy?" He squeezed her butt, and she swatted his hand away.

"Stop! I'm all grubby." She propped Drew on her hip as she opened a cabinet and took down a box of Cheerios.

"Hey, Matt."

"Hey, Bay." He grabbed the mug Bailey had gotten out for Hannah and filled it with coffee. "You're up early."

"I'm headed to work. Just thought I'd drop in."

Hannah sank into a chair and settled Drew in her lap, and he immediately reached for a stack of dish towels. She moved them out of his grasp and distracted him with a handful of Cheerios. Drew wore the green T-rex pajamas Bailey had given him for his birthday. He carefully picked up a Cheerio and put it into his mouth, getting slobber all over his fist.

"Bailey's on the front page this morning," Hannah told Matt.

"Way to go."

"Thanks."

Hannah bounced Drew on her knee. "You working later?" she asked Matt.

"Have to stop by the job site, see if the tile guys finished."

Matt was a contractor and spent most of his time renovating houses on the south side of town, where property values were soaring. He stayed busy, which was good, but he and Hannah never seemed to get a weekend off together.

Drew reached for another Cheerio. His intent little expression made Bailey's heart squeeze, and she took a last gulp of coffee. She didn't want to horn in on their limited family time.

"I'm heading out." Bailey hopped down from the stool and put her mug in the sink. "I've got to write a follow-up today." She planted a kiss on Drew's pudgy cheek. He smelled like baby shampoo.

"If you go to the lake, be careful," Hannah said, shifting into protective older-sister mode.

"Always am."

"I'll ask around about that detective. See if anyone remembers what that thing was about."

"Don't worry about it. I've got sources." Bailey winked at her. "Whatever it is, I'll track it down."

JACOB ARRIVED EARLY, with a full cup of coffee and an empty stomach, braced for the second-worst aspect of his job. As he crossed the parking lot to the ME's office, his phone buzzed and he pulled it from the pocket of his jeans.

"Where are you?" Kendra demanded.

"About to sign in. Why?"

"The post is wrapping up."

"*Our* post?"

"Yeah, Jane Doe. Postmortem's over, and his assistant is in there sewing her up."

"Where's Nielsen?"

"I don't know."

"Find out."

Jacob entered the building and was met by a wall of cold

air. They always kept this place freezing, even in the winter. Jacob peeled off his sunglasses and quickly signed in at the security desk, then grabbed his visitor's badge and went straight to the wing that housed the medical examiner's suite of offices. This wing was even colder and smelled of bleach and formaldehyde, a combination that always made him think of dissected bodies.

Jacob took a long swig of coffee and pitched the rest in a trash can as he made his way down the sterile white hallway. He passed a sheriff's deputy, then turned a corner and spotted Kendra. Even though it was Sunday, she wore her typical dark pantsuit, with her Glock 23 holstered at her hip under the jacket. Her straight blond hair was pulled back in a ponytail.

"What the hell?" he asked.

"He decided to start early." She rolled her eyes. "His assistant told me they got two traffic fatalities and a drug overdose in last night."

"So, he's done with her?"

"Yeah. Started at six."

A man in blue scrubs stepped into the hallway, and Jacob recognized Nielsen's wiry build.

"Doc, wait."

The man turned around. The pathologist had a buzz haircut and rimless glasses. A file folder was tucked under his arm and in his hand was an unopened can of Red Bull.

Jacob approached him. "You got a minute?"

He checked his watch. "I've got four."

"We're working the Jane Doe from the lake," Kendra said.

Nielsen nodded. "The water recovery. My preliminary report will be ready Tuesday morning."

"What can you tell us now?" Jacob asked.

The doctor gave him a long look. Nielsen was short and

lean, and probably in his late thirties, but the somber look in his blue eyes tacked on some years.

A young woman in green scrubs stepped from another doorway.

"A detective just called from Hays County," she told Nielsen. "He's asking about the tox screen from that boating accident."

"It should be in by tomorrow. Hey, send me those files from the Jane Doe autopsy, would you?" He turned and gave Jacob and Kendra a brisk nod. "This way."

He led them down another white hallway to a closed door. He opened it with a key code and ushered them into a small office with a wall of gray file cabinets and a black metal desk. No picture frames or clutter of any kind. The desk was bare except for a laptop computer and a mechanical pencil, and Jacob figured this guy was either type A or ex-military or both.

"Have a seat," Nielsen said, gesturing to a pair of gray plastic chairs identical to the ones sprinkled throughout police headquarters.

Nielsen dropped the folder onto the desk and took a seat. On the wall behind him was a topographical map of central Texas. The Travis County ME got cases from the multiple jurisdictions—all of them growing, population-wise—which was probably one reason they were swamped today. As a deputy ME, Nielsen caught much of the workload.

The doctor checked his watch again, then popped open his Red Bull and took a swig.

"We need to get the basics," Jacob said. "No ID at the crime scene, so that's priority one."

Nielsen cleared his throat. "Caucasian female. Sixty-four inches tall, one hundred sixteen pounds. Age twenty to twenty-five, I'd say, and I can narrow that down after I study her X-rays." He flipped open the file. "We printed her yesterday."

"She's not in the system," Jacob said.

"You try DPS?" he asked. Texas drivers were required to submit both thumbprints.

"No hits," Kendra said.

"Missing-person report?" he asked.

"Nothing that comes close to that description," Jacob said.

Nielsen flipped a page in the file. "Manner of death, homicide. Cause of death, sharp force trauma." He turned the file folder 180 degrees and slid it toward Jacob and Kendra, showing them a black-and-white diagram of a female body, front and back views. Handwritten notes surrounded the diagram.

"She had a wound measuring one point two inches in her upper back."

Kendra gave a low whistle as she took out her notepad.

"The wound is just left of the vertebral column if the assailant is positioned behind the victim." He pointed to several vertebrae. "The wound is between T-five and T-six."

"One point two inches is a wide blade," Jacob said.

The doctor nodded. "I understand there was no weapon recovered at the crime scene?"

"That's right," Kendra said as she jotted notes.

"What are these marks here?" Jacob asked, zeroing in on some cryptic notations beside the wound.

"Anterior fractures, eighth and ninth rib. In addition, she had multiple abrasions around her mouth, as well as a laceration inside her mouth near the left lateral incisor. Looks like she bit her lip." He looked at Jacob. "You want my take on what happened?"

"Yes."

"It looks like the assailant tackled her from behind, landed on her with his knees, and clamped a hand over her mouth during the struggle."

"So, he broke her ribs?" Kendra asked.

"Her injuries would be consistent with that, yes."

"Any defensive wounds?" Jacob asked.

"No parry wounds, no knuckle abrasions, no torn finger-nails."

Kendra looked at Jacob. "Sounds like he ambushed her."

"Or she could have been chased," Nielsen said. "She had scratches on her forearms consistent with someone running through some brush."

"What about sexual assault?" Jacob asked.

Nielsen shook his head. "No sign of that in terms of contusions or abrasions. We did a rape kit, but I don't expect that to be conclusive because she was partially submerged."

Kendra leaned forward, frowning. "But her clothes were all torn. It looked like—"

"That happened after she was stabbed." Nielsen pivoted to his computer. He tapped a few keys and brought up his email screen. He clicked open a file and scrolled through a series of grisly images, all showing the victim on a stainless-steel autopsy table, still wearing her ripped cloth-ing. He paused on an image of the victim facedown on the table. She wore black running shorts and a form-fitting white tank top made of stretchy synthetic material. Jacob had gotten a glimpse of the clothing at the scene, but leaves and debris from the lake had made it hard to see the details.

"We lined up her clothing with the wound. See here?" Nielsen used his mechanical pencil to point out a tear in the white shirt. The fabric around the tear was tinged brown from blood. "I measured the cuts, and the blade went through the fabric." He scrolled to another picture. Clothing had been removed, and the photo showed a close-up of the wound with a metal ruler positioned beside it.

"So . . . you're saying he tackled her from behind, landed on her back, breaking her ribs, then muffled her screams while he stabbed her, and *then* tore her clothing?" Kendra asked.

"That scenario is consistent with what I found."

"But no sexual assault?" Kendra sounded skeptical.

"No obvious evidence of that, like I said." Nielsen looked at Jacob. "But we don't have the lab results yet."

"Anything suggest that she was moved from another location?" Jacob asked, thinking about the cell phone in the field behind the juice bar.

"If you're asking if she was killed elsewhere and transported to the trail, I'd say no, not based on her livor patterns. But it looks like she was moved a short distance. Abrasions on her knees suggest she was dragged facedown, possibly by her underarms, and deposited in shallow water. That's where she was spotted by the jogger, correct?"

"That's right," Kendra said. "The caller first thought it was a drowning, then thought she'd been shot. Called 911 in a panic."

"What about time of death?" Jacob asked.

Nielsen smiled thinly. "Determining postmortem interval is difficult, imprecise, and often impossible, unless you've got a witness. Based on the water temperature and the condition of the body, I'd say she died between late Friday night and mid–Saturday morning."

Kendra blew out a sigh.

"Sorry. That's the best I can do."

Jacob pulled the file closer and examined the diagram, trying to decipher the notes scrawled in the margins. "What about any distinguishing marks on her body? Scars or birthmarks—anything that might help us with her ID?"

Nielsen leaned back in his chair. "No scars, breast implants, joint replacements—nothing like that. Her ortho-dontics were interesting."

"How?" Kendra asked.

"Perfectly straight teeth, evidence of bleaching treat-ments, a couple of porcelain crowns. She'd had good dental work, so if you track down those dental records, it shouldn't be hard to get a positive ID."

Jacob tamped down his frustration. He didn't have den-tal records. Without a missing-person report or a hit on fingerprints, they were no closer to getting an ID than they'd been at the crime scene fifteen hours ago. And time was ticking away.

"There is one thing." Nielsen turned to his computer again and scrolled through more photographs, and Jacob's stomach clenched as the victim's body went by in a blur. Nielsen paused on a photo of a bare ankle. The victim's shoes and socks had been removed.

"Some residual pigmentation," Nielsen said.

Jacob leaned forward.

"A ghost image." The doctor tapped the screen with his pencil. "See? She had a tattoo here at one point but looks like it was removed."

"Can you tell what it was?" Jacob asked.

"Not anymore."

Kendra leaned closer. "How does that work? I've been meaning to check into it. How exactly do they get rid of the ink?"

"The most effective way is using Q-switched lasers," he told her. "Basically, different lasers are effective at remov-ing different ranges on the color spectrum. Black is easiest to remove, but yellows and greens are harder. Takes numer-ous sessions, which can get expensive. It may never go away completely."

"So, she had a tattoo, but no telling what it was at this point." Kendra looked at Jacob. "Our fabulous luck continues."

"Back to the murder weapon," Jacob said. "What else do you know about it?"

"It was a deep wound," Nielsen said. "The blade penetrated all the way to the hilt—you can see the mark."

Kendra winced.

"Most interesting thing, though, is the location. Typically, we see knife wounds to the chest. Second most common is head, then neck. This stab wound"—he nodded at the diagram—"directly to the heart from behind like that? That's unusual. Haven't seen that since Afghanistan."

Kendra pulled the file closer and stared down at the diagram. "You said she bit her lip during the attack, when he clamped his hand over her mouth. Any chance she bit *him*, too?"

"I swabbed her teeth for DNA, just in case. But again, with the body being in water for several hours—"

"A long shot." Kendra heaved a sigh. "Got it."

Nielsen checked his watch. "I need to get back."

"Thanks for making the time," Kendra said as they stood up.

"No problem."

Jacob shook hands with the doctor. "Where were you in Afghanistan?"

"Asadabad."

"Heard it was rough over there."

"It was."

"Doctor?"

They turned to see the woman in green scrubs standing in the doorway. "Your nine o'clock is ready."

"Detectives." Nielsen nodded at them. "I'll send over that report Tuesday morning."

They parted ways in the hall, and Kendra watched him rush to his next appointment.

"I can't even imagine that," she said.

"What?"

"Cutting people open all day long." She shuddered. "I go to one of those things, I'm queasy for a week."

Jacob didn't comment as they made their way back through the maze of hallways.

"What happened with the cell phone you found last night?" Kendra asked.

"I took it to Luis. It's dead as a doornail, but he said he might be able to get it working."

Luis handled all the department's hardware evidence— laptops, tablets, cell phones. He was a wizard with anything electronic, but even he might not be able to get anything useful off a waterlogged cell phone.

"Bizarre case," Kendra said.

"In what way?"

"Every way."

"Yeah, but what jumps out most?" Jacob wanted her opinion. She sometimes noticed things he didn't, especially with female victims.

"I don't know." She paused beside the door where they'd first spotted Nielsen. It was a break room, and Kendra made a beeline for the vending machine, digging some cash from the wallet she kept in her back pocket. They'd worked together three years, and Jacob had never seen her carry a purse.

"We've got nothing whatsoever on ID," she said, feeding a bill into the machine. "No license, no keys, no abandoned vehicle. No missing-person report. This thing's been all over the news, and yet no one's called to say maybe it's their roommate or their girlfriend who hasn't been home all weekend." Kendra jabbed a button and a bottle of water thunked down. "Normally, I'd think maybe she's a transient."

"Evidence doesn't back that up," he said.

"Exactly. Expensive teeth, shoes, clothing. Hell, those designer running shorts alone cost eighty-five bucks."

Jacob shot her a look. "Eighty-five bucks for shorts?"

"Yeah, at least. I've got a pair just like them. I—" She halted. "Damn, I just thought of something."

"What?"

"I have an idea."

CHAPTER

FIVE

THE DRYING ROOM smelled better than the morgue, but the technician working there didn't look particularly happy with her job. Jacob didn't blame her. She worked in a windowless space surrounded by evidence of violence. On the rack behind her was a torn pink blouse and a pair of white jeans, both streaked with blood.

"This would have come in yesterday evening," Kendra was telling the technician, who wore a white lab coat and a rubber apron. Thick purple gloves covered her hands.

The woman tugged the paper mask from her face. "The water recovery?"

"That's right," Kendra said. "We need to examine the clothing."

"We don't usually let—"

"It's important," Kendra said.

The woman shifted her attention to Jacob, letting her gaze linger on his detective's shield. "Table three." She nodded toward the doorway. "Right in there."

Jacob followed Kendra into the adjacent room, where a series of numbered slate tables occupied the far wall. The victim's clothing and personal effects were spread out atop a piece of white butcher paper. Beside the shoes was the black zipper pouch that had been found with the body. Unfortunately, all the pouch had contained was a packet of orange-flavored sports gel.

"Everything's still drying," the woman said from the doorway. "When it's done, it goes to the lab."

This room smelled earthy from the leaves and dirt still clinging to the clothes. Jacob approached the table, feeling intensely frustrated as he studied the torn white shirt. In this light, the hole created by the blade was clearly visible.

"Glove up if you need to touch anything," the technician said, handing Jacob a box.

Kendra pulled on a pair of purple gloves and carefully picked up the shorts. She moved her fingers along the waistband, and her eyes brightened.

"I *knew* it," she said.

"What?"

"Inside pocket."

Jacob eased closer, holding his breath as Kendra tugged open the zipper. She pulled out a white plastic card with a black magnetic strip on the back.

"Check it out." She smiled and held up the card. "Our first break."

THE NEWSROOM WAS quiet, even for a Sunday night. Bailey hitched her laptop bag onto her shoulder and meandered through the desks with the vague hope of encountering another metro reporter working late. But the only people in tonight were a couple guys from sports. Bailey followed the sound of hip-hop to the lifestyle editor's office and leaned her head in.

"I'm out," she said.

Sophia glanced up from her computer. "You get your story in?"

"Yep."

"I saw the layout. It's running above the fold."

Bailey winced. She should have been elated to have a story running top of page one, but this one didn't merit that placement.

"What's wrong?" Sophia asked.

"I'm just surprised. I didn't turn up much, and I figured they'd bury it."

"Slow news day." Sophia shrugged. "Just be glad for the byline."

"I am. Don't work too late."

"Ha."

Bailey passed the elevator, where a janitor's cart blocked the door. As she stepped into the stairwell, her phone chimed, echoing off the cinder-block walls. She rummaged through her bag and cursed as she read the number.

"Rhoads," she snapped.

"It's Jacob Merritt."

"I know."

"You have time to meet up?"

She started to laugh. But then she remembered how annoyed she was with him.

"Where are you?" she asked.

"Outside the building."

Bailey stopped on the landing and peered out the window. The *Herald* parking lot was nearly empty—only a dozen or so cars, mostly belonging to production people.

"I'll meet you at the bench by the newsstand," he said.

"Fine."

Bailey tucked her phone away. She combed a hand through her hair and dug a lipstick out of her bag. But then she changed her mind. She didn't date cops. Even just flirting with a cop was a slippery slope.

She took her time descending the stairs and crossing the lobby, giving the security guard a wave on her way out.

She stepped into the sultry night air and spotted Jacob standing beside the bench. His gaze homed in on her, making her stomach do a little dance. As she approached, she saw that he wore the same scarred leather jacket he'd been wearing last night and had that same penetrating look in his dark eyes.

"Hi," he said.

She stopped in front of him and crossed her arms. "How did you know I was here?"

"Lucky guess."

Was it really? Maybe he'd pinged her phone to look up her location. She knew detectives could do that under certain circumstances. But she was probably being paranoid.

He smiled slightly. "You told me you had the weekend shift, remember?"

Bailey glanced around and spied his black truck parked at a meter along the street. "So, what's up?" she asked.

"I wanted to talk to you about the case."

"You're aware that my deadline has come and gone, right?"

"I figured."

She'd left him three messages, and he'd ignored every one. She didn't like being blown off.

But at least he was here. Better late than never.

"So, how'd it go today?" she asked, referring to the autopsy. Judging from his grim expression, he knew that was what she meant.

"Not like we wanted."

She tipped her head to the side. "What happened?"

"Still no ID. But I'm guessing you heard that."

"I did, yeah."

He looked out over the parking lot. "I'll walk you to your car."

She started walking, purposely not filling the silence with conversation. She wanted him to do the talking.

"I assume you've got a story running tomorrow?" he asked.

"Yep."

"What's your angle?"

"Who says I have an angle?"

"You always have an angle."

She looked at him. Was he saying he read her work? More likely, he was generalizing. Then again, she'd been covering the crime beat for almost a year, so maybe he'd caught a few articles.

"We went with trail safety," she told him. "I interviewed a bunch of regulars on the lake. Some of them talked about the emergency phones and the running buddy program. There's speculation that this could be related to the string of muggings last month. Maybe the murder was a robbery gone wrong." She looked at him. "What do you think?"

He didn't answer for a moment. "It's possible."

"But not likely."

"I didn't say that."

Bailey stopped beside her car. "You know, I really could have used your input this afternoon. Or this evening. I got stuck using a quote from your PR flack again."

He smiled. "I'm sure you made it work."

"Why are you being friendly all of a sudden?"

"All of a sudden?" He smiled again. "I bought you a Coke last night."

"Yeah, and then you ignored three messages."

His smile faded. "I need a favor. We have to get an ID on this victim. We've had some leads, but nothing's panned out, and meanwhile the trail's going cold." He paused. "Don't quote me on that."

"What is it you need?"

"We've decided to release a photo, hoping the public can help us."

"A photo of the *victim*?"

"No, her personal effects." He pulled his phone from his pocket, brought up a picture, and handed it to Bailey. The phone was warm from his body heat, and holding it in her hand felt strangely intimate.

The photograph showed a woman's shirt, shorts, and running shoes laid out on a nondescript background—maybe a bedsheet or a piece of white butcher paper. Bailey's stomach knotted. She owned a pair of sneakers just like the victim's.

"These aren't actually her clothes." Bailey glanced up at him.

"These are duplicates of the clothes she was wearing. Same brand, same style, same everything. We're hoping to jog someone's memory." He took the phone and swiped to a new picture. This one showed a drawing of a pair of earrings. "She was wearing these silver, leaf-shaped earrings, too."

"Those are lotus flowers."

"We're hoping someone recognizes the jewelry, along with her clothes and shoes. Maybe they'll give us a call." His gaze locked with hers. "Will you ask your editor to run this?"

"He's gone for the night. But text me the pictures and I'll call him at home. I'm sure we can at least get it in the online edition by tomorrow."

"I'd appreciate it." He looked relieved as he tucked his phone into his pocket.

"You guys must really be up against a wall."

"ID is critical. It's hard to move forward without it."

Jacob ran a hand through his hair, and Bailey thought he looked tired. He'd worked late last night, too, and—unlike her—he probably wasn't getting a comp day tomorrow to make up for losing his weekend.

"So, you headed home now?" he asked.

"Yeah."

So how about having a drink with me? Or dinner?

But he didn't say either of those things. He just gazed down at her with those serious brown eyes.

"Thanks, Bailey."

"Sure."

"I owe you one."

She opened her car door and tossed her bag inside. "Don't think I won't remind you."

JACOB SLID BEHIND the wheel and watched in his rear-view mirror as Bailey's white Toyota pulled out of the parking lot.

Guilt needled him. It was shitty to ignore her all day and then hit her up for a favor, but he couldn't worry about that now. His top priority was identifying his victim so the case could move forward.

Jacob started up his truck and pulled into traffic. After finding that keycard, he and Kendra had had it fingerprinted and then spent the better part of the day combing parking garages and apartment buildings near the lake, hoping to get a hit. The keycard didn't have a logo on it, so Jacob doubted it came from a hotel. But after striking out all afternoon with every apartment building and garage within half a mile of the hike-and-bike trail, he'd decided they were wrong to rule out hotels.

It was also possible the victim didn't live near the lake at all. Maybe she'd taken an Uber to the trail or had a friend drop her off, and the keycard went to some building on the other side of town.

Jacob cruised through traffic, trying to ignore the pounding in his head. He was hungry, tired, and more than a little frustrated after spending his day chasing down dead-end leads. Releasing a photo to the press was pretty much a Hail Mary, but he'd managed to convince his lieutenant that a tip from the public was their best chance of getting an ID sooner rather than later. Most female homicide victims were killed by someone they knew, often a domestic partner, so ID was critical. And even if this was a case where the victim didn't know her attacker, Jacob needed to notify next of kin and learn everything he could about the victim's routine so he could piece together what happened to her. The case was growing colder by the hour, and he didn't even have a name.

Jacob's phone vibrated in his pocket as he pulled up to a stoplight. He recognized the number for the tech lab.

"Hey, what's up?"

"I'm working on that cell phone," Luis said.

Jacob heard music in the background and pictured Luis alone in the lab, surrounded by all his gadgets and listening to a concert on YouTube.

"You get it to work?" Jacob asked.

"Not yet. It's a cheap-as-shit phone. You know that, right?"

"Yeah, I noticed."

"No contract on this thing. It's prepaid, so even if I get it working, which I probably *can*, you may not be able to get much off it. It doesn't get email or anything."

"Okay."

"But here's the good news. We lifted a print."

"Who's 'we'?"

"Me and Marisa. I took the phone to her right after you brought it in here, and she dusted it and came up with a thumbprint."

"I'm surprised."

"I know, right? I mean, with the water and all, I thought printing it was a formality, but Marisa got this off the inside."

"The *inside*?"

"Yeah, the battery. And get this, the print matches your DOA. We just confirmed it with the ME's office."

"So, you're saying—"

"Your victim's print is on this phone. That's what I'm saying. Looks like she lost it right before she died."

T ABITHA DARTED ACROSS the busy street, ignoring an angry shout from a cabdriver. She stepped onto the sidewalk and passed another pub, sidestepping a pair of weaving tourists who'd just stumbled out. One of them called after her, but she pretended not to hear as she moved briskly toward the intersection. She hung a left at the corner and walked two more blocks, then checked over her shoulder for anyone following before ducking between two buildings. The dim alley smelled of urine. It was a gross shortcut, but she used it anyway because it spit her out near the bed-and-breakfast.

She passed under a streetlamp. The rest of the road was dark, with giant oak trees blocking out the moonlight. She passed the tall white Victorian, where a porchlight illuminated hanging ferns and an empty swing. She passed three small bungalows—pink, yellow, blue—lined up like Easter eggs, with matching flower boxes and glowing lights above the doors. Another glance over her shoulder before she turned up the driveway and breathed a sigh of relief. No lights on in the windows, so Frank wasn't home.

Tabitha approached the carriage house, passing a messy old oak tree dripping with Spanish moss. No pastels here or cheerful blooms—just peeling white paint and a creaky staircase leading to her one-room apartment.

The light above the door was out still, big surprise. She'd mentioned it to Frank, but he'd ignored her, of course.

"Freaking cheapskate," she muttered, digging through her backpack in the dark. She found her key, and it took her two fumbling tries before she got it in and unlocked the door. A slip of paper fluttered to her feet, and she grabbed it before the breeze could snatch it away. It was a message from Frank, no doubt, and she cursed him again for tromping all the way up here without bothering to bring a light-bulb. She tucked the message into her jeans pocket for later and stepped inside.

Her apartment was an oven. She flipped on the light and the ceiling fan and eyed the silent AC unit that had sputtered its last breath during her first month here. Under any sane lease agreement, the landlord would have been required to repair the damn thing by now, given the triple-digit heat enveloping the city. But Tabitha didn't have a lease agreement, only a spoken promise of discounted rent in exchange for work.

Tabitha closed the door and flipped the latch. She sniffed the air for any hint of tobacco that would indicate Frank had been in her place while she was out, but it smelled only of mildew. With a sigh, she kicked off her sandals and dropped her backpack on the futon. The back of her tank top was damp with sweat, and she stripped down to her bra as she crossed the room to open the window. The pane stuck, but she jerked it up a few inches and used the can of tomato soup on the windowsill to prop it open. A faint whisper of air drifted through the screen.

She returned to her backpack and retrieved the roll of cash from the inner pocket. Eighteen dollars. Pathetic. She opened the narrow closet and shoved the hangers aside to access the green peacoat she hadn't worn in well over a year. Carefully, she pulled open the Velcro seam in the lining and slipped her hand inside the hidden pocket to pull out a thin stack of bills held together with a binder clip. She counted the money, added her tips, and replaced the stash.

Tabitha flopped onto the futon and stared at the ceiling. The fan turned listlessly, barely stirring the air. For a minute she just lay there, listening to the cicadas outside as a bead of sweat slid down her temple and into her ear.

She tugged the folded paper from her pocket. As suspected, it was a page from one of the freebie notepads in each of the bungalows. *Sunset Oaks Bed & Breakfast* was printed in formal script above Frank's jerky scrawl: *#201 202 203 #101 LATE checkout!!*

"Shit," she hissed.

Four units. And 101 included the garden, which entailed sweeping the patio and picking cigarette butts out of the planters. Late checkout meant she'd be doing everything after noon in the suffocating heat, too. She felt sticky just thinking about it. And she had to be at the restaurant by four.

Eighteen dollars tonight. It was pitiful for a five-hour shift. Between both jobs, she'd put in sixty hours this week.

Once upon a time in a galaxy far, far away, sixty hours had seemed like a tough workweek. But that was a lifetime ago. That was back before she had any real appreciation for her salaried job or her 401(k) plan or her air-conditioned office, which she'd once lamented not having a *window*, for crying out loud. Her routine back then had included venti lattes and sushi lunches and occasional happy hours with fruity drinks served in delicate martini glasses.

Tabitha's chest tightened. She closed her eyes against the hot burn of tears. She couldn't give in to nostalgia. Or despair. She had to be practical.

Never look back. Never, never, never.

Her stomach growled, reminding her she hadn't eaten in six hours. She dug into her backpack again for the brown to-go box. The hamburger and fries were cold, and she got up and popped the box into the microwave of her apartment's tiny kitchen. Then she opened the mini fridge. The only contents were a blueberry yogurt and a half-finished bottle of chardonnay that had been left in 102 last week. She didn't even like chardonnay, but she pulled out the bottle and poured a few glugs into a plastic cup.

She took a sip and cringed. The sour taste lingered in her mouth as she tried to think. As of tonight, she had one hundred twenty-six dollars to her name. And it was time to leave. She'd meant to take off weeks ago, but the no-questions-asked waitressing gig combined with the daily perk of groceries left behind for the maid had made this place difficult to leave. So she'd given herself an extra week, then two, then three, even though she hated the heat and the never-ending bed linens and the drunken tourists with grabby hands.

The microwave dinged. She opened it and noticed a thin line of sugar ants crawling across the counter. She picked up a dish towel and followed the trail from a box of cereal to the electrical outlet near the microwave. She had a charger plugged in there, and her cheap black cell phone sat ready to go at a moment's notice. She hadn't touched the thing in months.

A little red light on the top of the phone was blinking.

Tabitha stared at it. Her pulse quickened as she unplugged the phone and looked at the keypad. Her mind drew a complete blank, but her thumb seemed to remember the passcode. Tabitha's stomach clenched as the screen brightened with the words *1 NEW MESSAGE*.

She tapped the button and lifted the phone to her ear, holding her breath and watching the line of ants for what seemed like an eternity. She heard a faint rustle. Then panting.

And the words she heard next turned her blood to ice.

CHAPTER

SIX

Bailey's muscles burned as she cut through the water. She leaned forward and pulled with all her might, huffing out a breath as she dug hard with the oars. Glancing over her shoulder, she spotted the red buoy marking the dock. She leaned forward and completed another stroke, and another, and another, determined to finish strong as she blocked out everything—the boats, the paddleboards, the green blur of trees. Closing in on the red buoy, she gave a last powerful pull and let the boat glide.

She tipped her head back and sighed. The morning sky was gray with clouds, and sweat seeped into her eyes as she stared up at it. Her heart thrummed. This was her favorite part, the part that made her get out of bed instead of hitting the snooze button. She liked the sky this time of morning. She liked the lake cool and peaceful, before the heat and the crowds and the traffic set in. She liked the feeling of being immersed in nature. *This* was her time. These few minutes on the water, feeling sweaty and spent, would power her through whatever challenges came her way throughout the day.

Bailey looked over her shoulder. Past the pedestrian bridge was a row of cypress trees, and she tried to pinpoint the spot where the victim had been pulled from the water just hours ago. Had this place been her refuge, too? Had she come out here to relax and recharge? To push her body to the limit?

What had she been thinking about in the minutes before she died?

Maybe she'd been distracted, thinking about work or sex or overdue bills. Maybe she hadn't been paying attention, and her killer had spotted her alone and vulnerable. Bailey liked it out here when there was no one around, and maybe the victim had, too. People always said never jog at night or in the dark, and especially not alone. But Bailey understood the allure.

Sure, blame the victim. It's her fault she came out here and got murdered.

A shrill whistle jerked Bailey from her thoughts, and she turned to see the UT women's rowing team slicing across the water. Their coach followed close behind them in a launch—one of the few motorized vehicles allowed on the lake.

She held up her megaphone. "In two, power ten!" she commanded as the boat razored through the water.

Bailey wiped her forehead with her arm. With a few quick strokes, she maneuvered to the dock, where a kid with a goatee and a blond ponytail waited to help her. Sam wore a blue Austin Rowing Club T-shirt and pink Hawaiian shorts today.

"Leave her in," Sam told her. "We're hot-boating."

"Oh, yeah?"

"We're booked solid till noon, and someone's right behind you. Here he is now."

Bailey unfastened her feet from the stretchers and stepped out of the boat. Sam held it steady as a skinny guy wearing a Texas Regatta T-shirt walked over. Bailey traded nods with him and headed to the boathouse to retrieve her gear from a locker and change into flip-flops. When she came out, Sam was at the water cooler dumping in a bag of ice.

"Saw you out there," Sam said. "You were really hauling."

"It's nice out."

Sam replaced the lid on the cooler. "Supposed to get hot later. Hundred and two by lunchtime. That's what the radio said."

Bailey filled a paper cone with water and took a cold gulp. She looked at Sam, glad to have a chance to talk to him alone.

"So, did you work Saturday?" she asked.

"Yep."

"You see anything unusual on the trail?"

His brow furrowed and he crossed his arms. "Like what?"

"I don't know. Any suspicious people or cars? Any unusual noises?"

"Like . . . maybe a scream for help?"

"Yeah."

He shook his head. "Couple of cops were just here, asking me the same thing."

"Really? When?"

"Just now." He nodded toward the parking lot.

Bailey turned and followed his gaze. Past a row of boat trailers, she spotted an unmarked police car. No detectives in sight. She looked around and noticed a blond woman in a dark pantsuit standing beside the trailhead, interviewing a guy in running shorts.

"Hard to believe it happened just up the trail," Sam said.

"I know."

"I mean, that's freaking creepy."

"Yeah." Bailey scanned the area for Jacob. Was the blond woman his partner or some other APD detective assigned to the case?

"They think it happened Friday night or early Saturday morning."

Bailey looked at Sam. "What's that?"

"The murder. That's what the detective said, anyway."

"And you were working both days?"

"Friday I was off. I was scheduled Saturday, seven to three. But we pulled all the boats out by one because of the rain."

Bailey spotted Jacob at the water fountains, and her heart rate kicked up. He wore dark pants and a dress shirt today, sleeves rolled up already, and he was interviewing a woman with a stroller.

What was it about this man? Maybe she was lightheaded from her workout. Yeah, right. That would definitely explain why the mere sight of him made her heart start to pound.

Bailey had done some asking around, and she was pretty sure she'd found the "something" Hannah had heard about Jacob. Last summer he and another off-duty officer had had an altercation in the parking lot of the Ice House, which was a cop hangout downtown. According to Bailey's dispatcher friend, the other cop had been talking trash about Jacob's partner. The dispatcher didn't know the details, but whatever was said must have been really offensive because Jacob had given the guy a split lip over it. He didn't seem like the type to lose his cool over something petty.

Bailey glanced at Jacob's partner again, wondering if maybe there was some sort of love triangle involved.

She turned back to Sam, but he'd returned to the dock to help someone launch a kayak. Bailey shouldered her backpack and started up the trail. Jacob was watching her now as she approached him. He had that intent look about him, and she could tell he was in cop mode. No hint of the smile he'd given her last night when he needed a favor.

"What brings you here?" he asked.

"Just finished my workout."

His gaze dropped to her flip-flops.

"I row," she said.

"With a team or—"

"Single scull."

He lifted an eyebrow. "Interesting."

"Why?"

"I figured you for a runner."

"Nope. Not for me. I like the water." She nodded at the trailhead behind him. "What brings *you* out here this morning?"

A pair of cyclists whisked past, and Jacob touched Bailey's arm to guide her to the side of the trail. Her skin tingled from the contact.

"We're conducting interviews," he said.

"You're looking for regulars?"

"People tend to stick to routines, especially when it comes to exercise. We're looking for anyone who saw something out of the norm."

She turned toward the boathouse. "Well, there's the boathouse staff, but I hear you talked to them already. There's also a running club that meets by the nature center every morning at six thirty. You could talk to them."

"We did."

She gazed up at him and was struck once again by those

serious dark eyes. He'd shaved since she last saw him, and she caught the faint scent of his soap or cologne. She suddenly felt self-conscious of her sweat-soaked clothes. She took a step back, and he gave her a quizzical look.

"We posted your photos," she said. "Any new leads?"

"Not yet. But the local news stations ran them, too, so that's good. We're hoping to get an ID soon."

"Give me a heads-up when you do."

He nodded, but it was noncommittal.

"That was our deal."

He smiled. "I don't remember a deal."

"It was unspoken. I agreed to get your pictures posted, you agreed to give me a heads-up if anything came of it." She put her hand on her hip. "Are you backing out now?"

"No."

He gazed down at her, and she got the impression he found her amusing. She should probably be annoyed, but his smile was too appealing, and she was glad to see him here, even though she was all sweaty from her workout.

"I need to go," he said.

"Keep me posted."

"I'll call you if anything big breaks."

"If *any*thing breaks."

JACOB LEFT THE lake without a single new lead. They'd interviewed dozens of regulars, but only a few had been there on Saturday morning, and the ones who had said they'd seen nothing suspicious or noteworthy. He walked across the parking lot beside the weathered wooden boathouse with the Texas flag painted on the side. A series of boat trailers lined the asphalt beside the building.

Single scull. He shouldn't have been surprised. Bailey had an independent streak. As Jacob crossed the parking lot, he imagined her pulling in here at the crack of dawn and walking alone past the canoe racks where anyone might be waiting in the shadows.

Two days ago, he had never so much as talked to Bailey Rhoads and knew her only by reputation. Now he couldn't stop thinking about her. And bumping into her. Whenever he saw her unexpectedly his mind went blank. Jacob needed to snap out of it and get focused on his case. He probably shouldn't have gone to her office last night, but he was running out of options, and he'd take any help he could get at this point if it meant getting an ID on his victim.

He approached the old gray Taurus he'd parked along the street near a bagel shop. Kendra was in her own car this morning, and she'd decided to stay to interview the nature center staffers for a second time, hoping to shake something loose. Jacob was ready to cut his losses and see if any forensic reports had come in yet.

He popped the locks and slid behind the wheel. He'd picked up the Taurus from the motor pool at oh-dark-hundred this morning and made it over here as the first of the early-morning joggers were beginning to trickle in. The lakefront was awake now, busy with runners and cyclists and dog walkers, even a few summer tourists on Segways. The coffee shops were busy, too, as commuters stopped in to load up on caffeine and carbs.

Jacob surveyed the sidewalks crowded with people, almost all of them with a phone in hand. A pair of women with matching blond ponytails and yoga mats tucked under their arms strode up the sidewalk together. They looked to be friends, except they didn't say a word to each other as they stared down at their devices. Another woman with a yoga mat under her arm walked past them going the opposite direction. She stopped at a wrought-iron gate and pulled a card from a little purse looped around her wrist. She swiped the card through a reader and opened the gate.

Jacob's pulse picked up. He reached for the accordion file in the back seat and fished out the envelope containing the white card with the magnetic strip on the back.

He got out and walked up the street, eyeing the building as he neared the gate. The ground level was a bank. Jacob had driven by here yesterday and noted what looked like offices on the upper four floors, but maybe he'd been wrong about that.

Jacob waited for a break in traffic and darted across the street as a thirtyish man stepped through the gate. He had a computer bag slung over his shoulder and looked to be headed to work. The gate clanged shut behind him.

Beside the gate was a small black card reader. Jacob swiped the keycard through. A light flashed green and the lock made a *snick*.

Jacob stared down in disbelief. He pushed the gate open and followed a narrow cobblestone walkway into a small courtyard with a gurgling fountain at the center. To his left was a tall glass door with *LAKEVIEW COURT* etched across it. Entering the air-conditioned lobby, Jacob took off his sunglasses. One side of the lobby had an elevator bank and a wall of mailboxes. On the opposite side was a windowed office. Photos taped to the window showed apartment interiors and views of the lake.

Jacob stepped into the leasing office, and a fiftyish woman with bottle-blond hair looked up from her computer.

"How may I help you?" she asked with a smile.

"Jacob Merritt, Austin Police." He flashed his credentials. "I need information about one of your tenants."

SEVEN

BAILEY CUT THROUGH the newsroom, hoping to get in and out before Max spotted her and started nagging her for updates that she didn't have. She walked through the sea of desks and workstations. Several years ago, the *Herald* had ditched the traditional cubicle setup and started clustering the desks together in "pods," which were designed to "facilitate information sharing." The staff hated the change, of course. Reporters were territorial enough about their sources without having to conduct phone interviews while directly facing colleagues who didn't even bother to pretend they weren't eavesdropping on every word.

Bailey dumped her backpack onto her desk chair. Her pod was empty at the moment. She shared it with several sports guys whose computers were decorated with Longhorn paraphernalia. Glancing across the newsroom, she was relieved not to see Max in his windowed office. But the conference room blinds were shut, and her chest tightened with apprehension. Were they letting someone go? She spotted Lance at the coffee maker. She dug some money from her backpack and darted over to catch him.

"Hi, Lance."

"Hey, Bay." He looked her over and lifted an eyebrow at her shorts and flip-flops. Lance was dressed for success in slacks and a blue silk tie, meaning he probably had a city council meeting later.

"Who's in the conference room?" she asked.

"Sophia."

She felt a stab of fear. *"Sophia?"*

"Relax." He sipped his coffee. "She's interviewing a new stringer for the lifestyle section."

"Oh."

Bailey stuffed a dollar bill in the glass jar beside the Keurig, then spun the coffee carousel and selected an extra-dark roast. She grabbed a chipped Snoopy mug from the drying rack by the sink.

"So, you're still working the lake trail murder?" Lance asked.

"Yep."

The machine whirred, and she watched her mug fill.

"They have an ID yet?" he asked.

"No."

"Suspects?"

"No."

He shook his head. "My girlfriend's down there all the time with her running club. She's really freaked out by this thing. Hope they make an arrest soon."

"Same." Bailey picked up her coffee. "I'll keep you posted."

She headed back to her desk, where she sank into her chair and scanned the newsroom as she waited for her computer to boot up. Still no Max, and she didn't see any other

metro reporters, either. Everyone was out, and it was un-
nervingly quiet.

Bailey checked the budget for tomorrow and saw that
her story had been planned for A-1 again. *RHOADS—
LAKE MURDER FOLLOW.* Just the words put a cramp in
her stomach. She checked her cell phone for the nth time
this morning. Her source at dispatch still hadn't responded
to her message.

"Thought you were off today."

She turned around to see Max looming behind her. Her
boss was tall and lanky and had a neatly trimmed beard.
He wore his typical starched shirt with jeans today, but his
eyes were bloodshot and his hair looked messier than usual.

"I just stopped in to see if anything came in on the scanner last night," she told him.

"Nothing interesting." He sat on the edge of her desk
with a sigh.

"Everything all right?"

"Yeah." He combed his hand through his hair. "The
twins are sick. We were up all night."

"I'm sorry. What is it?"

"I don't know. Some kind of summer cold. Selma's taking them to the doctor this morning." He glanced at his
watch, and she knew he would rather be with his wife than
working. He was a family guy, but his job required crazy
hours.

"Hey, thanks for getting those photos posted," she said.

"No problem. They get any tips yet?"

"Not that I've heard."

"You check with your PD source? The dispatcher?"

"I was just about to call her again."

"You know you're on for tomorrow, right?"

"I know."

He looked her up and down, and she sensed his disapproval. Not about her casual attire. Max didn't care about that, and he knew she was technically off right now because she'd worked the weekend. Although no one was every really *off* around here. They simply worked from home. But Max seemed uneasy, and Bailey got the feeling he didn't think she was up for this assignment. Bailey was the youngest reporter and the only woman to ever cover the crime beat, which made her doubly determined to prove herself.

"What's your plan if they don't come up with an ID?" he asked.

She didn't have a plan.

"I know someone in the ME's office who might have something," she improvised. "And I'll interview the lead detective and find out where everything stands. I heard they were going through parking lot footage looking for leads."

He nodded. "Have they scheduled a presser for today?"

"No."

He stood. "Well, try that dispatcher again. Just in case that detective blows you off. Who's the lead on this one?"

"Jacob Merritt."

Max scoffed. "You won't get crap from that guy. Try his partner. Kendra something."

"Porter."

"Yeah, try her. Merritt's tight as a drum. Expect him to stonewall."

DANA SMITH LIVED in a spacious one-bedroom unit on the fourth floor. The apartment faced west and had a narrow balcony barely large enough for a chair. If Jacob leaned out far enough, he could see a partial view of the lake, including the stretch of shoreline that had been a crime scene Saturday night.

Just one more strange circumstance in a list of strange circumstances that was growing longer by the minute.

Jacob stepped into the bathroom now and looked around. The counter was clean and uncluttered. With a gloved hand, he pulled back the shower curtain. A row of high-end hair products lined the tub, and a pink razor sat in the soap dish. He turned to the mirrored cabinet above the sink. Opening it, he found mouthwash, dental floss, and about a dozen bottles of vitamins. Under the sink he found a stack of beige bath towels and a teeth-whitening kit.

Jacob returned to the living room, where a dark gray sofa and matching armchairs were arranged around a wooden coffee table. Fuzzy pink throw pillows added some color, but the entire place had a bland, staged look, like an IKEA showroom.

Jacob poked through a stack of mail on the coffee table—all flyers and catalogs addressed to *Current Resident*. Set apart from the stack was a Lululemon catalog with several pages earmarked. It also was addressed to Current Resident but the street listed was Mockingbird Cove. Jacob took out his phone and snapped a picture of the address.

Stepping into the kitchen, he opened several cabinets to find plain white dishes. No coffeepot, but on the stove was a red teakettle. The kitchen drawers held the usual assortment of flatware and utensils. He opened another cabinet to find a hodgepodge of chunky ceramic mugs in different shapes and colors that looked like they'd come from a garage sale.

Jacob opened the dishwasher. The top tray held a cereal bowl and two wineglasses. Dirty or clean? He held one of the glasses up to the window, and sunlight illuminated several fingerprints. Either she'd used both wineglasses herself or she'd had someone over. A CSI could tell him.

Jacob replaced the glass and moved to the breakfast bar, where a short black charger was plugged into the outlet.

Jacob's phone buzzed with a call from Kendra.

"What'd you find?" he asked her.

"You said Dana Anne Smith, Anne with an e, correct?"

"That's what the paperwork says," he told her. "She's listed as the occupant, but the apartment is leased to an LLC."

"Okay, get this. The name 'Dana Smith' came in over the tip line."

"You're kidding."

"The caller saw the story on the news and recognized the pictures," Kendra reported. "She says Dana works for her, but she didn't show up today and hasn't answered her phone all weekend. This woman lives over in Hyde Park and says Dana's her nanny."

"Four sixty-two Mockingbird Cove."

Silence.

"Kendra?"

"How the hell did you know that?"

"There's some mail to that address here in the apartment." Jacob opened the fridge. An array of flavored soda waters filled the top shelf. Underneath was a six-pack of yogurt and a cardboard take-out container from Red Pagoda.

"Okay, so that's confirmation," Kendra said.

"Maybe."

"What do you mean? Everything lines up."

"Something feels off." He closed the door and zeroed in on a piece of paper stuck to the side of the fridge with a magnet. It was a drawing scribbled with green and pink crayon. Jacob had no idea what it was supposed to be. A tornado? A heart? Maybe the kid she took care of had drawn it for her. The magnet was from a local art museum.

"How do you mean 'off'?" Kendra asked.

"This apartment's odd. It's in a prime location and it's filled with nice stuff, but Dana Smith's name isn't anywhere. I'm not finding any bills, letters, check stubs, prescriptions. No financial paperwork, no receipts. No photographs in the place. No pictures on the walls. The closet's half-empty, and she only has four pairs of shoes."

"Five, counting the ones in evidence."

"Okay, five." Jacob stepped over to the window and parted the mini blinds. A line of clouds was moving in, and they might be in for some rain again today. "How many do you have?"

"What? Shoes?"

"Yeah."

"I don't know. Twenty pairs?"

"Right, and you don't even like clothes. I've been in a lot of victims' homes and this one is strange."

"Maybe it's a love nest, and she lives someplace else."

Jacob had considered that, too. "What's the employer say about Dana's social life? She know if she had a boyfriend? There's no evidence of a man here. No extra toothbrush or men's clothes or condoms."

"That was my first question, and no. This woman said she isn't aware of anyone."

"Friends?"

"Nope."

"What about family in town?" Jacob asked.

"I asked about next of kin, but she doesn't know. Said Dana had only been working there eight months."

"So, she knows nothing about this woman, yet she trusts her with her kid. What's this woman do for a living?"

"Her name's Celeste Camden, and she's an associate professor over at UT. Teaches cultural anthropology or something."

"And her husband?"

"She's a widow."

There went another potential suspect.

"We need to get her in for an interview," Jacob said.

"She's on her way, and I asked her to bring photos. She said she has some of Dana and her daughter."

Jacob combed his hand through his hair with frustration. He had a tentative ID, finally, but touring the apartment had teed up a whole new list of questions.

He returned to the kitchen and snapped a photo of the phone charger and a close-up of the cord. He wanted to see whether it was a fit with the phone recovered from the woods behind the juice bar.

"Jacob? You there?"

"I need to get back to the station and run some things," he said. "Then I want to get forensics in here. This could be a secondary crime scene."

"All right. Find me when you get here."

Jacob returned to his car with the leasing agent's key still in his pocket. He wanted to make sure he could get into the apartment again and didn't want anyone else sweet-talking the agent into granting access.

Rain started to come down as Jacob headed across town. Dana Smith's apartment felt off, and it wasn't just the lack of clothes. People's homes tended to have more personal touches, particularly women's homes. It looked like Dana had just moved in, but according to the lease, she'd been there eighteen months. He'd have to come back and interview some of the neighbors.

Jacob's phone dinged in the cup holder as he got a text from Bailey.

WORD IS U HAVE POSSIBLE IDENT?

He eyed the phone. Bailey clearly had some sources within the department. But they couldn't be very high-ranking, or she wouldn't keep hitting him up for info. He resolved to call her later when he firmed things up.

As Jacob pulled into the police station parking lot, his phone buzzed. The caller ID read *US GOV.*

"Shit," he muttered. He slid into a space and picked up. "Merritt."

"Hey, it's Morgan."

Of all the government numbers that might have called him, he'd somehow known this would be his ex. He didn't know whether she was in town or calling from the San Antonio field office.

"I've been trying to reach you," she said. "We need to meet."

"I can't do it right now. I'm in the middle of something."

"It's about Dana Smith."

Jacob looked at his phone, startled. "Where did you get that? We haven't even confirmed her ID yet."

"You won't," Morgan said. "It's an alias. She's one of ours."

EIGHT

THE COFFEE SHOP across from the federal courthouse was crowded, but Jacob spotted Special Agent Morgan Young immediately. At five eleven, she towered over the other people in line. As usual, she had her phone pressed to her ear, but she paused the call to place her order with the barista.

Jacob claimed a stool by the window. He had a view of the courthouse steps where a steady flow of prosecutors, paralegals, and harried-looking assistants streamed back and forth.

"Thanks for meeting me."

Jacob turned around. Morgan wore a navy skirt and heels, which told him she planned to be in court later. And she was using her business voice, which told him to forget about kissing her hello.

"Hi." He nodded at the empty stool beside him. She cast a glance at the coffee counter before taking the seat. Morgan had straight dark hair, and she'd chopped it since the last time he'd seen her almost a year ago.

"You plan to order anything?" she asked.

"No. Tell me about Dana Smith."

She checked her phone before setting it facedown on the wooden counter. Then she glanced around the shop and leaned closer.

"I can't tell you much," she said in a low voice.

"Then why'd you call me?"

She tipped her head to the side. "Don't get pissy. I'm doing you a favor here."

"Is she an agent or a CI?" Jacob asked.

"Neither."

A barista called out a skinny latte, and Morgan stood up. "Just a sec."

He watched her get her coffee, and she used the opportunity to check her phone again before returning to the stool. She took a sip and wiped lipstick off the lid, and Jacob tamped down his impatience.

Morgan eased close again. "She's WITSEC."

Jacob stared at her.

"But you can't act like you know that," she said.

"Right."

"I mean it. *I'm* not even supposed to know."

He leaned closer. "You're telling me my homicide victim is in the federal witness protection program, but I can't act on that information? Don't you think this is relevant to my case?"

She rolled her eyes. "Of course, but—"

"So, the murder was a hit."

Her eyes turned fierce. "You absolutely can*not* jump to that conclusion. It could have been a mugging gone wrong, like they've been saying on the news."

"Okay, potentially a hit. Either way, it's an avenue we need to investigate."

"No, you don't."

He laughed.

"I'm serious, Jacob. This isn't your case anymore."

He tensed. "How's that?"

"I heard Mullins is taking over."

"Like hell."

"He is." She glanced at her watch. "In fact, I wouldn't be surprised if he's already contacted your commander."

Richard Mullins was in charge of the FBI's satellite office in Austin, which had been expanding recently, along with the city's population. Jacob had crossed paths with the guy before on a human trafficking case, and he wasn't a fan.

Morgan glanced around and leaned close again. "The official line is that Dana Smith had a connection to an ongoing federal case, and therefore we're taking over the investigation."

"What about my team? We've already racked up a ton of hours on this thing, and it's been all over the news. They expect us to just drop it?"

"That's exactly what they expect. And that's what's going to happen. You guys will release her name, since it's already out there anyway—"

"You said it was an alias."

"That's what I mean. Dana Smith. You guys will release that, and there will be a flurry of reporting, and then we'll quietly take over from there, and the story will die down."

"And we never make an arrest."

"We'll handle it."

Jacob shook his head. "Not happening."

She smiled slightly. "You're not getting it, Jacob. It isn't up to you. This has all been decided already. I'm just telling you, in confidence and as a personal favor, because I can't stand for you to be kept in the dark. I know how invested you are with your cases."

He watched her. Was that the real reason, or did she have some other agenda?

"Why?" he asked.

"Why what?"

"Why are you doing me this personal favor?"

She huffed out a breath. "Because. I respect you, all right? And even though things ended, we had six good months together."

Jacob watched her, trying to read her eyes. She sounded sincere, but he'd learned she didn't always tell him the full story, especially when it came to her job. Morgan was a workaholic. So was he. If either one of them hadn't been, their relationship might have stood a chance.

She flipped her phone over. "I've got to get back. I'm supposed to testify in fifteen minutes."

"Wait. I need more. What's her real name?"

"I don't know," Morgan said. "And even if I did, I wouldn't tell you."

"How'd you guys hear about this?"

"I don't know, but I'm guessing when someone ran those fingerprints, it triggered an alert with the Marshals Office."

"What case was she a witness in?"

"I don't know that, either. Everything I just told you, I picked up from an agent friend here in Austin, and he'd kill me if he knew we were having this conversation right now."

"Where was the trial? Do you know that at least?"

She stared at him.

"Come on, Morg. Give me something."

She checked her phone again and stood up. "I'm going to be late for court."

"Morgan."

"This is out of my hands, and it's out of yours, too. You can't control everything all the time, Jacob. You need to let it go."

He held her gaze and waited. He saw the ambivalence in her eyes, and he knew she was well aware he wasn't dropping anything. He was a detective. This was *his* case, in *his* city, and he wasn't about to shrug his shoulders and let the feds take over and hope maybe one day they came up with an arrest. A woman had been murdered, and someone needed to be held accountable.

Jacob needed to be put on the task force investigating this thing. He'd pitch it to his lieutenant. They were going to need local help in order to move quickly.

Morgan was still watching him, debating whether to tell him more. She sighed.

"I don't know for sure, but I heard something about Chicago."

Jacob nodded.

"I could be wrong about that, and I could definitely get in trouble for giving you any of this."

"Thank you."

She shot him a warning look as she grabbed her coffee. "Don't make me sorry I told you."

B AILEY OPENED THE oven to check her dinner, but it still wasn't ready.

"No hits," Nico said over the phone.

"Which platform?" she asked.

"All of them."

Bailey tossed the pizza box into the recycle bin. Her laptop computer was open on the bar, and she tapped the mouse to wake it up.

"What about Instagram?" she asked.

"I looked."

"Facebook?"

"I looked."

Thud.

Bailey glanced at the ceiling. Her upstairs neighbors had people over, and they were getting louder by the minute.

"How about Twitter?" she asked.

Nico said something, but she couldn't hear him over the ear-grating guitar chords.

"What's that?"

"I said, I checked everything, all platforms, even the ones no one uses anymore. Far as social media goes, it's like she doesn't exist."

Nico was the *Herald*'s tech reporter. He knew a lot more about social media platforms that Bailey did, and she'd hit him up for help when her original search came up dry. She trusted his expertise but found it hard to believe there was nothing whatsoever about Dana Anne Smith, given that she was a twenty-five-year-old living in a tech-savvy city. Bailey clicked into the file where she'd been keeping notes about the case. Earlier today she'd added a name to the Victim section. Beneath it she typed *social media—keep looking.*

"Hey, are you having a party?" Nico asked.

"It's my neighbor."

"Your neighbor's a Whitesnake fan?"

"He likes eighties hair bands."

The music grew louder, and she glared at the ceiling.

"I need to get *something*," she said, picking up her computer. She took it into the bedroom and closed the door, then sank onto the bed, where her cat was curled up beside her bathrobe. "Is she an undergrad? A grad student?

Is she local? I don't even know if this woman is from Austin. According to my police source, she doesn't have a Texas driver's license."

"Can't help you there."

"Max wants a profile, but so far I've got crap here."

"You sure she doesn't have a nickname?" Nico asked.

"I'm not sure of anything except what we got at the press conference, and it was totally bare bones. All I have is her name and age. I don't even have an address that would give me a place to knock on doors."

"Sorry."

"No, it's my fault, not yours," she said. "Thanks anyway for trying. I owe you a favor."

He snorted. "I'll add it to the list. See you tomorrow."

Bailey tossed her phone on the bed and sighed. She scratched Boba Fett's stomach, and he purred but didn't open his eyes.

"This is pathetic," she muttered as she scrolled through her notes. Tomorrow's article would give the victim's name and confirm that she'd been stabbed to death on Austin's most popular hike-and-bike trail. She had a canned "ongoing investigation" quote from the police department spokesperson, plus some local reaction. But in terms of a follow-up profile, she had zilch.

Boba Fett stood up and stretched. Then he rubbed his chin on the corner of her computer screen.

"You smell something burning, Boba? *Crap!*"

Bailey leaped up and raced into the kitchen. She snatched a dish towel off the counter and jerked open the oven.

"Damn it!"

Her pizza was burned, and a glob of cheese had turned into a smoking cinder on the bottom of the oven. The smoke alarm shrieked as Bailey grabbed a spatula. She scraped the pizza off the rack and dumped it into the sink, then grabbed a flimsy folding chair from the kitchen table. She dragged it under the smoke alarm, taking care not to collapse the damn thing as she climbed up. She poked the button on the alarm, but the shrieking continued. Stomping overhead let her know she was disturbing the neighbors.

Bailey jiggled the alarm but couldn't get it loose. Finally, she tore it from the ceiling and hopped down from the chair.

Stomp stomp stomp!

"Are you freaking kidding me?" she yelled at the ceiling.

They cranked the volume until her walls rattled.

Bailey stepped to the sink and examined the charred pizza. She hadn't been to the grocery all week, and her freezer was empty.

"Screw it." She dropped the smoke alarm onto the counter and strode into the bedroom. She pulled a tank top on over her sports bra and slipped her feet into sandals, then packed up her computer bag and locked the apartment. On the outdoor staircase she passed a college guy with a case of beer in each hand.

It was damp and muggy out, but at least the rain had stopped. Bailey passed a hamburger place with a line out the door and a busy convenience store with neon beer signs that glimmered off the wet sidewalk. The next two blocks were empty—just a long stretch of dark doorways. She held her computer bag close as she cast a wary look around.

Cause of death, sharp force trauma. Her source in the medical examiner's office had been brief and clinical, and Bailey's mind had filled in the gaps. Bailey hated knives, and the mere thought of coming face-to-face with a blade-wielding assailant made her queasy.

Her phone chimed, and she pulled it from the back

pocket of her jeans. Jacob. For some reason just seeing his name calmed her nerves a bit.

"Hi," she said.

"Are you still at your office?"

"I'm working from home today. Why?"

"We need to talk."

He paused. Bailey waited for him to suggest something, but he didn't. Maybe he didn't want to invite himself over. Too personal.

"Do you know Eli's?" she asked him.

"No."

"It's just west of campus, right by the Stop-N-Save." She wondered if she was making a mistake sending him to her favorite hangout.

"Pearl Street," he said.

"Yeah."

"Okay, I'll be there in twenty."

CHAPTER

NINE

JACOB FOUND HER in a candlelit booth in back with a laptop computer in front of her and a glass of red wine at her elbow. For a moment, he just looked at her. She wore a loose pink top over a black sports bra, and her hair was up in another messy bun. Her bare arms were tan and toned, and after seeing her at the lake that morning, he understood why.

She glanced up, putting an end to his gawking as he walked over.

"Any trouble parking?" she asked.

"Nope."

He slid into the booth, and a waitress stepped over.

"Something to drink?"

"Shiner Bock. Draft if you have it."

"You got it."

The waitress walked off, and he looked Bailey over. She had a coy expression on her face now.

"What?" he asked.

"You changed." She sipped her wine. "So, I take it you're off for the night?"

"Barring any emergencies."

She closed her laptop and zipped it into the bag on the seat beside her. She rested her arms on the table and looked at him, and her gray eyes looked smoky in the dim light.

"I never met a reporter who wrote in a pub," he said.

"I come here when my apartment's noisy."

"Why is your apartment noisy?"

"It's near campus." She rolled her eyes. "Not far from some of the frat houses. You know the red-brick walkup with the giant weeping willow in front?"

"Right down from Hud's Hamburgers?"

"That's the one."

"That place is retro."

The waitress stopped by to drop off his beer. When she was gone, Bailey lifted her wineglass.

"Salud," she said.

He clinked glasses with her and took a sip.

"If by retro you mean they haven't painted since 1985, you're right on."

He smiled. "Why do you live there?"

"I moved in my senior year. Then my roommate left, but by then I was kind of attached." She shrugged. "It's a good location. Walking distance to cheap food, shopping, parks."

So, she'd gone to UT. Jacob had been meaning to check her background, but the investigation had sucked up every minute of his time.

"Also, the landlord made an exception for my cat when he changed the pet policy, so that was nice of him."

Jacob smiled. "That's some loyalty you've got there."

"I'll move at some point, but right now it just seems like

a hassle." She tucked a dark curl behind her ear. "What about you? Where do you live?"

"South of the lake," he said. "I'm rehabbing a place in Travis Heights."

"You're doing it yourself?"

"When I have the time. Which isn't much lately."

"Sounds like a big project."

"Bigger than I thought when I bought it."

She sipped her wine and set the glass down, and the candlelight picked up the lip print on the rim. She was wearing pale pink lip gloss, and he was reminded of the pair of wineglasses in Dana Smith's apartment. Would the FBI's forensics team bag them up and test them? Jacob didn't know, and even if they did, he'd probably never see the results. As of two this afternoon, Richard Mullins was taking over his case, exactly as Morgan had predicted.

Jacob stifled a sigh and downed another sip of beer. He'd had a shitty afternoon, and the argument with his lieutenant hadn't helped. He'd flat-out rejected Jacob's request to be in on the task force and wouldn't even run the idea up the chain. His department was more than happy to be rid of a complicated case that could bring negative publicity. They'd handed it over without even putting up a fight.

But Jacob wasn't done trying yet. Not by a long shot.

"You look frustrated," Bailey said.

"Long day."

"Care to share? I'm a good listener."

His gaze locked on hers, and he felt tempted to tell her. He couldn't, obviously, because she was a reporter. But it would have been nice to vent, even though she was the last person he should open up with about any of this.

The waitress reappeared, this time with a pizza.

"Veggie supreme, extra jalapeños?"

"Thanks."

She set down the pizza, along with a pair of plates and a stack of napkins. Bailey slid one of the plates in front of Jacob.

He shook his head. "No, thanks."

"Oh, come on. I can't eat this by myself." She picked up a slice, dropping mushrooms and peppers as she stretched the cheese. She took a small bite, and he watched her mouth as she chewed.

"So, Bailey."

"Uh-oh." She dabbed her lip with a napkin. "That's your cop voice. Let me get out my notepad."

"This is off the record. I want to talk about the case."

She leaned back against the booth. "Here we go."

"What?"

"The old bait-and-switch. Ask me to meet you, and then tell me I can't use anything you say."

"You can use it," he said. "Just don't quote me. This is on background."

"Okay." She leaned her elbows on the table, and her gray eyes turned serious. "What's up?"

"You got the ID."

"We did," she said.

"I assume you're running it in a story tomorrow?"

"Given that the local networks have been running it since five o'clock, you assumed right. We also confirmed it was a stabbing."

"Where'd you confirm that?"

She smiled. "You're not asking me to reveal my sources, are you?"

He sighed. "What else do you have?"

"Some stuff about park safety. I heard your investigators are going over surveillance footage from the parking lots near the trail."

"You have a source in the department?"

She sipped her wine but didn't comment. Jacob wanted to know, and not just because he was curious about where she was getting her information. He wanted to find out if she'd heard about the FBI's involvement. Only a few people knew about it, but if the public became aware, it would be much harder to keep control of the story.

She dropped the crust on her plate and dusted her hands. "You know those aren't the only cameras, right?"

"Which ones?" he asked.

"The parking lot cams. There are also some at the nature center and the boathouse."

Jacob lifted an eyebrow.

"You didn't know?"

"I knew about the nature center. The boathouse is news."

"They installed one several months ago after some kayaks got stolen. It faces the boat racks, but I wouldn't be surprised if it captures footage of the trail as well."

"I'll look into it. Thanks."

She shot him a look. "No problem."

"Anything else coming out tomorrow?"

"That's more or less it," she said. "It's pretty thin, to be honest with you. I'm working on more for Wednesday."

"What happens Wednesday?"

"My editor wants a profile of the victim."

He frowned. "He wants you to profile Dana Smith?"

"Yeah. Why?"

"I wasn't aware."

"Well, what did you expect? A young woman was stabbed to death at the city's most popular park. People are riveted by this thing."

"What do you have on her?"

"Not a lot." She took another bite of pizza and chewed

thoughtfully. "She's not registered at any of the colleges, but I haven't been able to track down much. What do *you* know about her?"

"Not nearly enough."

"Is it looking like a random act of violence or—"

"We don't know yet."

It came out sharper than intended, and she gave him a suspicious look.

"Why do I get the impression there's something big you're not telling me?"

"I can't give details of an ongoing investigation. That's standard." He picked up the slice of pizza and chomped into it, and his mouth was instantly on fire from the jalapeños. He gulped his beer as Bailey watched him with a peeved look.

"Is there *any*thing you can tell me that might be useful?" she asked.

"So far, no eyewitnesses. I'm hoping you'll give me a heads-up if you come across anyone."

"I will."

"And no murder weapon."

"You don't really expect to find one with the lake right there, do you?"

"You never know."

Bailey sighed. "This is frustrating. I mean, who was this woman? And what was this murder about? All I've got are bits and pieces, but no big picture."

"Welcome to my world."

Jacob felt guilty now for holding so much back. Which didn't make sense. Of course he couldn't tell a reporter everything he knew. But he wasn't exactly helping her here. Everything he'd given her he was pretty sure she'd already known anyway.

He picked up his beer. "So, how'd you get into rowing?"

"Nice change of subject," she said dryly.

"I'm interested."

She smiled. "No, you're not."

"I am."

She sighed and pushed her plate away, as if she was willing to play along. "I grew up in Corpus. My dad loves boats and he taught me and my sisters how to sail when we were kids. We had this big catamaran that he kept at a marina on Laguna Madre." She smiled. "Actually, it wasn't that big, but to me it seemed huge. He named it the *Mary Alice* after my mom."

"Your family still there?"

"Not anymore. My parents retired to Padre Island." She twisted her wineglass. "My dad's got RA now. Rheumatoid arthritis. He doesn't sail anymore, but they still love being on the coast. Wouldn't want to be anywhere else."

He nodded. "I've spent some time on the island. Good fishing."

"So I hear." She shrugged. "I've never had the patience for fishing. The beaches are nice, though. I love the dunes."

He watched her in the candlelight. Her cheeks looked pink and she seemed more relaxed now that they weren't talking about work. He wished—again—that he'd met her under different circumstances. He could be on a date with her right now instead of sitting here trying to manipulate her into revealing her sources.

She smiled. "What's that look?"

"Nothing."

"You know, I used to go out with one of your colleagues."

"Oh, yeah?" He'd heard, but he hadn't expected her to bring it up.

"You know Skip Shepherd?"

"Not well."

Jacob knew him well enough to question her tastes in men. Shepherd was closer to Bailey's age—probably twenty-eight. He was smart and ambitious, but he was also an ass. Jacob couldn't see Bailey putting up with him.

Jacob's phone buzzed, and he pulled it from his pocket to check it. It was Kendra, so he let it go to voice mail. If it was urgent, she'd text him.

Bailey watched him put the phone away. "Anything important?"

"It can wait. What happened with Shepherd?" Jacob wasn't sure he wanted to know, but she'd brought it up, so maybe she wanted to tell him.

"You know, the usual. Compatibility issues."

"That covers a lot of ground."

"Yep."

Bailey gave him a long, steady look, and he wondered what she was thinking. Was she warning him off, in some way?

Jacob didn't need to be here, and they both knew it. All of his questions about the case could have been asked over the phone, and yet here he was, seeking her out after work again. He liked being around her, liked talking to her. He liked looking at her across the scarred wooden table. He watched her trace the stem of her wineglass with her finger, and his pulse thrummed in a way he'd almost forgotten about. The candlelight flickered in her eyes as she looked at him, and he knew it wasn't one-sided. She felt the attraction, too.

The waitress dropped off the check, breaking the mood, which was probably for the better.

"I should get home," Bailey said.

She let him split the bill with her, and they walked out into the humid night air. The sidewalks were wet again, and he realized it had rained while they'd been inside. Jacob's truck was parked right out front.

"You walk or drive?" he asked.

"I walked."

"Can I give you a ride?" He popped the locks.

"It's only four blocks."

"And you've got a computer with you."

She surprised him by not arguing. Instead, she reached for the passenger door and climbed into his truck. He closed the door for her and went around the front. As he slid behind the wheel, she was looking around with blatant curiosity.

"Pretty clean for a cop."

He started the engine and pulled out. "What'd you expect?"

"Oh, I don't know. All the stereotypes. Fast-food wrappers. Half-eaten doughnuts." She picked up the APD hang tag from the cup holder. "Damn, I'd kill for one of these things. You know how many tickets I rack up?"

He drove the short distance to her building, and an SUV was leaving just as he pulled up.

"Well, *that* never happens," she said.

Jacob pulled into the space and parked, then turned to look at her. She held his gaze, and the air between them felt charged suddenly. Every time she looked at him with those cool gray eyes, Jacob's pulse kicked up a notch.

She turned and glanced out the window. The door to one of the third-floor apartments stood open, and someone's party had spilled onto the breezeway.

She sighed. "My lovely neighbors."

"Want me to walk you up?"

"No."

It was a firm *no*, as if he'd been angling for an invitation inside.

Maybe he had.

Her eyes locked with his, and the silence stretched out. "I'm glad you called," she said.

"Me too."

Her gaze dropped to his mouth, and he felt a surge of lust. Who was he kidding? He wanted her to invite him in. He wanted to kiss her right now and find out how she tasted. He'd been thinking about it for days.

She leaned in and kissed him, shocking the hell out of him. Her mouth was warm and soft, and she rested her fingers on the side of his neck. Jacob slid his arms around her and pulled her closer.

He coaxed her mouth open, and she tangled her tongue with his as he leaned over the console and slid his hands over her hips. He wanted her in his lap. She seemed to want that, too, and she eased closer, hitching herself onto the console as she combed her fingers into his hair, and her nails bit into his scalp. She tasted amazing. Her mouth was hot and eager, and he wanted more. He slid his hand up to cup her breast through her shirt, and she arched against his palm. Her soft moan sent another shot of lust through him, and he pulled her even closer.

Jacob's phone buzzed, and she jerked back. Her cheeks were flushed, and she looked as surprised as he felt. She slid back into her seat.

The phone buzzed again, and he bit back a curse as he took it from his pocket. "Sorry."

"Better get that." She reached for the door handle.

"Wait."

"No, it's fine. I should go." She smiled and pushed open the door. "Good night, Jacob."

CHAPTER

TEN

KNEW IT."

Jacob glanced up from his work to see Kendra standing in the doorway.

"What?"

"You're hiding out down here." She stepped into the windowless room known as Cold Storage. Metal filing cabinets packed with cold case files lined the walls, leaving barely enough room for a desk and chair.

Kendra pulled the door shut behind her. She had a roll of evidence tape in her hand and a folder tucked under her arm.

"You're still working the Dana Smith case, aren't you?" she demanded.

Jacob looked up from his computer. "Why do you ask?"

"Because I haven't seen you all morning."

"Yes, I'm still working it."

"Good. Me too." She dropped the folder on the desk, along with the tape roll.

"What's in the file?" he asked.

"Copies of the police reports. I made them yesterday before Mullins carted everything off. And my notes from the Camden interview." She glanced behind her, probably for a chair.

"Behind the cabinet by the door," he said.

She pulled a metal folding chair from behind the cabinet and sat down across the desk from him.

"Anything from Luis on the cell phone?" she asked.

"Not yet."

"Okay, so where are we? Show me what you're working on."

He just looked at her.

"Come on, Jacob. I want in."

"Don't come crying to me when Schneider busts your ass down to patrol."

"What about *your* ass?"

"I've been a detective longer than you."

"Whatever. Tell me what you've got."

"I'm working on who wanted Dana Smith dead."

Kendra scooted closer. "Whoever she flipped on when she turned state's evidence."

"That's assuming it was a hit."

"You're not assuming that?"

"I'm strongly leaning that way, but it could have been random. Except . . ." He shook his head.

"Except what?"

"The knife thing," Jacob said. "I keep thinking about what Nielsen said, that he hadn't seen a wound like that since Afghanistan."

"Stabbed from behind, straight through the heart?"

"Right. So, say it's a professional hit. Maybe the perp has some kind of military training. Maybe black ops."

"How do you jump to that?"

"Those guys are trained to locate bad guys and take them out," he said. "Some of them come home, have problems with reentry. Maybe sell their skills on the black market. They're trained to get in and get out without leaving a trail, and that fits with our crime scene."

"Okay. So . . . let's work backward. Let's figure out who contracted it. He's the one ultimately responsible anyway."

Jacob shook his head. "I want the doer."

"Same for me. Let's get both."

"We need more on the victim," Jacob said. "What's her employer say? Did Dana give any hints about where she's from originally? I heard it might be Chicago, but that isn't confirmed."

Kendra's eyebrows arched. "You *heard*? Is that from Special Agent Sexytimes?"

Jacob didn't say anything, and Kendra shook her head.

"Hey, as long as Morgan's talking to you, maybe she can tell us what all this is about, save us a lot of trouble."

"She's out of it."

Kendra rolled her eyes. "Perfect. So, we're working in the dark here, while the feds keep everything under wraps."

Kendra had never been a fan of his relationship with Morgan, and Jacob wasn't sure why. But whatever the reason, he couldn't focus on it now.

"How did Celeste Camden hire Dana? Let's start there," he said.

Kendra flipped the file open. "She said she found her through a message board at the university."

"She got her nanny from a message board? How did she vet her?"

"She calls her an 'au pair.'" Another eye roll. "And the vetting was pretty weak. Evidently, Dana offered a reference from someone she'd done some babysitting for, and Camden called her and got a big thumbs-up."

"You think it was a phony reference?"

She shrugged. "Could have been a friend of Dana's. Who knows? Anyway, she hired her eight months ago and said Dana was great with her kid. She doesn't know anything about her friends or family." She flipped through the notes. "Also, she was always punctual and had nice handwriting."

"Nice *handwriting*?"

"That's what she said."

"What about money? Camden do any withholding on her?"

Kendra lifted an eyebrow. "That's where she got a little squirrelly. They had a cash arrangement."

"Did she have anything on file? A driver's license or social security card?"

"No. Dana told her she didn't drive and that she'd lost her social security card. Camden said she didn't want to make her jump through hoops to get a new one, so she agreed to pay her in cash."

"No taxes. Win-win for everyone."

"That's what it sounds like." Kendra blew out a sigh. "So, what's next?"

"We need Dana's real name, and we need to figure out what case she was involved with, possibly in Chicago, possibly not. Once we know who might have wanted revenge on her for testifying, we can see where that network leads."

"You're thinking organized crime?" Kendra asked.

"Could be a lot of things. Maybe she worked somewhere, and her boss was running drugs or embezzling money. Or maybe she was having an affair with a guy and stumbled across some illegal shit he was into."

Kendra's brow furrowed. "Whatever it is, is probably the feds' jurisdiction."

"She was murdered in ours."

Kendra watched him for a long moment. "What about that reporter?"

He bristled. "What reporter?"

"Bailey Rhoads from the *Herald*. I saw you talking to her at the lake yesterday."

"What about her?"

"Well, did you tell her the FBI's taking over?"

"No."

"Be careful talking to her. If the media sink their teeth into this story, it's going to be much harder to investigate anything on the down-low."

He thought of Bailey and the determined look in her eyes. She'd already sunk her teeth into the story.

He should have known Kendra would call him out for talking to Bailey. They were trying to keep their involvement with this case quiet, and the last thing they needed was for people to notice him talking to a reporter covering the story and assume he was not only still working the case but leaking to the media.

Kendra was watching him, looking worried. She had reservations about what they were doing. She would never admit it, but Jacob knew her too well.

"You don't have to do this with me, you know," he told her.

"You're saying you'd rather work alone?"

He would, and not only because he didn't want her to get in trouble.

"If Schneider finds out, there will be blowback," he said. "If the feds find out, there will be blowback. And if we solve the case and want to make an arrest, there will be blowback."

She folded her arms and looked at him. "So why are you doing this?"

"I could ask you the same question."

"Richard Mullins is a dick," she said. "I've never liked the guy."

Jacob felt the same.

"The minute he opened his mouth yesterday, I could tell that for him this is all about damage control." She shook her head. "Someone whacked an FBI source, and they don't want people to know, so he's been told to find a way to sweep everything under the rug. You know the Marshals claim that they've *never* lost anyone in the WITSEC program? At least no one who"—she did air quotes with her fingers—" 'followed the rules of the program.' It's a point of pride for them."

"So, you're thinking what?"

"I don't know." She shrugged. "Maybe one reason the feds were so eager to wrestle this thing away from us is they want to prove the victim screwed up somehow, and this whole thing is *her* fault. Then they can save face and maintain their bragging rights."

"That was my read, too," Jacob said. "Getting an arrest is secondary."

"And getting justice for this victim is even lower on his list, if it's on there at all."

Jacob nodded. "We're on the same page. But we have to work fast and under the radar. As soon as we catch another homicide case, it's going to be much harder to dedicate time to this thing, and the trail is growing colder by the minute."

"So, we'll work it fast and quiet with no resources to back us up," Kendra said. "Easy peasy."

"Say the word if you want out."

"Forget it. I'm in."

B AILEY RUSHED ACROSS Guadalupe Street as the light flashed red. A glance at the clock tower told her she was late for her interview. She'd overslept this morning and been late to the staff meeting, which had gone by in a blur. Everything felt off-kilter today, and she couldn't stop thinking about that kiss with Jacob in his truck.

She needed to focus. She needed to nail this interview and get back to the newsroom with the ingredients for a kick-ass story. Max had let her devote four full days to this thing to the exclusion of everything else, and he wanted results.

Bailey sliced through throngs of summer school students and took the concrete steps two at a time when she reached the student union. She hurried across the grassy mall, passing the flagpole where a woman had huddled in terror one hot August day as a sniper at the top of the tower aimed a hunting rifle at students, picking them off one by one. Bailey's grandmother had been on campus at the time, strolling down Guadalupe with her girlfriends when the first shots rang out and people started dropping. Dede had taken shelter in a shop and ripped up dresses to bandage the wounded as they waited for ambulances that couldn't get through the barrage of bullets. The gunman killed sixteen people before being taken out by a pair of Austin cops, and to this day—more than fifty years later—Dede got a tremor in her voice whenever she talked about it.

The story had made an impression on Bailey. It had prompted her to comb through newspaper clippings and yellowed *Life* magazines and ultimately sparked her interest in journalism.

She didn't look at the clock tower now as she rushed across the mall to the gnarled oak tree in front of Mezes Hall. A woman with long auburn hair and a loose cotton dress stood beside a stroller. She waved at Bailey.

"Dr. Camden?"

"Call me Celeste."

They shook hands, and Bailey smiled at the chubby-cheeked girl in the stroller. She clutched an Elmo sippy cup in her hands and regarded Bailey with big brown eyes.

"This is Jillian. She just turned two." Her mom beamed down at her, but her look turned wary as she glanced around. "The sitter's meeting us here before my 1:10 class, so I'm afraid I don't have much time."

"Thanks for meeting me. I'm so sorry for your loss."

Tears welled in her eyes, and she looked down at Jillian. "I almost didn't come. It's been so awful, but . . ."

She swiped her cheeks, and Bailey waited for her to compose herself.

"She was such a sweet person. I can't believe this happened."

A pair of students vacated a bench and Bailey stepped over to claim it. She set down her messenger bag, and Celeste pushed the stroller over. She set her big leather tote bag on the bench but didn't sit.

"I understand you called the police on Monday morning," Bailey said. "Do you remember what time?" Bailey had this information already, but she'd found it was better to start with easy questions.

Celeste took a deep breath and nodded. "I was getting ready for work. The TV was on in the kitchen, and Jill was eating breakfast. I was annoyed because Dana was late, and I needed to be in early. I'd called several times on Sunday to let Dana know, but she hadn't returned my calls, and that's very unlike her. Then I saw the pictures on the news."

"You recognized the personal items?"

"Yes, but I knew before that. I was pouring my coffee and they were talking about a woman found near the jogging trail, and I just *knew*. Dana was down there every single morning. She was obsessive about her exercise." Celeste rolled the stroller back and forth. "I saw the details in the paper this morning." She glanced at Jillian, and Bailey could tell she didn't want to elaborate about the murder. "It's just awful."

The tears welled again, and Bailey scooted over on the bench. "Do you want to sit down?"

She sat. Jillian squirmed against her straps, and Celeste unbuckled her. She scrambled out, dropping her sippy cup as she climbed onto her mother's lap and rested her head on her shoulder.

"I know, love. It's naptime." Celeste kissed her forehead.

Bailey picked up the cup and put it in the stroller. She felt uneasy talking about Dana in front of Jillian, but Celeste didn't seem to mind.

"As I mentioned in my email, I'm working on a profile." Bailey took a notepad from her messenger bag and cast a glance at Jillian. "I was hoping to get some background info? I haven't been able to find anything on social media."

"I doubt you will. She's not a social media person. Actually, that was one reason I hired her. She didn't even have a cell phone when I met her, if you can believe that. She doesn't like technology. *Didn't*, I should say."

"Mommy, I want Flopsy."

"Flopsy's at home, love. Remember? We forgot her on the sofa."

"I want to go home."

"Rosa's coming, and then you can go snuggle with Flopsy and take a nap, okay?"

Jillian plugged her thumb into her mouth and looked at Bailey.

"Oh, here she is. Thank goodness." Celeste stood and shifted Jillian to her hip as a young woman strode up the path. She had long dark hair pulled back in a ponytail, and she waved excitedly as she neared them.

"Hey, *chiquita*!" She gave Jillian a kiss on the cheek. "I

get to see *you* today!" Then she looked at Celeste. "Sorry I'm late. I had to park by the library."

"It's fine."

Rosa looked at Jillian. "You want to ride in the stroller, or walk and help me push?"

"Push!"

"She had a PBJ at eleven." Celeste set Jillian down. "There're strawberries in the fridge for snack. I should be home by six."

"I got it." Rosa held her hand out, and Jillian took it.

Celeste leaned over and planted a kiss on the top of her daughter's head. "Be good for Rosa, sweetie."

Bailey watched them walk away and felt a pang of sympathy. She shifted her attention to Celeste, who was weeping openly now that her daughter wasn't there to see her.

"Sorry." She pulled a crumpled tissue from her tote bag. "I'm a mess right now."

"I understand."

She shook her head. "It's horrible. *Horrible*. I still can't get my mind around it. Stabbed? I can't even imagine. Makes me never want to leave the house." She blew her nose and gave Bailey a watery look. "Sorry."

"Take your time."

Celeste took a deep breath and blew it out. Then she tucked a lock of hair behind her ear.

"Okay, so you're doing a profile."

"I'd like to know more about what Dana was like. What was her background? What were her interests? Did she have any hobbies?"

"Well, she didn't go out much. Which was good for *me* because I could call her up at a moment's notice. She had a few girlfriends here and there, but I never met them."

"She mentioned them to you? Do you happen to know their names?"

"No."

"What about a boyfriend?"

She shook her head. "Not that I ever knew about. And I was glad, to tell you the truth. I told her in the interview, I didn't want any men around Jillian, and she said that wouldn't be a problem. Of course, she could have been seeing someone and never said anything."

"How did you meet her?" Bailey asked.

"I got her name from a bulletin board in the anthropology building. You probably think that's strange, looking for a nanny that way, but most people who post there are grad students or spouses of people who work here. Anyway, it all worked out. I interviewed her, and it was a great fit."

"You mentioned she didn't have a phone at first? But then later she did?"

"I gave her one the first week. She couldn't afford a plan, but I had to be able to get hold of her, so I got her a cheap one. She didn't use it much, though. It was one of the reasons I hired her. Some of my colleagues have au pairs, and all they do is park the kids in front of a screen and sit on their phones all day. It's really atrocious."

"What about interests? Hobbies? I'm trying to get a picture."

She smiled. "Well, she was very pretty. I'm surprised she didn't have a guy in her life. And she was creative and energetic. Jillian adored her. She was very engaging."

"What about education?"

She shook her head. "No college. She said her parents couldn't afford it."

"And are they here in town?" Bailey already knew they weren't, but she wanted to see what Celeste said about it.

"She didn't talk about her family much. I got the impression they were estranged."

"Do you know where they live?"

"I don't know. St. Louis, maybe? She said something once when we were talking about baseball."

"Baseball?"

"She was over on a Saturday, and she wanted to watch a game. I remember, it was the Cardinals playing at Wrigley Field." She gave a wobbly smile. "My late husband was a Cubs fan."

"Okay, so . . . do you know what brought Dana to Austin?"

"No. But she seemed to love it here." She looked around at the sidewalks streaming with people. "What's not to love, right? It's sunny all the time. Friendly. It used to be safe, too, but not anymore. Just last week one of our TAs was robbed at a gas station. She was standing right there gassing up her car, and boom, someone reached right into her car and grabbed her purse off the seat. She's lucky she wasn't shot."

Bailey had written a brief on the incident, but she didn't say anything.

"The whole thing was caught on video, but has anyone made an arrest? No. The police are too busy handing out traffic tickets." She looked at Bailey. "Do I sound bitter? Maybe I am."

"The city's changed a lot."

She took a deep breath. "But back to Dana. She loved crafts. She and Jillian painted all the time together. You should see our fridge—it's covered with artwork. Oh, and she worked at the art museum down on the lake. Villa Paloma."

Bailey's ears perked up. "When did she work there?"

"Tuesdays and Thursdays after school. Come to think of it, they'd be a good source for you. She was friends with some of the other teachers there."

"She taught art lessons?"

"That's right. They have an after-school program for underprivileged kids. And they do camps in the summer, too. She was over there a lot."

A heavy gong sounded, and Celeste looked over her shoulder at the clock tower.

"My class starts soon. I wish I had more time." She dug a business card from her tote bag and handed it over. "Feel free to email me, if you have any more questions. Oh, and you said you needed a picture. I found this." She handed over a small snapshot of Dana on a grassy lawn with a white cat in her lap. She had thick, wavy brown hair and a wide smile. Her arm was draped around someone outside the shot.

"That was taken in our backyard. Jill was in it, too, but I cropped her out, obviously."

"Thank you. I can get this back to you."

"Keep it. It's a copy."

She stood up and shouldered her leather bag. "Like I said, I almost didn't come today. But then I read your piece about trail safety, and I appreciate what you're trying to do. Women need to be aware." She shook her head. "I told Dana over and over that she should jog later in the day when there're more people around, but she didn't listen." She gazed out at the grassy lawn. "When I moved here ten years ago, it felt like such a small town. Now it's like Houston or Dallas." She looked at Bailey. "But I guess that's everywhere, isn't it? No place is safe."

CHAPTER

ELEVEN

JACOB SLID INTO a no-parking zone and hooked his APD hang tag on the mirror.

I'd kill for one of these things.

He thought of Bailey in his truck last night. He'd been thinking about her all day—which was nothing new, really. He'd been thinking about her since he first met her. But today was worse, and memories of her soft mouth kept running through his mind.

Jacob couldn't get involved with her. Full stop.

It would be beyond stupid to get involved with a reporter covering one of his cases. He'd never be able to trust that she was with him for him, and not for the information he could give her.

The thing was, she didn't seem like a user. She seemed genuine. Yes, she was persistent about her job, but who could fault her for that? If she weren't, she wouldn't have the job in the first place. Jacob was good at judging people, and Bailey seemed trustworthy.

Still, there was no getting around the fact that she was a reporter. And if he couldn't get things back on a professional footing, he was going to have to stop seeing her altogether.

The thought depressed him way more than it should have.

Jacob slid from his truck and walked half a block to Red Pagoda, which occupied a narrow storefront between a dry cleaner's and a day spa. Parked in front of the restaurant was a motorcycle with a small red cooler mounted on the back.

Jacob opened the door and was hit with the smell of egg rolls. All six tables in the restaurant were empty. A row of brown take-out bags lined the top of the counter. Jacob approached the smiling man behind the register. Short black hair. Fifties. Jacob introduced himself, and the man's smile disappeared. Jacob took out a photo of Dana Smith that her employer had given Kendra before the FBI swooped in and took over the investigation.

"This woman placed an order here last week," Jacob said. "Do you happen to remember her?"

"No."

"Probably Thursday or Friday? Take a look."

He glanced down at the photo for maybe a nanosecond. "No."

"Are you sure?" He held out the picture, hoping he'd look again, but the man shook his head.

"We get lots of orders. Hundred a day."

The man's clipped tone told Jacob he had zero interest in talking to a cop. Jacob glanced around the restaurant for a security camera, but he didn't see one, so he thanked the clerk for his time and left.

Jacob waited in front of the dry cleaner's, and it didn't take long for a teenager in a helmet to exit the restaurant with a paper bag in each hand. He loaded the bags into the cooler on the back of the motorcycle.

Jacob approached him and flashed his creds. The kid looked wary but curious.

"This woman placed an order here sometime last week." He held out Dana's picture. "Maybe a delivery?"

The kid cast a look over his shoulder at the restaurant before taking the picture. "The apartment on the corner. Lakeview Court." He handed back the photo.

"You remember the delivery?"

"Yeah, it was Thursday night. It was raining, and she gave me a good tip."

Jacob studied the kid's face, gauging his credibility.

"Did you deliver to her door, or did she meet you in the lobby?" Jacob asked.

"She buzzed me up."

"Do you remember if she was alone or if there was anyone else in the apartment?"

"No idea, man."

"How did she pay?"

"Cash."

"Was she a regular customer, do you know?"

"I don't know. Maybe once every few weeks?"

"And did you ever see anyone in her apartment?"

He cast another glance at the restaurant before moving for the bike. "I don't think so." He threw his leg over the seat. "She was nice, though. Good tipper."

The kid fired up the bike, and Jacob stepped back to let him leave. Surveying the block again, he noted the day spa.

REJUVENATIVE TREATMENTS. FACIALS, BOTOX, TATTOO REMOVAL.

Jacob walked over and opened the door. Cold air wafted out as he stepped inside and let his eyes adjust to the dimness. The air smelled like tropical flowers. He approached the counter, where a white candle burned beside a bowl of

smooth gray stones with words etched on them. *RELAX.*
LOVE. POSITIVITY.

A woman stepped through a gray curtain. "May I help
you?" she asked with a smile.

"I hope so."

She wore a purple sports top and black yoga pants. Her
face was perfectly smooth, but Jacob put her age at fifty.

"You guys do tattoo removal?" he asked.

"That's right."

He flashed his creds, and her smile faded.

"I'm investigating a case, and I wanted to see if this
woman might have been a customer." He held out the picture of Dana.

The woman took it. She had a pair of reading glasses
hooked into her cleavage and she put them on. "I remember
her." She handed the picture back. "What about her?"

"Was she here getting a tattoo removed or—"

"Our client records are confidential."

"I understand. But this is a homicide investigation."

Her mouth dropped open. "She—"

"She's the victim."

The woman glanced at the picture again and stepped
over to the computer on the counter. "What's her name?"

"Dana Smith."

She tapped at her keyboard, and Jacob looked around
the waiting room. Two black leather chairs sat in the far
corner beside a small table where another perfumed candle burned. Working in this place would give him a headache.

"Looks like she came in back in February," the woman
said.

"Just one time?"

"No, then again in April and June. She bought a package. Four sessions, and we schedule them seven to eight weeks apart to allow for healing. She has one left. *Had* one left." The woman shuddered and glanced up.

"And can you tell me what she was getting removed?" Jacob asked.

"What, you mean her tattoo?"

"That's correct." He was hoping for Greek letters, or a name, or a maybe a significant date that would give him a lead on Dana Smith's previous identity.

The woman watched Jacob silently. Her forehead was smooth, but her eyes seemed to frown. "Well, we take before and after photos." She glanced over her shoulder at the curtain before pivoting the screen to face him.

"Mind?" Jacob walked around the counter to get a better look at the computer, and the woman stepped aside.

"That was taken February ninth before her first session."

The other photo Jacob had seen of Dana's ankle had been taken on an autopsy table, and her skin looked gray and lifeless. This picture showed Dana's ankle against a lavender sheet on what looked like a massage table. Her skin tone was warm and healthy, and she had her toes pointed as someone snapped the shot.

The tattoo depicted was a small bird on a branch. Beneath it were three characters in black calligraphy that appeared to be Chinese.

"Does that help, Detective?"

He glanced up. "I'm going to need a screen shot."

B AILEY KEPT HER eyes peeled for Jacob as she made the rounds at the police station. But she didn't see him. She didn't see his partner, either, so maybe they were out on a case together. Bailey tried to convince herself that she felt relieved as she crossed the busy lobby. If she *had* bumped into him, she wasn't sure what she would have said.

I really don't make a habit of jumping my sources, but the way you were looking at me . . .

"Bailey."

She turned around. Jacob strode across the lobby toward her. He had his sleeves rolled up and a file in his hand, and the intent look on his face put a flutter in her stomach.

He stopped and gazed down at her.

"Hi," she said, trying for cheerful.

"Everything okay?"

"Yeah. Just, you know, making the rounds."

He frowned slightly, and she realized he didn't know her routines.

"I swing by here every afternoon," she said. "Check with sources, see what's come in."

He glanced down at the notepad in her hand. "Get anything interesting?"

"Nothing much. Just a purse snatching and another car theft near campus." She watched him, searching his eyes. "How's the Dana Smith case going?"

Something flickered across his face. Then it was gone.

"Anything new?" she asked.

"Not really."

"So . . . is that a yes or a no?"

"Neither. Are you headed out now?"

"Yeah."

"I'll walk you."

He stepped over to push open the door and politely held it for her, as if that would distract her from the way he'd dodged her question.

She stepped into the heat and immediately began to sweat. He spotted her car parked along the street and started walking toward it, and she tucked her notebook into her purse.

She'd ask him again later. Maybe if she found him after hours or away from the station, she could get him to open up.

Bailey caught some curious looks from several cops she knew as she and Jacob walked to her car, which was in a reserved space.

"You're going to get a ticket," he said.

"I know." She popped the locks and pulled the door open, then turned to look at him.

He was much taller than she was, and she felt the inexplicable urge to go up on tiptoes and kiss him again, just to see if he'd look as shocked as he had last night. But she resisted this time. Probably the last thing he needed was to be seen kissing a reporter in front of the police station. Just being seen talking to her could raise a few eyebrows.

He rested his hand on the top of her door and looked down at her. A worry line appeared between his brows, and she got the feeling he wanted to tell her something.

"What?" she asked.

He shook his head.

"There's something new with the Dana Smith case, isn't there? What happened?"

"Who says something happened?"

"Did you make an arrest?"

"No."

"Do you have a suspect?"

"No."

Her phone chimed and she pulled it from her pocket.

"I have to grab this."

"I'll talk to you later," he said, looking relieved as he stepped away.

"When later?"

"I'll call you."

* * *

VILLA PALOMA PERCHED on a bluff overlooking Lake Austin. The mansion had once been the home of a wealthy philanthropist but now housed an extensive art collection and a library that included rare books. Several outbuildings around the property had been renovated and turned into an art school.

Bailey passed through the wrought-iron gate and parked in a lot beside a van with rainbow-colored handprints painted on the side. She got out of her car and looked around. After tucking a fresh notebook into the back pocket of her jeans, she walked into a wide courtyard filled with sculptures on concrete pedestals. A line of kids in matching yellow T-shirts tromped through the space, led by a pair of counselors with lanyards around their necks.

Bailey stepped out of the traffic flow and watched the counselors load the kids into the van. Then she turned to check out the courtyard. At the center was a large concrete fountain with a statue of a toga-clad woman holding a dove in her upstretched hand. At the far end of the courtyard was a white stucco mansion with a red-tile roof. Bailey followed signs to a row of low stucco buildings that housed the art school.

The first door was propped open with a green ceramic frog. Inside were four long tables, each with a chunky ceramic mug filled with paintbrushes in the center. A rotating fan circulated the air in the room, making art paper flutter on one of the easels.

"May I help you?"

Bailey turned to see a smiling young woman in a black apron. She had long blond braids and looked to be in her twenties.

"I'm Bailey Rhoads with the *Herald*." She smiled and

held up her press pass. "Do you work here at the art school?"

Her smile disappeared. "You're here about Dana."

"That's right. I'm writing a profile on her."

The woman bit her lip. She had a lanyard with an ID badge around her neck, and Bailey stepped closer.

"I'm Tish Brown." She reached out a hand but seemed to change her mind because her fingers were smeared with paint. She tucked her hand in her pocket. "I teach advanced painting and life drawing."

"And did you work with Dana?"

"Not a lot." She blew out a sigh. "She mostly worked with our Rainbow Kids."

Bailey took out her notepad, and Tish immediately looked uneasy.

"Rainbow Kids?"

"Our after-school program for underprivileged youth. In the summer, it's a day camp."

"I see." Bailey jotted it down. "And you didn't teach the program?"

"My classes are all adults, so Dana and I didn't overlap. I actually didn't know her very well at all. Still, it's . . ." She seemed to search for a word. "Tragic. Beyond tragic, really. I can't quite believe what happened to her. You're not quoting me, are you?"

"This is just background. Do you know who might have known Dana better? Or do you happen to know who hired her?"

"Oh, she was a volunteer."

"She was?"

"Yeah, there are only three of us on faculty. You could try the volunteer coordinator. Or maybe talk to Alex, our librarian. They were friends. Dana spent a lot of time in there. It's through the courtyard in the main house. Go under the curved staircase and hang a left."

Bailey followed her directions, but the front door was locked. She found a cobblestone path shaded by vibrant pink crepe myrtle trees and followed it around to a side courtyard. Branches rustled, and a giant blue bird swooshed down onto a patio table.

Bailey jumped back. The peacock was huge. It turned, sweeping its tail feathers over the table. It stared at Bailey for a long moment and then slowly fanned its shimmery plumage. Bailey held her breath, awestruck. Suddenly, the bird hopped down onto the ground.

"Vile creatures."

She turned to see a bald man with an armload of books. She looked back at the peacock as he flounced away, dragging his feathers over the cobblestones.

"I was just thinking how beautiful they are," Bailey said.

"Looks can be deceiving. They defecate all over everything and scream loud enough to wake the dead." The man's gaze dropped to the notebook in her hand. "Are you a reporter?"

"I'm with the *Herald* and I'm—"

"I know why you're here. Come in."

She followed him to a French door, where he balanced the books in one arm as he entered a passcode. The temperature in the building was a good thirty degrees cooler than it was outside. He led her down a hallway with arched windows and into a spacious library with bookshelves that had to be twelve feet tall.

"Wow," Bailey said, looking around.

She followed him past a row of computers, where several people were spread out with backpacks and papers.

Stopping at a large mahogany desk, the man set down his armload of books.

"I'm Alex Mendoza." He offered her a handshake.

"Bailey Rhoads."

The man was younger than she'd first thought, now that she saw him up close. He had a shaved head and thick dark eyebrows. Like Tish, he wore a lanyard around his neck with a photo ID on it. Bailey read the title beneath his name.

"You're a research librarian?"

"I don't know about the 'research' part. But I'm in charge of the books." He glanced around the room. "More than ten thousand volumes, many of them first editions." He nodded at the row of workstations. "We get grad students in here who use our collection."

Bailey took out her pen. "So, I understand you were friends with Dana?"

He tipped his head to the side. "Friends?"

"You weren't?"

"I didn't know her very well, really. She was quite an introvert."

Bailey sighed. She'd been all over town today, and she was striking out. Meanwhile, her profile was due in a few hours.

"She *did* spend a lot of time here." He gazed out at the room. "She liked books. And she loved our Rossetti."

"Rossetti?"

"The painting by the alcove there. Dana called it 'the Sunshine Girl.'"

Beside a windowed alcove was a large painting in an ornate gold frame. Bailey stepped closer. The picture showed a woman in a billowing yellow dress reclining on a sofa. Her cascade of blond curls spilled over her shoulders and swirled around her arms.

"Are you familiar with Rossetti?"

Bailey turned around, and Alex was standing closer now.

"No. But that looks like nineteenth century."

He nodded. "He was the star of the Pre-Raphaelite movement in England. It's really an exceptional piece. Collectors contact us all the time, wanting to acquire it, but we'd never part with it."

Bailey stepped closer to the painting. The woman had delicate features and smiled coquettishly, as though trying to tempt someone to join her on the sofa.

"She looked like her."

Bailey turned to Alex. "Who? Dana?"

"Except for the blond." He lifted an eyebrow. "Dana's hair was much darker, you know."

She studied the picture again. Then she turned to face Alex, determined to get something she could use before she had to rush back to the newsroom.

"What was Dana like?" she asked. "Besides introverted?"

He seemed to think about it. "Smart, I would say. She asked good questions."

"About what?"

"Whatever." He gave a shrug, and Bailey felt a surge of impatience.

"Do you know anything about her family? Her background? Where she went to school?"

"No, no, and no." He gave a slight smile. "Sorry. Like I said, she wasn't very talkative."

"Do you know where she was from?"

He looked up at the painting and sighed. "Everywhere and nowhere."

"Excuse me?"

He glanced at Bailey. "I asked her once, and that's what she said. 'I'm from everywhere and nowhere.' I have no idea where she was from originally, but it wasn't here."

"How do you know?"

"She complained about the weather all the time. Didn't understand how anyone could take the heat." He shrugged. "The classrooms aren't air-conditioned, so it *does* get pretty oppressive. But nothing like the heat wave we had a few years ago."

Bailey stifled a sigh. She'd been out all afternoon, and she hadn't gleaned anything substantive for her article. She looked at the Rossetti again.

"Wish I could help more, but I really didn't know her outside of the museum," Alex said. "Did you check her Instagram account?"

"I don't think she had one. I understand she didn't like computers."

"Who told you that?"

"Her employer."

He laughed. "Dana loved computers. She was in here all the time using ours." He nodded at the row of workstations by the door. "She parked herself in that chair every Tuesday and Thursday from after class until closing."

CHAPTER

TWELVE

THE POLICE DEPARTMENT'S technology lab occupied a remote corner of an underground warren of offices that Jacob typically tried to avoid. But some of his favorite people worked down there, so every so often he had to make the trip.

"I was wondering when you'd turn up," Gabby said as he stepped into the lab. They kept the lights dim, and Gabby's face was a ghostly blue in the light of her computer screen. Jacob couldn't tell for sure, but it looked like her short brown hair was streaked pink today. It changed week to week.

"Where is everyone?" he asked, glancing around. Someone had a Muse concert playing at one of the workstations, but Gabby was the only person in sight.

She plucked out her earbuds as he walked over. "Brian took off for the night, and Luis is grabbing dinner." She nibbled on a red gummy worm and regarded him with a suspicious look. "Where have you been? I was expecting you hours ago."

Jacob sat on the edge of her desk and set down his case file. "I've been slammed."

"What's that?" She nodded at the photo clipped to the folder.

"The victim had this tattoo. I've been trying to find someone to translate the words."

She pulled the file closer and studied it. "Looks like Chinese. You should ask Luis. He speaks Mandarin."

"He does?"

"One of his hidden talents." She held out the bag of candy. "Want some?"

"Sure." He dug a worm from the bag and popped it into his mouth as he looked at her screen. "What're you working on?"

"The footage from the nature center camera. Camera two, to be precise."

"How many do they have?"

"Three." She sighed. "So far, nothing resembling our victim."

"Did you get the footage from the boathouse camera?"

"It's next on my list."

Gabby tapped her mouse to pause the video and swiveled to face him. "You know, some feebie called today and asked for copies of all this."

That was news to Jacob, but he wasn't surprised. "What'd you tell him?"

"What do you think? I gave him what he wanted. He made it sound like they were taking over the case."

"And yet you're still going through footage."

"Yup."

Gabby handled video evidence for the department's high-priority cases, which might include anything from hit-and-run accidents caught on film to sex abuse. She had an eye for detail and an uncanny ability to spot hidden clues in even the most mundane surveillance footage. Gabby's work had provided a key break in more cases than Jacob could count, and he never missed a chance to hit her up for help.

But this time, helping him could get her in trouble.

She crossed her arms. "Look, you asked me to comb through and look for our victim. That's what I'm doing. I figured if you wanted me to stop looking, you would have said so."

Jacob watched her, trying to read her expression.

"Do you *want* me to stop looking?"

"It's a sensitive case," he said.

"That's not what I asked."

"No."

"Then I plan to keep going," she said matter-of-factly. "If I find something useful, you'll be the first to know."

Luis walked into the room. "Hey, you're here. I just left you a message."

"I got it," Jacob told him. He stood up and gave Gabby a hard look. "Let me know if you get sidetracked." In other words, if another case fell into her lap and demanded her attention. "And keep me posted on that security footage."

She put her earbuds in and shooed him away. "Go. You're distracting me."

Jacob joined Luis at his cubicle, which was actually two cubicles combined into one. Luis had two desktop computers and a laptop, plus numerous power cords. One entire side of his workspace was dedicated to cell phones, and he had chargers of various shapes and sizes plugged into a power bar.

Jacob recognized the black cell phone he'd rescued from the muck behind Jay's Juice Bar.

"You won't believe what I got." Luis sank into his chair.

"What'd you get?"

"I got it *working*, for starters. You believe that shit? This thing was *dead*. I thought it was hopeless."

"So, you were able to turn it on?"

"Yes." He leaned back in his chair, lacing his hands behind his head as he smiled at Jacob. "*And* retrieve the call history."

This was why he loved working with Luis. When he set his mind to something, he was tenacious as hell.

"Tell me about the call history." Jacob pulled a chair from a neighboring cube and sat down.

"Well, it was weird." Luis frowned and leaned forward, hunching over the phone.

"Weird how?"

"Like, sporadic. I only found two outgoing calls."

"Two since when?"

"Since ever. Like I told you, this thing is a burner. She only ever made two calls on it, and nothing incoming."

"Nothing? Did you confirm the number I gave you?" Jacob had texted Luis with the number of Dana's phone, according to Celeste Camden.

"Yeah, that's the other thing. That number doesn't match."

"It's not her number?"

"Not on this phone it isn't." Luis slid the device across the counter. "This is a different number."

"What's the area code?"

"Nine three seven. But that doesn't necessarily tell you anything because these burners are sold in batches to stores like Walmart, Target, Best Buy. It could have come from anywhere."

"Can you track down the batch?"

"Maybe, but you're missing the point. She had two outgoing calls, and one of them was made Saturday."

"As in three days ago?"

"Yeah, that's what I'm saying. Saturday at 6:26 a.m.

Based on the timeline the ME gave us, that sounds like she called someone right around the time she was murdered."

Jacob stared down at the phone. This lead sounded too good to be true, and maybe it was. Luis slid a slip of paper in front of him. It had two ten-digit numbers scrawled across it.

"Top number is her phone," Luis said. "Bottom number is the one she called."

"What about the first phone call?"

"Both outgoing calls were to the same number."

"Interesting."

"Yeah, no kidding."

"Have you tried—"

"I called this number from another phone, but it's out of service. I'm still working on this, though, so I'll let you know when I have more." He nodded at the file folder in Jacob's hand. "What's that?"

"A picture of the victim's tattoo. I'm looking for someone who can translate the words." He handed him the folder.

"That's easy." He tapped each of the characters. "Love, strength, happiness."

"You sure?"

"Yep."

Jacob sighed. "I was thinking it might say a name. Or something about flight."

"Because of the robin?"

"Yeah."

"Birds are pretty common, as far as women's tattoos go. Maybe she just liked the design." He handed back the file.

"Thanks for the language help. I didn't know you were an expert."

"My mom is from Hong Kong. I spent ten years in Saturday school."

Jacob's phone buzzed in his pocket and he pulled it out. Bailey. He stood and stepped into the neighboring cubicle, where Muse was playing.

"Hey, I'm tied up right now," he told her.

"I figured, or you would have called me." She didn't sound irritated, but he definitely caught something in her tone.

"Can I call you later?" he asked.

"When?"

"When I get off work."

"It's better if you come by. I need to talk to you face-to-face. It's about the case."

Jacob didn't say anything. Going to her home was a bad idea, for many reasons. But he didn't want to say no.

"When do you get off?" she asked.

"I don't know. Probably seven or eight."

"Come by my place, even if it's late."

Jacob paused. "Which unit?"

"Two fifteen."

He was committed now. Unless he made up an excuse.

"And don't blow me off," she said. "It's important."

B Y NINE O'CLOCK, Bailey decided he'd blown her off. She sat cross-legged on her sofa, stroking Boba Fett's ears while she read through the autopsy report on her computer for the third time.

Murder cases were the worst ones she covered, partly because of ME's reports. She hated the dense passages filled with clinical prose that distilled a life, a person, down to a few stock phrases. It was the same thing she hated about funerals. People issued emotional clichés that, at best, gave a snapshot of someone's life but didn't come close to giving a full picture.

Bailey closed out of the document and sighed. Glancing up at the ceiling, she wondered about her upstairs neighbors. Not a sound tonight, which probably meant they were out. It was nice to have some quiet, but they could come home stumbling drunk at any time.

Boba Fett got up and rubbed his chin against her arm.

"What's up with you?" she asked, scratching his neck.

Usually, he was sacked out in her bedroom by now, not wide awake and clamoring for attention. Maybe he sensed her nervous energy tonight. Bailey was wired. She felt like she'd had three cups of coffee, but she hadn't had a drop since the morning.

Her cat settled back on his haunches and watched her with those sea-green eyes, and his look of concern reminded her of Hannah.

How do you do your job, Bay?

Her sister had asked that once after reading a three-part series Bailey had written about online sex predators grooming kids as young as nine.

It was a strange question coming from someone who dealt with blood and sickness every day, and Bailey had tossed the question right back at her. Neither of them had ever really answered. Both of their jobs definitely had their dark sides, not to mention crazy hours. But Bailey loved her work anyway. She wasn't sure why she did what she did, only that she couldn't imagine doing anything else.

Three sharp raps on the door made her heart skitter. She got up and checked the peephole. Jacob still wore his work clothes, and it looked like he hadn't been home yet.

She opened the door. "Hi," she said, trying for nonchalance.

"Hi."

They simply stood there for a moment, and she stepped back to usher him in. She looked him over, noting his badge and holster. He seemed so official, and she was standing there in a tank top and running shorts, with bare feet.

"Long day?" she asked.

He raked his hand through his hair. "Yeah."

"How about a drink? I've got beer, wine."

"I'm still on call."

"Water, Gatorade—"

"Water's good."

She walked into the kitchen and grabbed a bottle from the fridge. Boba Fett had vanished. He was shy with visitors.

"Thanks." Jacob unscrewed the top from the water and watched her as he took a swig. He had that five o'clock shadow thing happening again, and she remembered how the stubble had felt under her fingertips.

She nodded at his gun. "Doesn't that thing get heavy?"

"No."

"I can't imagine wearing that all the time. What about when you're on vacation?"

"Depends. I've got a Glock 42 and an ankle holster when I want to travel light." He took another swig and set his bottle on the counter. They stared at each other across her kitchen, and Bailey felt a warm pull in the pit of her stomach. He was thinking about last night—she could tell.

He sauntered into her living room and looked around at the low bookshelves lining three of the walls. She'd made them last summer out of cinder blocks and wood slats after getting tired of the milk crates she'd used in college.

"Lot of books," he said.

"It's my indulgence."

"I see why you don't want to move." He stepped closer and tipped his head to read the titles. "Orwell, Atwood, Vonnegut." He looked at her. "Dystopian fiction?"

"And true crime. And horror. And politics. Of course, some people would tell you that's all the same."

Why was she babbling? Butterflies flitted in her stomach as she watched him checking out her living room. She wondered what he thought of her home. He lived in a house, not an apartment. It was another symbol of their age difference. He was thirty-four—eight years older than she was. She'd been looking into his background. She also happened to know his address and what he'd paid for his house two years ago. Amazing the info you could dig up with a simple Internet search.

He stepped closer to a shelf with framed photos along the top and zeroed in on a picture of Bailey with her sisters and their father at the marina in front of their catamaran.

"This the *Mary Alice*?" He looked at her.

"Yeah."

"You look like your dad."

She smiled. "People say that. I don't see it at all."

"The eyes."

He turned to face her, and again she felt that warm pull.

"I learned a lot today," she said. "Some of it I wanted to run by you."

He lifted an eyebrow. "You turn in your profile?"

"It's on hold."

"Why?" He looked concerned.

"There are some things I'm trying to pin down." She stepped back into the kitchen and grabbed a water for herself. He followed her and leaned back against the counter, and he was watching her now with a look she couldn't read.

"Let me ask you something." She took a sip of water and set down the bottle. "You think it's possible Dana wasn't who she said she was?"

"How do you mean?"

"I mean . . . do you think it's possible she misled people? Her employer, her friends, everyone."

"What makes you think that?"

"I've been researching the woman for days, and it's weird. No one can even tell me where she's from. She has no social media presence. She didn't drive or have a phone until Celeste Camden gave her one. She didn't talk about her background with her employer or her co-workers—"

"What co-workers?"

"At the museum."

His eyebrows tipped up.

"She volunteered at Villa Paloma two days a week. You didn't know?"

"No."

"She spent an average of eight hours a week there, but even her friends there don't know much about her, not even where she's from originally. Don't you think that's weird?" Bailey crossed her arms. "And then I was talking to Nico, our tech writer, who was trying to help me run down a social media account or even an email or any kind of digital footprint whatsoever, and Nico said, 'It's like she doesn't exist.' And I realized he's right."

Jacob didn't say anything. He just stood there, watching her with a guarded expression.

"I think she was on the run from something," Bailey said. "Or some*one*. Maybe an abusive husband or boyfriend or—who knows?—but I think she may have come here trying to start over and she was purposely keeping a low profile."

Jacob just looked at her. "This is what you wanted to talk about?"

"Yeah. I mean, if she was running from something and that's why she was killed, don't you think that's relevant to your investigation?"

"Possibly."

She watched him, trying to gauge his reaction. Or nonreaction.

"I heard the FBI is taking over the case," she said. "Is that true?"

Surprise flickered in his eyes. "Where'd you hear that?"

"Is it true?"

"I need to know where you're getting your information."

"I'll take that as a yes." She stepped closer and watched his eyes. "Why are the feds involved?"

"I didn't say they were."

She stepped closer again until she was standing right in front of him, close enough to see every little tick of his reaction. "Was she a protected witness?"

His jaw hardened.

Bailey stepped back. "Oh my God, she was, wasn't she?"

"I didn't say that."

This was why she'd wanted him here. She'd wanted to read every nuance of his expression, and she saw that she was right. And this was why he'd been acting weird last night when he'd met her at Eli's and tried to pump her for information without giving her a damn thing. And why he'd been evasive at the police station this afternoon.

"I'm right," she said. "I can see it in your face. You just confirmed it."

"Bailey." His voice had an edge now. "I'm not confirming anything. And you can't run that."

She leaned against the counter as the implications swirled through her head. "So that name is an alias. And her murder—it wasn't some mugging or some random sex crime. It was a *hit*."

"You have no proof of any of that, and you can't run that in your paper."

"If I get corroboration, I can."

His gaze sharpened. "That would be reckless as hell."

"But would it be accurate? Was she a protected witness? Is that why the FBI took over?"

"Who the hell are you talking to?" he asked.

"That doesn't matter."

"It matters to me."

"I'm not going to tell you my sources, so you can forget about that," she said. "And before you get mad, just know that also means I wouldn't betray *you* if someone asked me. You can trust me."

He laughed, and she felt a twinge of hurt.

"You can."

She watched him, waiting for him to calm down. He took a deep breath and rubbed his hand over his chin. Clearly, he was conflicted about this, and he probably regretted coming here.

She stepped close to him, and his gaze dropped to her mouth. And it was there again—that hot flare of attraction.

"Let's make a deal," she said.

"What kind of deal?"

"I'll hold off on running anything about this, if you'll answer some of my questions."

"No."

She took a deep breath. "Come on. You have to know you can't control this story, Jacob. It involves a lot of people not connected to you. The information is bound to get out."

His jaw tightened again, and she could see him weighing his options. She was being pushy. Yes. But she'd made a career out of being pushy. If she weren't pushy with people, she'd be out of a job.

"One question, off the record," he said.

"Was Dana Smith a protected witness?"

"Yes."

Holy hell.

"So, someone found her here?"

"That's two questions."

"But that's what happened, right?" She felt a surge of adrenaline. She'd been *right*. Up until now it had seemed like a slightly crazy conspiracy theory that had sprung from her vivid imagination. But Jacob was standing here confirming it. Off the record, but still.

"We don't know what happened for sure," he said, "but we're investigating. It's possible her murder is connected to a federal case she testified in. And if that *is* what happened, and you let it leak that the FBI is involved, whoever killed her will know we're onto him, and it will make it much tougher for us to apprehend him." He stepped closer. "Do you understand? Leaking this publicly could blow the whole case."

She watched him, heart thrumming. She didn't want to blow the case. But she couldn't sit on this forever, either.

Jacob stared down at her, and her heart thumped harder for a different reason. She could feel his tension. See the heat in his eyes. He was frustrated, and it wasn't just about the case.

"I have to go." He moved for the door.

"Wait. *Wait.* We're not done talking! I want to know more about what's going on."

He shook his head. "I've told you as much as I can."

She followed him to the door as he pulled it open and turned to look at her. "And we made a deal, Bailey, so I better not see this in the paper."

His words stung, but she tried not to let it show.

"You won't," she said. "I told you, you can trust me."

CHAPTER

FOURTEEN

Kendra poked her head into the file room. "You're working down here again?"

"It's quiet."

She stepped into the room and closed the door behind her. Jacob noted the laptop under her arm.

"I have to show you something," she said, and he caught the excitement in her voice. He slid his computer aside, and Kendra pulled over the folding chair she'd used last time and opened her laptop.

"I think I may have found it," she said.

"Found what?"

"Dana Smith's court case."

Jacob's pulse picked up. He'd been looking on and off for days for the case, but he hadn't come up with anything.

"I found three possibilities in Chicago over the last two years," she said.

"Why two years?"

"You said her apartment lease started eighteen months

ago. I figure she's been in WITSEC since around then. First two cases were straight-up financial crimes. Looks like the witnesses were all bankers and forensic accountants. I don't really see Dana fitting into that scene."

"Okay."

"But look at this." She clicked open a window and turned the computer to face him.

The screen showed an article in the *Chicago Tribune*. *STEEL MOGUL'S SON TARGETED IN FEDERAL PROBE*. Jacob skimmed the first paragraph. The photo alongside the story showed a young man in a suit surrounded by a throng of reporters in front of a courthouse.

"That's Will McKinney." Kendra tapped the picture. "Looks like a *GQ* model, doesn't he? Used to be one of the most eligible bachelors in Chicago. Now he's wearing an orange jumpsuit and cooling his heels at the federal penitentiary in Marion, Illinois."

"What'd he do?"

"Got busted for embezzling money from his family's company," Kendra said. "The family's old-money Chicago, and they're rumored to be connected to organized crime. One of his uncles went away on a tax evasion charge fifteen years ago. Now fast-forward a generation, and this guy Will is charged with two counts of bank fraud and one count of witness tampering."

"Tell me about the witness tampering. Anything physical?"

"McKinney's stockbroker was beaten to a bloody pulp in his parking garage. We're talking brass knuckles and steel-toed boots. Guy lost three teeth and had to have his jaw wired back together. Security camera got the license plate of the assailant, and the vehicle traced back to a PI that McKinney had hired. So, it's clear McKinney doesn't mind playing it rough. He went to trial and ended up getting eight years. And get this, his *girlfriend* testified against him in court, along with one of the company's in-house accountants. A woman, by the way."

Jacob skimmed the article. "Where'd you get all that? I'm not seeing it."

"The article is mostly about McKinney, who was being groomed to take over his dad's company when he started stealing from it. I mean, what a bonehead, right? If he'd just waited, he probably would've inherited everything."

"What kind of money are we talking about?"

"Two million dollars over three years."

"He didn't think they'd miss it?"

"Guess not." She shook her head. "Or if they did, maybe he thought they'd keep the problem in the family? I'm guessing they would have handled it themselves, but his wire transfers caught the attention of the feds, and they opened an investigation. They ended up getting several employees to testify."

"Employees? I thought you said it was an accountant and a girlfriend."

"It was." Kendra pulled out a spiral notebook and flipped a few pages. "But according to the transcript, the girlfriend started out as a temporary receptionist at McKinney Steel's downtown headquarters in Chicago. That's where they met."

"What are the witnesses' names?" Jacob asked.

"The accountant is . . ." She flipped another page. "Tabitha Walker. Age twenty-eight. I looked, but I haven't found anything on her yet. And the second one is Robin Nally."

"Her name's Robin?" Jacob scooted closer.

"Yeah. Why?"

He grabbed the folder beside his computer and flipped it open to the photograph. "That's the tattoo Dana Smith had removed."

She glanced at the picture, then at Jacob. "That's a robin redbreast."

"I know."

"Where the hell did you get that?"

"A day spa next to Dana's apartment building had a record of her," Jacob said. "She was in the process of having this ink removed when she was murdered."

"What do the words say? The calligraphy?"

" 'Love, strength, and happiness.' "

Kendra sat back in her chair and smiled. "Holy *crap*, Jacob. We found her."

"Probably."

"What do you mean, 'probably'? She had a *robin* tattooed on her ankle, and she got it removed after she went into WITSEC and changed her name."

"I'd believe it when I see a picture of Robin Nally."

"Since when are you such a skeptic?"

"Since always."

Kendra shook her head. "It's her, Jacob. Think about the odds. The city, the age, the tattoo, the organized-crime connection—that's way too many coincidences for this not to be our victim."

"Let's get proof," he said. "But in the meantime, we need to move on this."

"What do you mean, 'move'?"

"I mean, someone with inside knowledge and knife skills tracked down Dana Smith. We don't know how he did it, but what's to stop him from doing it again?"

"You're worried about Tabitha Walker?"

"Yes."

Kendra nodded. "If she testified, too, we need to find her before McKinney's hit man does."

"It's been four days since Dana's murder," Jacob said. "He may have already found her."

FIFTEEN

B AILEY LEFT HER office in a rush, late for her three
o'clock appointment at the Sunrise Café on Congress.
She crossed against the light, prompting honks from several cars. Stepping into the restaurant, she spotted the man
she was meeting at the back in a corner booth.

"You're late," he said as she slid into the seat.

"Sorry. Our staff meeting ran long."

John Colt had a coffee mug in front of him, and it was
already half-empty. He leaned back against the booth and
draped his long arms over the seat. Colt was tall and muscular, and his black T-shirt fit snugly over his pecs. He had
the body of a twenty-five-year-old, but the gray at his temples told Bailey he was closer to forty.

"What's up?" he asked.

"Thanks for taking the time to meet me."

He didn't respond. Colt wasn't into niceties. It was one
reason Bailey liked using him as a source. She'd first met
Colt when she was doing a story about bail bondsmen near

the courthouse. He was said to be the best skip tracer in town. He'd refused to be interviewed, Bailey had convinced him to talk to her on background only, and they'd met for omelets at four in the afternoon, Bailey's treat. Colt kept weird hours.

"I need help with a story," she said now.

He just looked at her.

"It involves skip tracing."

"What about it?"

"Generally speaking, how does it work?"

"Depends. Who are you looking for?"

"No one. But if I *were* looking for someone—someone who really didn't want to be found—what's the first thing I'd do?"

A young waitress stopped by with a steaming platter of eggs and hash browns. She looked at Bailey. "Something for you?"

"Just water, thanks."

She walked off, and Colt shook Tabasco over his food. He scooped up a bite, and Bailey watched him eat. She wondered, as she always did, what he was thinking. Colt was an enigma. She knew very little about his professional background, except that he'd once been in the Marines, and she suspected he might have been some sort of special-ops badass. She knew zilch about his personal life—not even whether he was married. She couldn't imagine him with a wife, though. He seemed like too much of a loner.

"Depends on the target," Colt told her. "Are we talking about an ex-con? An ex-wife? A fugitive? People skip town for a lot of reasons."

And sometimes Colt refused to find them, even if he could. During the course of her reporting, Bailey had learned that Colt checked out all his clients beforehand. If the client had a history of violence or wanted him to track down a wife or girlfriend who'd left, Colt turned down the job. She had even heard of him helping women skip town to get away from a violent partner. Of course, she'd asked Colt about that, but he wouldn't discuss it.

"In this case . . . I don't know," she said.

"You don't know?" He sipped his coffee.

"The details are unclear. All I really know is the person was a witness in a trial and doesn't want to be found."

Interest sparked in his eyes at that. "A protected witness?"

She nodded.

Colt squinted as he chewed. He swallowed and took another sip of coffee. "Now, that's a more interesting challenge. If the target's in WITSEC, the feds will set him up with a new identity, new place to live, possibly a job. All that stuff would be traceless, too. Program like that, it'd be much harder to locate someone."

"But not impossible."

He just looked at her.

"You could do it, right?"

"Maybe."

"How?"

The corner of his mouth ticked up. "You think I'm going to tell you my methods so you can put them in the paper?"

"This is strictly for background. If I wanted to find someone in the witness protection program, what would I do?"

He watched her without talking, and Bailey tried not to show her impatience. Colt was one of her best sources, but she didn't use him much because she didn't want to pester him. In fact, she'd only used him twice before now—which was probably one reason he'd agreed to meet her.

The server stopped by to drop off Bailey's water. She refilled Colt's mug, and he watched her walk away. Then he looked at Bailey.

"It would be tough," he said.

"Hypothetically, where would I start?"

He folded his arms over his chest. "Everyone's different. Again, it would depend on the target. You research the target and zero in on a potential vulnerability."

"Say the target is a twenty-five-year-old woman."

"What else you know about her?"

"Very little."

"You need to do some more legwork, then. That's not much to go on."

"I don't need all your methods," she said. "Just give me a direction. What would you do first if someone hired you to track down someone like that?"

"Social media, no question."

"Really?" That sounded a little basic to Bailey. "Isn't that the first thing federal agents would warn you to stay away from?"

"Yeah, but people are bad at resisting temptation. Also, there's the ID. A driver's license or passport could be a weakness."

"How?"

"Facial recognition technology. Those pictures go into a database. Now, if it's a federally protected witness, they probably keep the pictures out, but you never know."

"What if she doesn't have a driver's license?"

"Then I'd focus on social media," he said. "Twenty-five years old? I wouldn't be surprised if she has a dummy profile, just so she can follow what some of her friends are doing. Like I said, people are bad at resisting temptation. They want to reenter their lives, even if only to observe what's going on without them. She probably has a profile on one or more platforms. With enough research, someone could find it. From there, it's not hard to narrow down a location."

Bailey thought about all the time Dana Smith had spent on the computers at Villa Paloma. Was that what she'd been doing? Checking up on her old life, her old friends? Watching people move on without her?

"What about phones?" she asked. "I heard about a case in Milwaukee where a stalker tracked down a woman by paying a bounty hunter to ping her cell phone. Did you hear about that case?"

Colt nodded.

"How does that work?"

"It doesn't. It's illegal, for one thing."

"But if someone was willing to break the law?"

Colt waited a beat before answering. "Bail bondsmen are treated like quasi law enforcement agencies in some ways. They're given more access than the general public when it comes to databases. But anyone who did what you're describing could lose his license."

"Still, you've heard of this happening?"

He nodded.

"WITSEC is a buttoned-up program, though," he said. "One of the most secure in the world. I doubt they'd provide a witness with a phone that could be traced, even if someone had the means to ping it." He emptied his coffee and reached for his wallet. "I need to go."

"This is on me. Thank you for meeting me."

"No problem," Colt said. "So, I take it the victim at the lake was a witness?"

Bailey cursed inwardly. She should have known he'd figure out what she was working on, but she hadn't thought Colt read her stories.

"I'm just doing some research," she said vaguely.

"Understood."

"This is purely for background."

"Relax, Bailey. I get it." He scooted from the booth.

"One more question."

He watched her expectantly.

"Given what you know, would you describe WITSEC as impenetrable?"

He smiled slightly. "Nothing's impenetrable."

TABITHA WHIRLED FROM table to table, dropping off food and picking up empties. She collected a stack of baskets from a high-top, then spun to the neighboring table to deliver beers.

"This is a light."

She glanced up at the customer. The man was tall and heavyset. His T-shirt had a swoosh with the words *Just Do Me* under it.

"I'm sorry?" she asked.

"I ordered Genuine Draft." He held up his glass as if it had piss in it. "This is light."

"Oh. You're right." She glanced at his friend, who was staring at her boobs. They weren't that impressive, but she'd discovered a Wonderbra did wonders for her tips. "I'll bring you a new one. You want to keep that or—"

"You can have it." He plunked it on her tray, throwing it off balance, but she caught the side an instant before it tipped.

"Be right back."

She whirled around and darted a glance behind the bar. No sign of Theo, her manager, and she'd been watching for him all afternoon, panic growing inside her as the hours ticked by.

She'd been a wreck for three days, jumping at shadows and constantly looking over her shoulder. She'd had to close last night, and she'd practically sprinted home, clutching her tube of pepper spray in her hand.

"Miss? Waitress?"

She turned around.

"We're still waiting on those nachos." The woman looked tired and annoyed as she pointed at the tray. "And is that my wine?"

"Yes. Here you go. Sorry for the—" Tabitha tripped, sloshing wine on the table. "*Oops!* My bad, I—" She looked down and saw that she'd stepped on a tote bag someone had left on the floor. "Sorry." She set the half-empty glass down in front of the customer, who looked even more peeved now as Tabitha mopped up the spill with a stack of napkins. "I'll bring you a new one." She turned away before the woman could reply.

And spotted Theo walking into the kitchen.

Tabitha hurried to catch up with him, unloading her tray at the bar before entering the kitchen. It was hot, crowded, and noisy, with dishes clattering and music playing on a radio somewhere. She caught sight of Theo as he ducked into the office next to the supply room.

Tabitha stashed her tray in a corner and rushed over before he had a chance to close the door.

"Theo?" She stepped into the cramped room, which was barely big enough for his desk and the putty-colored computer that took up most of it.

He stood at the file cabinet and tossed a glance over his shoulder. "Not now, Red."

"I just needed to ask—"

"Not now. A food delivery just pulled up, and I've got ATC here."

"ATC?"

"Alcohol and Tobacco Control." He jerked a file from the cabinet and turned to slap it on the desk. He flipped the folder open and grabbed the reading glasses from the top of his bald head.

Would ATC be looking at employment records? Tabitha's stomach did a somersault as Theo read the file, ignoring her.

She'd selected O'Shea's carefully. It was one of a dozen bars and restaurants she'd scoped out when she first came to town. None of the kitchen staff spoke English, and she had a hunch some didn't have papers. When she'd turned in her job application, she'd waited until Theo was looking at her breasts to mention that she'd lost her social security card. His response was a shrug, and it hadn't come up again. As far as she knew, he had no idea that Rachel Moore was an alias, and since everyone called her Red, he might have even forgotten her full name. Theo seemed happy to have an off-the-books employee, and every other Friday he paid her wages in cash, no questions. It was all very wink-wink.

He glanced up. "*What?* I told you, I'm busy."

"I just wanted to see if I could get a small advance on my next payday."

"What, do I look like a bank?"

"I've been working a lot of doubles and—"

"I don't do advances. *Shit.*" He turned back to the file cabinet and started thumbing through the drawer again.

"I wouldn't normally ask, but my car is in the shop and it turns out it needs new brake pads and—"

"Not happening." He slapped another folder on his desk and ran his hand over his bare head. Then he looked at her and his eyes softened. This was why she liked him. One of the reasons, anyway. He talked with a lot of bluster, but he had a generous streak, too. He was protective of his employees, and she'd seen him turn a blind eye when people took home leftover food.

"I'll think about it," he said.

Her stomach did another somersault. "You mean . . . today?"

"Today's not happening." He darted an anxious look at the door. "Maybe tomorrow. You're working, right? We've got that wake tomorrow at four. I need everyone."

Tabitha's heart sank. The pub would be packed tomorrow, and there was no way he'd make time to pay her. A sour lump clogged her throat as she thought about waiting another day or maybe two. She'd hardly slept since that phone message. She couldn't eat. Her nerves were raw, and her stomach seemed to be filled with battery acid.

He glanced up from the file. "Don't flake out on me, Red."

"No, I'll be here."

But she knew she wouldn't.

CHAPTER

SIXTEEN

JACOB DUCKED UNDER the yellow tape and pulled open the door to the liquor store. Kendra stood beside a display of mini tequila bottles near the cash register. She had a notebook in her hand and was interviewing a middle-aged guy on a stool behind the counter as he rubbed his forehead and looked distraught.

Jacob caught Kendra's eye, and she walked over.

"What do we have?" he asked.

"Two men, both in ski masks. One gun."

"What kind?"

"A black pistol. Big, according to the clerk."

Jacob glanced at the man. Any pistol looked big if it was aimed at your face.

"Our witness here says they came in through the back. Someone had left the door propped open, so there could be a third accomplice. They made him empty the register at gunpoint and bumped into his stock boy on the way out and took a shot at him, getting him in the arm. He's at Seton

Hospital. Stock boy says they took off in a dark gray sedan. We don't have the make and model yet."

"Cameras?"

"Trujillo's in the back office working on that. He says the whole thing's on tape."

"Good."

"You see Bailey?" Kendra asked.

"No. Where?"

She nodded toward the door. "Outside. She was talking to some bystanders when I pulled in. Must have caught it on the scanner."

Jacob resisted the urge to go looking for her.

"She asked me if you were here," Kendra said pointedly. Then she looked back at the witness, who was bent over the stool, clutching his knees. "I need to finish getting this guy's statement before he loses his lunch. Meet me in back and we'll go over the security footage."

Jacob left the store and ducked back under the scene tape. He spotted Bailey at the side of the building, leaning against the trunk of her white Toyota and talking on her phone as she flipped through a notepad. She ended her call as Jacob approached.

This evening she wore cutoff shorts and flip-flops, and her press pass dangled on a lanyard around her neck. Jacob made an effort not to stare at her legs.

"Hi," she said.

"They call you back in for this?"

"I was out grabbing dinner. Max picked it up on the scanner." She looked at the store entrance.

"Is the clerk okay?"

"He will be."

"I hear the guy at the hospital has a flesh wound," she said.

She didn't ask him to confirm, and he didn't.

"Listen, can you talk for a minute?" she asked.

"Sure."

She glanced at the patrol officer who was stationed beside the door. He was close enough to eavesdrop, and Jacob followed Bailey to the passenger side, where she rummaged through the glove compartment for a fresh notepad. She set it on the roof of her car and held her pen poised, as though she were interviewing him about the crime at hand.

Apparently, she didn't want the other cops on the scene to think they had a personal relationship.

"I went back to Villa Paloma," she said in a low voice.

"Why?"

"Dana Smith spent a lot of time in the library there, using their computers. I checked all the caches."

Jacob's irritation battled with his curiosity. He'd been by Villa Paloma and interviewed several people, but he hadn't thought to check the library computers. Bailey was one step ahead of him, and that didn't sit well. What if she stumbled into something dangerous? It could have happened already.

"I thought you were done with this story," he said.

"I didn't say I was done. I said the story was on hold. At least the profile is. Now it could be scuttled altogether."

"So, why are you still working on it?"

She tipped her head to the side. "Don't you want to know what I found?"

"What did you find?"

"*Nothing.* She cleared all the caches after each use, apparently. So there's no way of knowing if she visited social media sites that might have tipped off someone searching for her."

Clearing caches wasn't a permanent way to erase someone's tracks, but he didn't bother saying that. He wanted Bailey to drop the story, not get more immersed.

She eased closer. Just a fraction, but it was close enough for him to smell her shampoo. "But you want to know what I *did* learn?" she asked.

"What?"

"The name of the museum's security company. Granite Tech Enterprises. They're a local start-up with a head-quarters on Lake Austin."

Jacob frowned. "What does that—"

"They provide IDs to all the museum employees and handle security on the grounds. And I got to thinking, what if that's how Dana's name and photo and possibly her fingerprints ended up in some database that may have been compromised and—"

"Whoa. Whoa. Whoa. You're investigating WITSEC now?"

"Yeah," she said. "What did you think? If someone penetrated the witness protection program, that's a huge story."

"I thought we agreed you were dropping this."

She frowned. "I agreed to no such thing. We agreed I wouldn't run anything without corroboration, and I agreed not to use you as my source."

"So, what are you using?"

"I'm investigating. That's what investigative reporters *do*. I've got an interview lined up at Granite Tech tomorrow so I can learn more about their operation and—"

"Are you serious? You think you might want to slow down?"

"Why?" She looked genuinely confused.

"Because a woman was stabbed to death less than a week ago. And we don't know who's responsible. Or have anyone in custody. And now you want to go snooping around, turning over rocks and asking questions all over the place? I guarantee you whoever killed Dana Smith is monitoring this investigation, and that includes the news coverage."

Her phone chimed and she looked annoyed as she pulled it out. "That's my boss. I need to get this story in. Chill out, okay? Tomorrow's just an interview. I haven't written anything yet that would flag anyone's attention."

"You don't know *what* might flag someone's attention. That's the whole point."

She looked around, and Jacob realized their conversation was attracting notice from people in the parking lot, including the patrol cop stationed by the door. Jacob didn't want to be seen getting into it with a reporter, for either of their sakes.

He stepped away from her. "I have to get back to work."

"You're overreacting, Jacob."

"No. I'm reacting to the facts."

B AILEY ROLLED THE windows down and let the wind whip around her as she crossed the bridge. Moonlight shimmered off the inky lake. The cypress trees along the banks looked tall and protective, guarding secrets most people would never know about. But Bailey knew. And Jacob. Covering crime had given her a view of the city's dark side. She still loved it, but she'd never see it the way she had before her job had taken her into squalid apartment buildings and vomit-scented alleyways.

After the bridge, Bailey passed the shiny restaurants and nightclubs of South Congress. She turned into a neighborhood with tree-lined streets and cars parked along the curbs. Glowing porch lights revealed a hodgepodge of architecture—thirties-era cottages, midcentury bungalows, bloated new construction. She surveyed the street numbers and slowed in front of a modest one-story with a flat roof and a black Chevy pickup in the drive. A light on the porch illuminated a black front door flanked by two large windows, both dark.

Bailey parked and checked her reflection in the mirror. Not great, but not bad, either. She pulled the elastic band from her hair and ran her fingers through it. She had on the same clothes as earlier, minus the press pass.

She got out and glanced up and down the block as she made her way up the concrete walk. The thick lawn needed mowing, but the flower beds beneath the windows were devoid of plants. A thin strip of light outlined a shade covering one of the windows, indicating someone was home, and Bailey felt a surge of nervousness as she approached the door. She hoped he didn't have company.

She rang the bell and waited, listening to the muffled sound of a television inside.

She rang again. The TV noise ceased. A moment later the peephole went dark briefly, and the door swung open.

Jacob stood there in faded jeans, no shirt. Bailey's mind went blank. His hair was mussed, and his slick skin was covered in a thin layer of . . . something.

"Hi," he said, clearly surprised.

"Hey. I hope it's not too late."

He stared at her for a second, then stepped back to let her inside.

The spacious room had gleaming wooden floors and no furniture. The air smelled of sawdust.

"You're working?" She turned and smiled, trying to seem more relaxed than she felt.

"Yeah." He looked down at her for a long moment, and those deep brown eyes made her nerves flutter. She kept her focus on his face, but it was hard not to gape at his muscular arms and perfectly sculpted torso. His feet were bare, too. He rested his hands on his hips and watched her curiously, but she didn't explain what she was doing here.

"I was about to take a beer break," he said. "Want one?"

"Sure."

He turned and led her across the room, and she noted a ladder in the corner beside a wall of floor-to-ceiling bookshelves. Squares of sandpaper littered the floor.

"You really are doing it yourself," she said.

He glanced over his shoulder. "You thought I lied?"

"No, it's just people say that. But what they really mean is they've hired a crew."

Hannah's husband made his living off people like that, and Austin was getting more of them each day as people moved down from the Bay Area and New York to take advantage of a lower cost of living. The tech sector was thriving, and the city had been nicknamed Silicon Hills.

Jacob led her past a laminate bar and into a kitchen. Or what could have been a kitchen. Tile had been pulled up to expose a concrete subfloor, and there was an empty space where a stove should have been. A white bucket sat in a sink beside a brown refrigerator that looked older than Bailey. Jacob pulled open the fridge.

"Shiner Bock or Shiner Blonde?"

"I'll take a Blonde."

He grabbed two with one hand, then regarded her warily as he twisted the tops off. He handed her a bottle and leaned back against the counter.

"How'd you find my address?" he asked.

"Way too easily."

His eyebrows tipped up.

"There's no such thing as privacy anymore."

He tipped his beer back, watching her as he took a sip. He set the bottle on the counter and reached for a dish towel. He wiped down his neck, and the towel came away yellow with sawdust.

"Nice shelves," she said, nodding at the living room.

"They will be."

"You're sanding them by hand? Isn't there a power tool for that?"

"By hand's better. And better for working out frustration at the end of the day."

"Why are you frustrated?"

He wiped his neck again and tossed the towel in the sink. Then he stepped closer and gazed down at her. She tilted her head back to look at him, trying not to seem intimidated even though her heart was thrumming.

"What's on your mind, Bailey?"

His voice had an edge, and she knew she was the source of his frustration. At least, some of it.

She cleared her throat. "Robin Nally."

His jaw tightened. "Where did you get that name?"

"Guy Elliott with the *Chicago Trib.*"

"Who?"

"He covers the courts beat. I called him up and asked him if he knew of a federal case about two years ago in which a woman in her early twenties had testified against someone and become a protected witness."

"Where'd you get Chicago?"

"I didn't originally," she said. "Celeste Camden told me she thought Dana was from St. Louis because they once watched a Cardinals-Cubs game together. The court reporter in St. Louis didn't have a case in mind, but he remembered something in Chicago that fit the timing, so I tried the *Tribune.*"

She set her purse down on the counter and took out two folded pages that she'd printed out at her office. The first was a copy of the *Tribune* story about Will McKinney's conviction.

Jacob closed his eyes and cursed under his breath.

"There are two of them, Jacob. *Two* civilian witnesses testified in this trial. And check this out." She unfolded the second article. It was from the lifestyle section and showed a couple on a red carpet outside the Art Institute of Chicago. The museum's famous lion statues stood on either side of the carpet.

She had Jacob's interest now. She pointed at the woman. "That's Robin Nally at a charity gala with Will McKinney six months before he was indicted."

Jacob's brow furrowed as he stared down at the picture. Robin wore a shimmery yellow gown that was backless. She looked over her shoulder to smile at the camera, and a cascade of curly blond hair tumbled down her shoulders all the way to her elbows. Her boyfriend rested his hand possessively on her hip as he gave the photographer a cool stare.

"Beautiful, isn't she?"

Jacob glanced at her but didn't comment.

"Now, look at this." Bailey took out her phone and opened a photograph she'd taken during her second visit to Villa Paloma. It was the Rossetti painting.

Jacob frowned. "What's this?"

"That's a painting hanging in the library at Villa Paloma. It was Dana Smith's favorite. She called it 'the Sunshine Girl.'"

The resemblance between Robin Nally and the woman in the painting with the yellow dress and hair was striking. Bailey looked at Jacob to gauge his reaction. She could tell he saw the resemblance, even if he didn't admit it.

"Uncanny, isn't it?"

"Dana Smith had brown hair."

Bailey rolled her eyes. "She dyed it. Brown hair was part of her cover. The blond would have been too conspicuous— I mean, look at her. She looks like a movie star. But I bet she missed the blond."

Seeing the photo of Robin Nally had made Bailey view the Sunshine Girl painting in a whole new light. And she'd also thought about some of the cryptic things Dana's friend Alex had said. *Looks can be deceiving.*

"You know, when I interviewed one of Dana's friends at the museum, he even pointed out that she looked like the woman in this painting. 'Except for the blond,' he said. 'Her hair is much darker.'"

Alex had also made a point of saying Dana was evasive about her background. *I'm from everywhere and nowhere.* Bailey had a hunch Alex knew that Dana wasn't who she'd said she was.

Jacob was watching Bailey now with a look she couldn't read. He definitely seemed tense, as though he had something he wanted to say but couldn't.

"I'm not asking you to confirm, Jacob. I know I'm right."

The muscles in his jaw bunched.

"And I also know there are *two* witnesses who testified. Where's the other one? Where's Tabitha Walker?"

He didn't respond.

"Someone needs to find her and warn her that her life's in danger. Assuming it's not too late."

His look darkened, and she felt the tension coming off him, but still he didn't say anything.

She stepped closer, close enough to see the tiny bits of sawdust in his hair. His skin was slick, and she wanted to slide her hands over his muscular shoulders. Instead, she just looked up at him, watching the conflict burning in his eyes.

"I'll be right back." He stepped around her.

"Where are you going?"

"To shower."

"You don't need to *shower*. We're having a conversation."

But he ignored her and disappeared down a hallway.

She huffed out a breath and scanned his empty kitchen, annoyed by his abrupt exit and his lack of reaction to her discovery. This wasn't going as she'd expected.

She sipped her beer in an effort to relax and then stepped into the room just beyond the kitchen. As opposed to the front room, this space looked finished. More rich golden floors, plus some brown leather furniture and an intricate rug of deep reds and blues. The furniture faced a huge TV where the Rangers game was on, but muted, and she guessed he'd been watching it when she rang the bell.

Bailey crossed the room to check out the big windows that looked out on a wooden deck illuminated by floodlights. She glanced back at the hallway and heard the pipes running. Then she opened the glass door and stepped outside.

The deep yard sloped down, and the back was shadowed by towering pecan trees. Cicadas droned in the distance, luring her across the deck. She took a few steps down to the lawn, then turned around to look at the house.

It glowed like a lantern, warm and inviting. She skimmed her gaze over the ladder and the bare light fixtures in the front room. It was a work in progress, an endeavor that absorbed his spare time and energy, and she felt a sharp prick of envy. She couldn't remember the last time she'd had that. Outside of rowing, she'd let go of all her hobbies. Basically, she worked. And when she wasn't working, she was thinking about work. And when she wasn't thinking about work, she was catching up on laundry or cleaning or maybe stealing a quick coffee at Hannah's. Ever since the first round of layoffs at the newspaper, her life had become an endless quest to rack up bylines and hang on to her job.

She sat down on the wooden step, facing the darkness of the trees. Acoustic guitar music drifted over from the neighbor's yard, along with the scent of marijuana. She tipped her head back and looked at the sky. The stars were out, along with a full moon. She closed her eyes and realized how good it felt to sit and just *be*. Jacob's yard was an oasis, removed from the hustle and noise only a few blocks away.

The floodlights went off. Then a dim light came on beside the back door as Jacob stepped outside.

"You getting eaten alive?" he asked.

"Nope."

He wore a gray T-shirt with his jeans now, and his hair was damp from the shower. She stood up to join him on the deck, setting her beer on the railing.

"Did you build this yourself?" she asked.

"With some help from my brother."

"Does he live here in town?"

"In Fort Worth. We got the posts and piers done together, then I finished the rest."

He rested his beer on the railing and settled his gaze on her. He smelled amazing. Not like cologne or aftershave, but something subtle and masculine that made her want to bury her face against his chest.

She thought of their kiss again, how everything had ramped up in an instant. Physically, they clicked. It was the rest of it that seemed off. She kept getting mixed signals, as though he liked her, but then he didn't. Or maybe he didn't *like* that he liked her.

"Are you mad that I looked you up?" she asked.

"No."

"Are you pissed that I'm on this story?"

He took a sip, watching her, and set his bottle down. "Not pissed."

"What then?"

He hesitated, seeming to carefully choose his words. "I'm concerned."

"Why?"

"You're digging into something you know nothing about."

"Not nothing."

Irritation flickered across his face.

"We may as well be honest," she said. "I know more than you thought. I've managed to find a lot in only a few short days. You never thought I'd find any of it, did you?"

"You're resourceful." He turned to look at her, leaning against the railing. "And, yeah, I underestimated you. But that doesn't change anything."

"It changes things for you."

"How?"

"You're not my only source on this. I have others. Many, in fact. So you can relax. None of this is going to blow back on you."

He dipped his head down. "*That's* why you think I'm pissed off? Because I might get blowback over a fucking news story?"

She flinched.

"I couldn't give a shit about that."

She gazed up into those dark eyes, and again she saw the conflict. The frustration. And in her heart, she understood what was really bothering him. He didn't want her getting hurt.

She went up on tiptoes and kissed him.

Last time had been hot but controlled. Not this time. He dug his fingers into her hair and pulled her against him as he delved into her mouth. The kiss was hard. Demanding. And she slid her hands around his neck and kissed him back the same way. His warm fingers dipped into the back of her shorts and cupped her buttocks, bringing her close against him, and she felt the hard ridge of him through his jeans. Desire surged through her, and she arched her back, pressing her breasts against him. He answered by pulling her in tighter.

She loved the way he kissed. The way he tasted. She loved the way he smelled and the way he touched her, like some forbidden temptation that might be snatched away if he lingered too long.

His hands moved, and she felt them close around her waist, and suddenly she was up off her feet. She gasped as he set her on the wooden railing. They were at eye level now, and she saw the desire burning in his deep brown eyes. She kissed him again, wrapping her legs around him and pulling him in close, and he made a low moan. She slid her hands up his sleeves, over those muscular shoulders she'd been wanting to touch, and his skin felt warm under her fingertips. She wanted his shirt off. Hers, too. He seemed to read her mind as his fingers slipped inside her T-shirt and glided around her back.

A faint buzzing noise penetrated the haze. It blended with the cicadas and then was gone. But then it came back again.

Bailey pulled away. "Your phone."

He blinked at her.

"Inside," she said.

He muttered a curse, and she slid down from the railing.

"I have to get that. Don't move."

He went into the house, and she watched him grab his phone off the breakfast bar.

Bailey shook off the daze. Her flip-flops had fallen, and she slid her feet back into them. She looked up. Jacob was watching her through the window, but his expression was a million miles away. She knew what that meant.

She picked up both of their beers and went inside. From his clipped words, she could tell it was work-related, and she set the bottles on the bar and went to her purse to see if she'd missed anything from Max. No new messages, so whatever it was hadn't gone out over the police scanner.

Jacob ended the call.

"Sorry. Something's come up."

"No problem." She searched his face, and his tense expression didn't change.

"I should go."

He nodded.

She grabbed her purse and walked to the door. Without a word, he followed her out to her car and opened the door for her.

"Sorry," he said again as she slid behind the wheel.

"It's fine." She smiled. "It's probably better, actually, if we put the brakes on."

His expression darkened, but he didn't argue, and she felt a twinge of disappointment. She pulled the door, but he caught it.

"Nothing's changed, Bailey. I don't want you on this story. You don't understand the risks involved."

"Well, I'm on it, so you'll just have to deal." She sighed. "Maybe if we worked together instead of butting heads, it would be easier for both of us."

"How do you mean?"

"You help me. I help you. Collaboration? I'm helping you already, you just haven't acknowledged it yet."

He frowned at that idea, as she'd expected he would.

"No one has to know you're talking to me, Jacob. I can be very discreet."

His frown deepened.

"Think about it," she said, and pulled the door shut.

J ACOB WATCHED HER drive away, frustration churning inside him. Collaboration. Right. He didn't want to collaborate with her. Not on this case or any other.

Especially not on this case.

He wanted her way the hell away from it, and he didn't want Will McKinney or any of his hired guns to know Bailey Rhoads even existed.

We're talking brass knuckles and steel-toed boots. Guy had to have his jaw wired back together.

Jacob went back into his house and eyed his phone on the bar. Talk about shitty timing.

Or maybe not. Maybe it was good that his phone had stopped him from doing what he'd been dying to do for days now, which would have been a mistake for both of them. Why did she have to be a reporter? And not just any reporter—a reporter covering *his* case, one of the thorniest cases he'd worked, a case that he shouldn't even be working at all if he valued his career. But—just as with Bailey—he couldn't seem to resist.

Jacob scrubbed his hand over his face and checked his watch. He walked over to switch off the baseball game and heard his front door opening and closing behind him.

"Well, well. Progress."

He turned to see Morgan standing in the front room. She wore a skirt and heels again, which meant she was probably in town for another trial.

"Thanks for seeing me," she said.

"You said it was urgent. What's up?"

She crossed the room to his kitchen, where she leaned

her hands on the bar. "You're still working the Dana Smith case."

"That's right."

She huffed out a breath. "Jacob."

"You knew I wasn't going to hand it over to Mullins from the second you told me about it."

"What? I asked you—no, practically *begged* you—to let this thing go. And now days later, I hear you've been withholding evidence and talking to the Marshals Office?"

"I haven't withheld a damn thing." He crossed his arms. "But while we're on the subject, why didn't you tell me about Tabitha Walker?"

"Who?"

Jacob just stared at her, waiting. Morgan was an exceptionally good liar. But she had one tell, and he'd figured it out the first month they were together. She always asked a question to stall for time while trying to make something up.

"The second witness in the McKinney trial," he said.

"What McKinney trial?"

He waited, and it turned into a staring contest. She looked away first.

"She's not safe," he said. "Someone has to pull her out of wherever they put her—"

"We didn't put her anywhere."

"The Bureau, the Marshals, *someone* has to step up and do the right thing for this woman. She trusted you guys. You used her as a witness. And now someone with a federal badge fucked up, and your program's been penetrated. A woman is dead, and Tabitha Walker could be next."

Morgan tipped her head back and stared at the ceiling. She muttered something under her breath that Jacob didn't hear. Then she glared at him.

"You're impossible, you know that? I knew I never should have called you."

He waited, watching her. He had no patience for games right now. Or relationship bullshit. He needed information.

"Where is she?" he asked.

She scoffed. "I have no idea."

"You haven't warned her, have you?"

"*I* haven't? This isn't my case. It's got nothing to do with me."

"Mullins hasn't. The Marshals haven't."

Guilt flickered in her eyes, and he knew that he was right.

"Goddamn it, Morgan. Are they just going to stand by and let her get whacked? What the fuck's wrong with you people? She trusted you guys."

"No, she didn't."

"She stuck her neck out and—"

"She never trusted us. She never trusted anyone, from what I've heard. Yeah, she testified, but that was it."

"What do you mean?"

"That was *it*. She disappeared. Dropped off the radar. Tabitha Walker was never in WITSEC."

"Was she killed?"

"No."

"How do you know that?"

Morgan sighed. She walked around the bar and pulled open his fridge. He knew she wouldn't like the contents, but she stared anyway for a full ten seconds.

"I don't know why I'm talking to you about any of this," she said.

"I do."

She looked at him, and in the light of the refrigerator he saw that she looked tired. The stress of her job was taking its toll on her and had been for a long time. She closed the fridge and leaned back against the counter.

"She testified, as planned," Morgan said. "Then she disappeared. Evidently, she withdrew money from her bank account in advance and packed, so we know she planned to leave."

"Or someone wanted it to look like she did."

"I can't confirm that one way or another. But I can tell you she's not under federal protection. We don't know *where* the hell she is. So if anyone's going to warn her it's not going to be us."

Her tired gaze settled on Jacob, and he felt a deep uneasiness in his gut. But it wasn't new. He'd felt it since he first ducked under that crime scene tape and crouched in the mud beside a young jogger with a knife wound in her back. He'd known instantly this wasn't a typical homicide. He hadn't realized just how strange and complex it would turn out to be.

But it didn't matter. It had happened in his backyard. Someone had come into his jurisdiction and carried out a cold-blooded killing, and Jacob planned to figure out who it was and hold him accountable. It was as simple—and as complicated—as that. Jacob wasn't wired for diplomacy or office politics or interagency chess games. He was a cop. He'd taken an oath to protect and serve, and that was what mattered to him.

Morgan knew it, too, which was why she'd contacted him in the first place and why she continued to drop these nuggets of information on him. She believed in him. And she knew Mullins would be all too happy for this whole case to just disappear, solved or not.

"What will you do now?" she asked.

"Same thing I was doing before. Investigate. Track down a murderer. Hopefully, before he tracks down anyone else."

SEVENTEEN

TABITHA INSERTED THE keycard and let herself into the bungalow. The air was still and silent, and she knew right away that she was alone.

She moved quickly, positioning her cleaning cart in front of the door so she'd have advance warning in case someone came in. The guests were out for the morning, but Frank was a wild card, always lurking around the property and popping up unexpectedly.

She went straight to the bedroom. The dresser was a prime spot for jewelry and cash, but today there was nothing, not even a pile of loose change. Same for the bathroom. She checked the safe in the closet, on the off chance someone had left it open, but it was empty, too.

"Damn it," she whispered. "Damn it. Damn it. *Damn it.*"

Tears stung her eyes as she stared at the dresser. She wasn't a thief. Or she hadn't been. For months, she'd cleaned these rooms from top to bottom without even *thinking* of stealing anything, no matter how much cash people left lying around. But now that she really, *really* needed the money, as a matter of survival, every last guest was suddenly being careful with their stuff.

A bitter lump of disappointment lodged in her throat. But Tabitha ignored it and got to work stripping the sheets off the king-size bed. Next she stripped the pillows—all six of them, different sizes, because reviews ruled the world, and God forbid someone might post a complaint about pillow thickness.

After wrapping the linens in a bundle, she went to the bathroom and doused every surface with disinfecting foam. Then she started scrubbing, working high to low, the way she'd been doing since she was eight years old. The work calmed her ragged nerves, and she imagined her mother looking down at her. She'd approve of the cleaning, sure. Tabitha had become a master at it. But she wouldn't be happy to see her daughter scrubbing toilets for a living after all the sacrifices she'd made.

Tabitha's mom had worked two jobs so they could afford an apartment within a good school zone in the suburbs. There hadn't been money for maids or dance lessons or private tutors, and her mom had set aside every spare dollar so that Tabitha could go to a four-year university instead of a two-year community college like her mother had attended.

Tabitha wiped her nose. She was crying again, damn it. She was going on day four of barely any sleep, and her nerves were frayed.

Never look back. She couldn't get bogged down in the past. She had to be strategic. She had to make a plan.

She finished the bathroom and stuffed the bundle of sheets into the hamper of her cart. She dragged the vacuum into the living room and collected dirty mugs from the coffee table.

Her gaze fell on a silver corner peeking out from a magazine.

A laptop.

Tabitha's pulse skittered. She nudged the magazine aside. It was a Lenovo notebook, just like the one she used to schlep home every weekend from her job at McKinney Steel. Before she could think about what she was doing, she flipped open the notebook and powered it up. The familiar *whirr* and chime made her heart start to pound. It would probably be password protected. Of course it would.

The screen brightened and she was staring at a sunset desktop photo with a tidy row of icons arrayed across it.

No password. How lucky was that? It had to be a sign.

She glanced over her shoulder at the door. Frank was on the property somewhere. And the guest could waltz in here at any moment and get her fired.

But she had to look. She had to know. *Not* knowing what happened was making her insane. She clicked into a browser and stared at the screen.

Tabitha hadn't touched a computer in twenty-two months. The withdrawal had been excruciating, worse than giving up coffee for Lent. She'd had no idea how addicted she'd been to her devices. But she'd forced herself to stay away, because she knew the quickest way to blow her cover was to get online and take the teeniest, tiniest step back into her former life.

Now she stared at the screen and pondered what to search.

She had no idea where Robin had been living. They'd only spoken once since the day of their testimony when Robin handed her that burner phone and they'd made a pact only to use it if everything went to shit. But Robin, in typical Robin fashion, had broken the rules, calling Tabitha on her last birthday and leaving a message. Just the sound of her voice had made Tabitha realize how desperately *lonely* she'd become. Tabitha had always been a bit of a loner, but these last few months she'd felt utterly isolated.

A slamming door made her jump and turn around. It was the neighboring unit, where the guests had slept in.

Focus.

She turned back and stared at the screen, debating what to search. Back when life was normal, Robin had been obsessed with the idea of moving to California. They'd be trudging up Wacker Drive after lunch, with the icy wind off Lake Michigan freezing their noses and making their ears ache, and Robin had talked longingly about beaches and surfers.

Was that where she'd settled?

Tabitha's fingers hovered over the keyboard. Her hands trembled as she typed in the search terms: *CALIFORNIA AND MURDER AND WOMAN.*

A list of results appeared. Tabitha held her breath and skimmed them: *Elderly woman murdered during home invasion. Long Beach woman killed by stray bullet. Chico woman arrested in husband's murder.*

Tabitha scrolled through page after page, but none of the dates fit.

She bit her lip and reconsidered. The Marshals were footing the bill, so California was probably out in terms of relocating a witness. Too expensive. Ditto New York.

She tried broader search terms: *MURDER AND WOMAN AND UNIDENTIFIED.*

She hit enter and held her breath as a slew of new headings appeared.

Unidentified murder victim exhumed. Boise woman unidentified six years after murder. Police release name of woman murdered on bike trail.

Tabitha's stomach clenched. The date on the last story

was Tuesday and the reporter was Bailey Rhoads of the *Austin Herald*. Tabitha skimmed the first few lines.

The search continues for suspects in the murder of 25-year-old Dana Smith, who was stabbed to death over the weekend at Lady Bird Lake . . .

Tabitha's breath caught and she reread the words: *stabbed to death*. She clicked to read the full article.

The photo that appeared hit her like a sucker punch. The woman in the picture had dark hair and sunglasses, but there was no mistaking that dazzling smile. Robin had a cat in her lap and her arm around someone outside the picture.

Tabitha clutched her stomach. She felt dizzy. She stared at the screen, and all her deepest, darkest fears stared back at her.

CHAPTER

EIGHTEEN

BAILEY DROVE UP the curving driveway, catching glimpses of Granite Tech through the trees. The building perched atop a sheer limestone cliff facing the lake, a shiny glass fortress overlooking the city.

She curved around a giant water fountain at the top of the hill and parked in a visitor's space near the building's grand entrance. Tall glass doors silently slid open as she approached. A pair of spherical security cameras peered down at her like eyeballs as she stepped into the building. Taking off her sunglasses, Bailey looked up at the soaring atrium.

"Ms. Rhoads?"

She turned around, and a man fitting the description of Nico's friend approached her. He had short brown hair and a muscular, compact build like a gymnast. Chunky black glasses added a touch of computer-geek to the look.

"Seth Cole," he said, giving her a firm handshake. He

wore dark jeans and a green polo with the Granite Tech logo on the front.

"Call me Bailey. And thanks for meeting me."

"Let's get you checked in."

He ushered her to a round reception desk, where an auburn-haired woman wearing a headset glanced at Bailey's ID and handed her a green visitor's badge that resembled the badges she'd seen at Villa Paloma.

"I thought I'd show you around before we talk." Seth led her across the atrium to a bank of elevators. "You ever been here before?"

"No."

"You don't usually cover tech, do you? I don't recognize your byline." He smiled sheepishly. "I mostly read the business section."

"I'm on the metro desk. Tech is Nico's domain."

They stepped into a glass elevator that reminded her of her favorite Roald Dahl book. The doors slid shut and an awkward silence settled over them.

"How's Nico doing?" Seth asked. "Tell him he owes me a pint."

"He told me you'd say that. Nico's good. Busy."

"Yeah, I haven't seen him in a while. Probably since the spring."

"He's been slammed. We all have."

The elevator stopped, and they stepped into an open hallway overlooking the atrium. Bailey took a tentative step toward the long glass wall.

"What floor are we on?" she asked.

"Ten. All of our executive suites are up here."

Music to Bailey's ears.

"I was hoping to get some time with Lucinda Oberhoff. Do you know if she's in today?"

He lifted an eyebrow. "She is, but she's probably booked up."

"I'd really like to talk to your CEO. Even just a few minutes would be great."

"This way." He held his hand out to usher her down a long hallway overlooking the atrium. "I'll see what I can do. I'm in charge of operations, so I should be able to answer most of your questions."

They reached an open space with three glass offices facing a seating area. A receptionist sat in the center at a wide glass desk. He had a shaved head and rimless glasses. Instead of a company polo he wore a lavender button-down and black slacks.

"Levon, this is Bailey Rhoads from the *Herald*."

Levon's face brightened in a way she wasn't accustomed to, and he reached across the desk to shake her hand. "Delighted to meet you. Welcome to Granite Tech."

"Thank you."

"Any chance Lucinda has an opening?" Seth asked.

"Doubtful." Levon lifted a pencil-thin eyebrow. "Board meeting Monday. You know what that means."

"I would only need a few minutes," Bailey said.

He winked at her. "I'll see what I can do."

Seth led her past the middle office, a huge room with glass on two sides. "That's Lucinda's. I'm next door." He paused beside another spacious office, also with windows facing in and out. Bailey's workplace had glass offices, too, but they all had cheap mini blinds that could be snapped shut for sensitive meetings. Or, more recently, for Friday afternoon firings.

"Tell you what, we don't need to sit in there," Seth said. "Let's go to the Skydeck. You drink tea?"

"Coffee."

He led her down a corridor to yet another hallway overlooking an atrium. A coffee bar stood off to one side beside a cluster of high-top tables. The ceiling was all skylights, and people perched on stools beneath the streaming sunlight. Everyone had a laptop in front of them or was scrolling through a phone.

Seth stepped up to the counter and ordered a chai tea. Bailey asked for plain drip coffee and tried to pay, but Seth waved her off.

"It's free for employees."

"Really? Wow."

"Hey, there's Lucinda. One sec."

Bailey turned to see a rail-thin woman in a charcoal suit talking on her phone as she collected a frothy green drink from the end of the counter. She wore a pale pink blouse that should have softened the severity of the suit, but didn't, possibly because of her three-inch black stilettos. She ended her phone call, and Seth approached her.

"Lucinda, this is Bailey Rhoads from the *Herald*."

Her gaze narrowed and she turned to Bailey with a tight smile. "Hello." She stabbed a straw into her drink.

"Bailey's hoping to sit down with you briefly—"

She turned her tight smile to Seth. "Today's impossible."

"I would only need a minute or two," Bailey said.

Irritation flickered in her eyes as she looked from Bailey to Seth. "Have Levon set something up for next week." She grabbed her phone off the counter and nodded at Bailey. "Enjoy your visit."

She strode away with her cup, and Bailey noticed she had the calves of an Olympic athlete. She kept her gaze straight ahead, ignoring people's nods and greetings as they passed by.

Bailey glanced at Seth. He seemed a bit embarrassed by the brush-off as he led her to a table overlooking the atrium.

"Free coffee is a nice perk," Bailey said, taking a sip.

"Yeah, it's good for morale." He smiled. "Cheaper than stock options."

Bailey pulled out her notebook. "So, you know Nico from college?"

"Not really. I met him there. We were both CS majors. But I didn't really know him until he joined our Ultimate team."

"Ultimate Frisbee."

"Right. We've got about twenty people. Most of them work here or at Dell. We have a few from Google, too. Nico's the odd man out, working for the paper." He smiled again. "You play?"

"No."

"It's fun to watch. You should come out sometime." He nodded at her notebook, where she'd jotted his name and title. "Nico said you're writing about data security?"

"Sort of. I'm interested in the background checks you do for people. What information you collect and how you keep it private."

He nodded. "We take privacy very seriously. It's one of our three bedrocks."

"Bedrocks?"

"Bedrock tenets. Security, privacy, liberty."

She jotted down the words.

"Those principles are ingrained. Literally." He nodded at the atrium, and Bailey followed his gaze. "They're engraved on the granite floor down there. Bedrock. See?"

She peered over the railing at the granite floor ten stories below where employees streamed back and forth. The design showed a globe surrounded by the words *SECURITY * PRIVACY * LIBERTY * GRANITE TECH.*

"Interesting. Aren't those concepts kind of . . . contradictory?"

"What do you mean?"

"I mean, how does liberty go with privacy?"

He nodded. "Freedom from worry. We keep your life secure, so you don't have to." He smiled. "Or something like that. I sound like a commercial, don't I?"

"A little. Your main business is background checks for clients?"

"And increasingly we're getting into storage solutions. Cloud storage, that sort of thing. We take extraordinary measures to secure digital data for all our clients. That includes sensitive documents, emails, telecommunications, biometric data."

"Such as?"

"Fingerprints, faceprints, everything. Also, social security numbers, tax information."

She flipped a page. "I read about a data breach several years ago."

He winced. "Yeah, we got some bad press on that one. It was overblown, though."

"What happened?"

"Your basic phishing scam. Someone posing as one of our executives sent an email to an assistant in HR, asking for a list of social security numbers."

"And they provided it?"

"Yeah. The email looked legit. It was only off by two letters from a real Granite Tech email address. *But* it was phony, of course, so the list got sent to someone outside the company. We found out what happened when April rolled around and people started discovering someone had filed fraudulent tax returns and claimed refunds." He shook his head. "Like I said, it could happen to any company. It happens way more than you would think, but when the press got a hold of it, we took a real beating."

"That was three years ago?"

"Four."

"And now?"

"Well, that coincided with a rough patch, financially." He paused. "Can we talk off the record for a minute?"

"Okay." She put down her pen.

"Tensions were running high here at that time. We'd just had a round of layoffs. I know you know what that's like."

She nodded. "It sucks."

"Right. I had to do some of the firing myself." He rubbed his forehead. "Worst experience of my life. And, you know, it was stressful on a personal level, too. I kept my job, but I'd just forked over savings to pay off my student loans." He shook his head. "They say you're supposed to have something like six months' expenses in reserve? I had, like, six weeks, maybe, and we were doing layoffs everywhere. I was sweating it, thinking I was going to show up for work one day and find out I didn't have a job."

"I know the feeling."

He nodded. "So, you escaped the cuts at the *Herald*?"

"Barely." She smiled. "That's the beauty of being new and cheap."

Seth was watching her now with a certain eagerness that felt a little intense. She peered over the railing and watched the employees rush back and forth ten stories below.

"What's it like to work here now?" she asked.

"Better. But still, everyone works insane hours and does the job of two people." He shrugged. "But we have a young workforce. They can take it. You ready?" He nodded at her coffee.

"Yeah."

"I'll show you our Infinity Studio. Another new perk we added."

They walked down a glass catwalk, and Bailey got slightly dizzy overlooking the side.

"On the record again," she said, "have there been any more data breaches since the phishing scam?"

"No. And I say that definitively."

"How do you know?"

"We reviewed all our security procedures, tightened up everything, held training seminars to eliminate the human error angle."

"How do you eliminate human error?"

"Well, 'minimize,' I guess I should say."

They reached a window looking out on a two-story fitness room. "This is our Infinity Studio. Another benefit everyone is enjoying."

She looked out over rows and rows of weight machines, treadmills, and ellipticals, all with a view of Lake Austin, the iconic Pennybacker Bridge, and the city skyline in the distance. The studio was packed with thin, sweaty young people.

"It's busy," she commented.

"Like I said, it's a popular perk here."

Bailey counted twelve Peloton bikes, all in use and all tuned to different scenic ride channels. The views included a rain forest, a beach, a rugged coastline with waves crashing against the rocks.

"Plus, it fits in with our wellness program, so people get points."

"Points?"

"It's part of our company health plan," he said. "You accrue points and get a cash bonus if you meet certain standards like, say, not smoking or eating a plant-based diet, or working out one hundred twenty minutes a week."

"They monitor your *diet*?"

"We have an app that does it. You're laughing."

"I'm just imagining the *Herald* implementing a program

like that. Most of us eat a Whataburger-and-coffee-based diet."

"It's popular because people get cash for it. The program's very innovative."

"Sounds intrusive."

He shrugged. "People love it. Especially the boss. It's her brainchild."

"Lucinda Oberhoff came up with it?"

"Oh, yeah."

"Her name's quiet a mouthful. Does she have a nickname? Maybe Lucy or Cindy?"

"I've never heard anyone call her anything but Lucinda or Ms. Oberhoff."

"What's it like working for her? She seems a bit uptight."

Seth made a pained face. "She comes off that way."

"But she isn't?"

"No, she is. But she didn't use to be so . . . driven, I guess you'd say. That came after."

"After what?"

He looked surprised. "You don't know about what happened?"

"No. What happened?"

"I figured you would have read about it." He sighed and took a moment to sip his tea. "Her family was on a vacation in California. Lucinda and her husband and their two daughters. Her eight-year-old was abducted from a water park."

"When was this?"

He tipped his head to the side. "I guess it's been five years now."

"I missed the story. Did they ever find her?"

"No. Not a trace of her. It was horrible. Lucinda took a six-month leave while they searched, but the police never found anything."

"I'm surprised she came back."

"She had to. I think it kept her sane. She plunged into work, and it distracted her from Avery being gone. And there was a divorce, too. She's really been through hell. She's a survivor, though."

Bailey heard the empathy in his voice, and his affinity for his boss made a little more sense now.

He kept walking and they neared a solid black door. A pair of women paused and turned to look into a small glass window before opening the door.

"What's that?" Bailey asked.

"One of our labs. Our biggest one, actually."

"Mind if I see?"

"I'd show you, but it's strictly employees only."

"Just a look? I don't need a walk-through."

"Sorry. We don't even take recruits there."

A man paused at the door and turned to peer into the small glass window.

"What's he doing?"

"Iris scan."

Wow. Now she really wanted to see inside the lab. But Seth was already moving on, steering her back to the executive offices. Bailey realized they'd made a full loop.

"Seth?"

They turned to see Levon race-walking up to them, cell phone in hand.

"I was just looking for you two." He gave Bailey a beaming smile. "Ms. Oberhoff has an opening at four forty-five. I squeezed you in."

LUCINDA'S OFFICE HAD the same view as the Peloton brigade—hills, lake, bridge, and the distant Austin skyline. When Bailey stepped into her office, the CEO stood beside the wall of glass talking on her phone, and Bailey noted that she'd changed clothes. Instead of a suit and stilettos, she wore a form-fitting tank top and bike shorts. She had a hand planted on her hip and an elbow jutting out. Silhouetted against the glass that way, she looked like a scarecrow.

Levon led Bailey to a black leather seating area.

"She'll be right with you," he whispered.

Bailey sat down on the sofa and pulled a fresh notebook from her purse as she glanced around the austere office. No framed photos or diplomas. The desk was a huge sheet of glass balanced on a slab of granite. The only knickknacks on the desk were a trio of smooth stones, and Bailey craned her neck to read the words engraved on them: *SECURITY. PRIVACY. LIBERTY.* She managed not to roll her eyes.

Lucinda ended the call and dropped her cell phone on the desk. "Ms. Rhoads." She strode over and reached out a hand. "Glad to have you here."

The handshake was firm and bony. Lucinda had her hair back in a stubby ponytail. Up close, Bailey saw the lines on her tanned skin. Clearly, she spent a lot of time outdoors, and Bailey wondered how that fit in with her workaholic lifestyle.

"Excuse the clothes," she said. "I'm on my way to a ride."

"Do you go on the lake or—"

"I ride home every night. That's nine point two miles. I'm training for a triathlon in Napa." She perched on the arm of the sofa, looming over her, and Bailey resisted the urge to scoot away. "I understand you're writing an article about data security?"

"Not exactly. I'm interested in one of your clients in town. The Villa Paloma Museum?"

"Our clients are confidential."

"I understand."

"But I can tell you the list includes an array of Fortune 500 companies, as well as several universities, museums, hospitals—"

"What about government clients?"

She paused a beat. "No, actually. We're in the exploratory stages right now, but nothing's come through yet."

"I understand your main service is background checks?"

"That's one of our services. We also provide cloud services, document security, and on-site security guards in some cases—although we outsource that to a third party. We facilitate drug screening. The list goes on. I can have Seth provide you with a comprehensive list."

"I think I saw one on your website. How does all that work, exactly, when it comes to data security? People provide you with such sensitive information."

"We have strict procedures in place to protect any and all information that comes to us, I can assure you."

"Do you ever share client data with third parties?"

"Never. How would we stay in business?"

"What about selling client data to marketers?"

"Never. And we don't sell data that has been stripped of identifiers, either. Some companies do, but Granite Tech doesn't engage in that practice. Security and privacy are our top priorities, which is one reason we're going on three quarters of double-digit growth in market share. Write that down."

Bailey did as instructed. "Have you ever had issues with data being targeted by hackers?"

"No."

Bailey paused to give her a chance to expand. "I thought I heard about a phishing scam from several years ago."

"Oh, that." She waved her hand. "That was minor. I think maybe twenty people were affected by that. Really, nothing worth noting, even though the local press made hay with it. We did a comprehensive security review and changed our internal email procedures after that incident."

Bailey scribbled a few words, conscious of Lucinda's gaze on her notepad. She used a shorthand barely anyone could read, but it was entertaining when they tried.

"And since then?" Bailey asked. "Have there been any data breaches, to your knowledge?"

"No."

"None at all?"

"None."

Levon stepped into the room. "Ms. Oberhoff, it's five o'clock."

She stood up. "I'm sure Seth can answer any further questions. Oh, there he is. Seth, Ms. Rhoads needs a comprehensive list of our services for her article."

"Absolutely."

Lucinda grabbed her phone off the desk and zipped it into the back pocket of her bike shorts. Levon handed her a silver water bottle with the Granite Tech logo on it.

"Nice meeting you, Ms. Rhoads. Seth will show you out." She gave him a flinty smile. "Make sure you give her the full tour. Don't miss the Infinity Studio."

CHAPTER

NINETEEN

Jacob watched the trail, getting more and more impatient as the minutes rolled by.

"It's been an hour," Kendra said. "How long can he go?"

Jacob didn't answer.

"Figure an eight-minute mile, we're at seven and a half, at least." She glanced at him. "That's some stamina."

He didn't bother saying what they were both thinking. The man might have spotted their unmarked police car and wanted to dodge them, for any number of reasons.

"We should have come in your truck," Kendra muttered.

Jacob downed the last of his lukewarm coffee.

"What, no comment?"

He looked at her. She'd draped her jacket over the seat, and her white button-down shirt already looked wilted. It was barely after seven a.m.

She turned to face him. "Okay, Merritt. Enough. What's the deal with you?"

"What deal?"

"You've been sullen and quiet for two days now. What gives?"

Jacob adjusted the vent. The engine wasn't on, so the fan was just circulating warm air at this point.

"It's Bailey, isn't it? You're seeing her."

Jacob looked at her.

"Shit, I knew it."

"I'm not seeing her."

"Right."

Jacob *wasn't* seeing her, not the way she meant. And he didn't know what Bailey was up to right now, but he was pretty sure it involved wading deeper and deeper into the shitswamp that had become this case.

The case he'd been officially removed from.

The case that was no longer his, or Kendra's, but that they were working anyway against the explicit instructions of their boss.

Kendra laughed and shook her head.

"What?" he asked.

"It's funny, really. You usually hate reporters."

"I don't hate reporters."

She snorted.

Jacob wasn't going to argue with her.

"You know, she once dated Skip Shepherd."

He looked at her. "What's that got to do with anything?"

"This was right before her paper did that big exposé about the vice squad. I'm just saying."

"Those guys were dirtbags. If the *Herald* hadn't exposed them, someone else would have. Good riddance."

"I agree. I'm just saying, don't forget she's a reporter."

Jacob didn't comment. It was impossible to forget that about Bailey. She lived and breathed her job. It was part of who she *was*, and he respected that. He only wished it didn't make it harder for him to trust her. Whenever their conversation shifted to work—which was often—he always got the sense she was holding information back. He recognized the signs because he did the same to her.

Objectively, it was a bad idea to get involved with Bailey. But he couldn't get her out of his head. He'd been thinking about her since that first afternoon, and his interest had only ramped up after that kiss in his truck. He should have shut her down. He should have, but he hadn't. Pushing her away had been the very last thing on his mind.

"Jacob?"

"What?"

"Do you hear what I'm saying?"

"Yes."

She sighed, not sounding convinced. He wasn't surprised she'd picked up on his interest in Bailey. Had anyone else?

Jacob fixed his attention on the trail again as a woman plowed up the path, pushing a jogging stroller with one hand while texting on her phone with the other.

A man sprinted up behind her and came to a sudden halt. Six-two, brown hair, medium build.

"Heads up," Jacob said.

The man bent at the waist, catching his breath. Then he veered off the trail and walked to the drinking fountains, stretching his arms above his head as he went.

"That's him," Kendra said, grabbing the scrolled paper she'd stashed in the cup holder. They'd printed out the DPS record for twenty-nine-year-old Christopher Reynolds, who had been caught on a security camera entering the hike-and-bike trail from the parking lot around six a.m. all five days prior to Dana Smith's murder. Last Saturday, he'd arrived at 6:02 and departed at 7:10 in a black Jeep Renegade with Texas plates. The last call made on Dana's phone had been at 6:26, and the phone had been dropped—likely by her or her attacker—in the woods behind the juice bar several miles up the trail.

Jacob watched Christopher Reynolds as he made his way across the parking lot.

"He's big enough," Kendra said.

True, but it didn't take much to overpower a 116-pound woman, especially one who was unarmed and taken by surprise.

"The fact that he's here today shrinks the odds he's our guy," Jacob said.

"That's if you buy the hit-man-from-Chicago theory."

He looked at Kendra. "You don't?"

"It's the best we've got so far, but we certainly haven't proved it."

"Either way, he might know something. He could be a witness."

Reynolds crouched beside the Jeep and untied something from his shoelace. A key fob. He unlocked the Jeep and opened the door, then stripped off his T-shirt and tossed it in the back.

Kendra gave a deep sigh. *"Wow."*

Jacob looked at her.

"What? The man's hot. Look at him."

Jacob pushed open his door. "We doing this, or what?"

"You talk. I'll observe."

A suspect interview was like a dance, and he and Kendra had their choreography down pat after years of partnership. They moved together through the conversation, communicating silently as they sussed out weaknesses and zeroed in on the best way to exploit them. Working in tandem, they almost always extracted more information than they would have working alone.

They crossed the parking lot as their witness-suspect took a long swig from a bottle of water and set it on the

Jeep's roof. Then he grabbed a new T-shirt and pulled it over his head.

He caught sight of Jacob and Kendra and instantly went on alert.

"Christopher Reynolds?" Jacob held up his ID.

"Yeah." His gaze went to Kendra, whose hand rested on the butt of her Glock.

"We'd like a word," Jacob said.

"About what?"

"Is this your vehicle?"

His gaze narrowed. "Yes."

"Do you jog here every morning?"

"It's free parking. I'm in a space."

"Do you jog here every morning?" Jacob repeated.

The man watched him, and Jacob saw the moment he realized that he and Kendra weren't here to issue parking tickets. He'd probably seen something about the murder on the news.

Jacob watched the man's eyes, gauging his reaction, and he knew Kendra's attention was on his hands. Reynolds didn't look panicked or threatened. His blue eyes showed wariness. And just enough curiosity to wipe out Jacob's slim hope that this might be their guy.

"I jog here most days." He rested his hands on his hips. "Why?"

"Does this woman look familiar to you?" Kendra held out a paper. It showed a photograph of Dana Smith that Celeste Camden had provided to police.

Reynolds glanced at the paper. "No."

"Look again, please."

He took the paper and gave it a longer look. "I don't recognize her."

"What about this one?" Kendra handed over another photograph. The shot was more candid, and Dana was smiling and had a cat in her lap.

The man's expression changed as he studied the picture. "I don't know her, but she looks familiar." He glanced at Kendra. "Why?"

The tone of his voice told Jacob he knew who this was.

"This woman was murdered on the trail Saturday morning," Kendra stated.

Reynolds held the picture out to her. "Well, I don't know her. I might have seen her around, but—"

"Did you see her Saturday?" Jacob asked.

"No."

"When was the last time you saw her?"

"I don't know." He shot a worried look at Kendra. He was getting nervous now. But it was the mild kind of nervous, the kind anyone might get from being approached out of nowhere by a pair of homicide cops. Not the kind that reeked of guilt.

Kendra took back the picture. "Relax, Mr. Reynolds, this is a routine canvass. We've talked to dozens of people on the trail this week. We're trying to find out if anyone saw anything suspicious or out of the ordinary on Saturday or any other day, all right?"

He nodded.

"Now, can you look again?" She held up the second photo. "You said you've seen her around. Do you recall if that was Saturday?"

He took a deep breath and blew it out, then settled his gaze on the photo.

"Maybe," he said.

"Maybe?"

"I saw her recently. I think it was Saturday."

Kendra nodded. "Do you remember what time?"

"No." He wiped the tail of his T-shirt over his mouth. "Sometime before my run. She might have been over there by the lamppost."

"Doing what?" Jacob asked.

"Stretching. I think she started behind me."

"And you're sure this was Saturday?" Kendra asked.

"Yeah. I remember now because I didn't have my Airpods in. Usually, I do, but I left them at home."

"What else do you remember about Saturday?" Kendra kept her tone low-key, but she and Jacob were both on high alert now.

"I don't know." He raked his hand through his shaggy brown hair. "It was a regular day. Hot. And humid, too. We had that rain later."

Jacob waited, watching him, looking for anything off— even the slightest hint that he was lying or making something up.

"Who else did you see on the trail that morning?" Kendra was pure chill, no urgency at all. She'd taken over the questions, because the witness seemed more comfortable directing his answers at her.

"I don't know. The usual."

"What's the usual?" she asked.

Jacob had a pretty good idea already, because they'd spent two mornings canvassing this place.

"There's a running club. Some people with dogs. You know."

"What about individuals?" she asked. "You remember anyone specific?"

"I passed a couple track guys. UT track." He paused. "There was someone near the nature center."

Jacob's pulse picked up.

"A man?" Kendra prompted.

"Some guy. He was crouched near a tree, tying his shoe."

"What did he look like?"

"I don't know. Dark hair? He was looking down. I didn't see his face."

"Was he white? Black? Hispanic?" she asked.

"White. And he had gloves on."

"Gloves?"

"Golfing gloves. I noticed his hands when he was tying his shoelace."

Kendra shot Jacob a look. *Holy shit.*

"Did you think that was odd, someone wearing golf gloves to run?" Kendra asked.

"I thought it was random, yeah." He darted a look at Jacob. "But so what? Some guy out here rides his bike in a G-string. People are weird."

Kendra lifted an eyebrow at Jacob. He was right about the biker. Police called him Captain Butt Floss, and he was known to shout at tourists and pass out religious flyers on Sixth Street.

And so far, everything Christopher Reynolds said seemed credible.

Jacob looked at his partner, and he could tell she was feeling the same rush of adrenaline he was. After six long days, they had a potential eyewitness. It was a huge break. Maybe they could get him with a sketch artist and get something solid.

"What about his height? His build?" Kendra asked.

"I don't know. He was kneeling."

"And his hair?"

He sighed. "Dark. Short. That's all I remember. I really barely noticed him." He wiped his forehead with the back of his arm. "Look, I need to get to work soon. Are we almost done here?"

"Uh, no," Kendra said. "Not even close."

CHAPTER

TWENTY

BAILEY FOUND NICO in a conference room with his computer and stack of file folders. He plucked out his earbuds as Bailey walked in.

"You writing?" she asked.

"Transcribing an interview. What's up?"

She set a cold can of Dr Pepper in front of him, and his look turned suspicious.

"Thanks for setting up the interview with Seth," she said. "He says hi, by the way."

"I talked to him. He thinks you're hot."

"He does?"

The corner of Nico's mouth curved up. "You sound so shocked."

She perched her hip on the conference table. "I just didn't get that read from him." Well, maybe she had a little. At certain points in the interview, he'd seemed like he wanted to impress her, but that was pretty standard for people talking to a reporter.

Nico folded his arms over his chest. "So, is there a story there?"

"Nothing yet. I'm just doing background on something, like I said." She studied Nico's face. "What's that look?"

"You sure you're not poaching?"

"No. I told you."

"I thought you liked the crime beat," he said. "You got nominated for that AP award after the vice squad exposé."

"I love the crime beat. And I'm not poaching."

"But you can't tell me what you're working on."

"Not yet. But if it turns into anything big, we can work on it together."

He watched her for a long moment and seemed to believe her. He pulled the soft drink toward him and popped it open.

"So, what's up?" He took a long swig. Dr Pepper was his favorite, and she'd brought it as a goodwill gesture because she knew he was sensitive about her treading on his turf. Reporters were territorial.

"I've been reading about this FBI program. Next Generation Identification."

"Yeah, NGI. There's a company in town that developed some of the software. I wrote a piece about it last year."

"I know. What can you tell me about iris scans? Your article didn't go into much detail."

"Well, they're building a criminal repository of iris images. But that's just a small component of the overall project. NGI also includes fingerprints, palm prints, faceprints. The thing they love to talk about the most is the fingerprint database. The faceprint database is kept a lot quieter."

"How come?"

He leaned back in his chair. "Fingerprints are less controversial. They've got public opinion on their side. People generally figure if you're being fingerprinted for some reason, you must have done something wrong. Faceprints are a whole other matter."

"Why?"

"A lot of the images in the database are taken from noncriminal contexts, like state driver's license databases or passport applications or military records. We aren't just talking about mug shots here, and that's one thing that has privacy advocates up in arms."

"Tell me about the technology involved."

His gaze narrowed. "What are you writing about, exactly?"

"I don't know yet."

He didn't look like he believed her, but he let it go. "Well, originally some of the best tech was implemented by the big casinos. They were trying to spot people counting cards and running cheating scams. Since 9/11 the federal government has been in on the action, too, using the technology for law enforcement, antiterrorism, that kind of thing."

Bailey crossed her arms. "One person's 'terrorist' is another person's 'peaceful protester.'"

"Exactly. You can see how the technology could be abused. It's already happening in China and Saudi Arabia, where they've deployed it all over the place to track dissidents."

"They're probably doing that here, too."

Nico lifted an eyebrow. "Paranoid much?"

She shrugged. "I don't trust institutions. Never have."

"I can't say I disagree with you. I read about some shit in Virginia a while back. Some cop who took a cell phone picture of a woman he thought was hot, then got a friend to track her down in the DMV database, found out where she lived, and started stalking her."

Bailey's skin chilled.

"The thing about this technology," Nico said, "is that most people have no idea how insidious it is."

"How do you mean?"

"Well, it's based on math. Distance between pupils, nostrils, earlobes. The length and angle of the nose. It's things that are near impossible to change, so it's not like you can just wear sunglasses when you go out if you want to avoid it. And these cameras are everywhere now. They're capturing your image when you don't even know it."

A knot of dread formed in Bailey's gut. "So . . . someone could just look someone up?"

"No, not really. It's way more complicated than that. These databases aren't all connected, and there are rules about not sharing images. Plus, there're firewalls."

She thought of John Colt's words. *Nothing's impenetrable.*

"What's wrong?" Nico asked. "You look sick all of a sudden."

"I'm just . . . I'm fine." She stood up. "I shouldn't have skipped lunch. Thanks for talking."

She left him sitting there, baffled, as she crossed the newsroom to her desk. She wanted to talk to Jacob. Now. Maybe she could catch him at the police station. She grabbed her keys and pulled her purse from her desk drawer just as her phone chimed.

She didn't recognize the number or even the area code.

"Bailey Rhoads," she said as she cut through the maze of cubicles.

"Bailey, it's Seth."

The voice surprised her. She reached the elevator and tapped the button.

"I got your voice mail," he said, and she heard traffic noise in the background. "How did you get my cell phone number?"

"Oh. Sorry. Nico gave it to me last week. I hope you don't mind. I called your office earlier, but you weren't there, so—"

"When?"

"I'm sorry?"

"*When* did you call my office?"

"I don't know." The elevator was taking too long, so Bailey headed for the stairs. "Maybe around ten this morning? I left a message with Levon."

"What was it you needed?"

"Just a follow-up question about Granite Tech."

Bailey hurried down the stairs, passing Max, who gave her a reproachful look. She'd skipped the staff meeting this morning and he'd put her on the budget for tomorrow. Some damn fluff piece she didn't have time for.

"Seth? Are you there?"

"My reception's bad," he said. "What was your question?"

"When we were talking yesterday, you mentioned a rough patch four years ago. The company was doing layoffs and you said tensions were running high."

"Yeah?" His voice sounded wary.

"What prompted the turnaround?"

"What do you mean?" he asked.

"I mean, things were looking bleak for Granite Tech financially. But now they're adding employees and coffee bars and fitness studios." She reached the bottom of the stairs and pushed through the door into the lobby. "I'm wondering about the turnaround. What changed?"

Silence.

"Seth?"

Nothing.

"Seth? You there?"

She looked at her phone. But the call had dropped.

* * *

JACOB HAD JUST left the police station when he noticed Gabby on the sidewalk waving him down. He pulled over and lowered his window. She wore workout clothes and had a computer bag over her shoulder, and her short pink hair was pulled back with a cloth headband.

"Hey, I was looking for you." She rested her arm on the door. "Everyone said you'd taken off for the day."

Jacob had spent the afternoon at Cold Storage poring over a copy of Dana Smith's autopsy report, which he'd finally gotten his hands on, despite Mullins hijacking the case.

"I've been in and out," he said. "What's up?"

"Want to give me a lift to my yoga class? I can fill you in on the way."

"Sure, hop in."

She slid into the truck and stashed the computer bag at her feet. "It's five blocks west, right by the post office."

Jacob pulled into traffic.

"I went through every minute of video from the trail Saturday, everything we have," she said. "No sign of a dark-haired man in golf gloves. Or any gloves, for that matter—which isn't surprising since it was ninety degrees out."

"He could have removed the gloves. I'm sure there were plenty of dark-haired men."

"Yeah, but not jogging on that particular stretch of trail when Dana Smith was there. I got a couple women with dogs, a blond cyclist, a stroller mom. And then your witness, Christopher Reynolds. But no sign of this mystery man with the gloves."

Jacob pulled up to a stoplight and looked at her. "You check the boathouse footage?"

"Yes."

"The nature center?"

"Yes."

"All three cameras?"

"*Yes.* I told you, I checked everything." She dragged her computer bag into her lap and unzipped it. "He's not in the parking lots and not on the trail with her—not the section that's picked up by security cameras. At least not the cameras we're aware of. There could be more."

"There aren't. I've been down there three times now looking."

She opened her computer and powered it up. "I have a theory about that."

"Oh yeah?"

"I'll show you."

She tapped open a file as Jacob neared the yoga studio. It was a narrow storefront, and he didn't see anywhere to park, so he turned into an alley.

"Check this out." She placed the laptop on his console, the same console that Bailey had sat on the other night when she kissed the hell out of him.

"This is a map of the trail, and I've got all the camera locations marked in blue. The green areas show the view they cover."

"Okay."

"There's no way to run any significant stretch of this trail and avoid all these areas."

"Unless he scoped it out ahead of time."

"Yeah, that's my theory. I think your guy did some serious recon before the crime. He knew where the cameras were, where the tree cover was. He knew how to get in and out of that stretch of trail without being seen."

Recon. Another military word. According to an expert with the ME's office, Dana Smith's stab wounds had likely been made with a seven-inch tactical knife that had a serrated blade on one side. A combat knife.

"You see what I'm getting at?" Gabby looked at him. "He had to know all about this area ahead of the attack."

Jacob studied the screen. "He knew her timing, too."

"Well, maybe. If you assume *she* was the target. He could have just been waiting there, looking for a target of opportunity, some woman running alone that maybe fit the type he wanted. She could have been in the wrong place at the wrong time, and it could have been random."

It wasn't, but Jacob didn't share that information with Gabby.

"Send me that map, would you?"

"No problem." She snapped the computer shut. "I'll do it after my class. Thanks for the ride."

"If you come up with anything else, let me know. Call me anytime, day or night."

She got out, and he watched her walk to the end of the alley. He backed up and made sure she got into the studio okay before he checked his mirrors and pulled into traffic. His phone buzzed, and he dug it from his pocket. Bailey.

"Hi."

"Where are you?" she asked. "I just went by your office."

"I've got to drive up to Round Rock to interview a suspect's girlfriend."

"A suspect? You mean—"

"Different case."

"Oh."

He heard the disappointment in her voice.

"I can meet later," he said. "Want to have dinner?"

"I've got this damn gala thing I have to go to."

"Why?"

"One of our feature writers is sick today, so they tossed it to me. It's for the lifestyle section. What about afterward? I have to file a story but it can be short."

He battled the urge to invite her to his house. He wanted to pick up right where they'd left off the other night, but he'd told himself he wasn't going to go there. At least not while she was still writing about his case. Bailey was a determined reporter in pursuit of a story, and he still didn't totally trust her motives.

"How about we meet at Eli's," she suggested. "Nine o'clock?"

It wasn't any better than his place. If he met her there, they'd probably end up at her apartment.

He wanted to see her. He'd been thinking about her all day, and just hearing her voice was turning him on.

"Jacob? It's not a marriage proposal. I'm talking about beer and pizza."

"I'll be there at nine."

"Good."

CHAPTER

TWENTY-ONE

BAILEY STEPPED INTO the courtyard, careful not to catch a heel on the cobblestones and fall flat on her face as she entered the party. A week ago, she'd never even seen Villa Paloma, and now this was her third visit to the museum in four days.

The marble Greek goddess presided over the sculpture garden, which had been transformed into a luxe party venue with cocktail tables, votive candles, and vases brimming with pink and yellow roses. Swags of delicate white lights created a festive glow, and misters offered relief from the heat as guests mingled and sipped cocktails, accompanied by classical music from a string quartet.

Tonight's party was a fund-raiser for Austin Hands, an umbrella charity that benefited children's causes across town. The purpose of the event was—ostensibly—to raise money for backpacks filled with school supplies for needy kids. It was also a chance for Austin's elite to rub elbows and compare notes about their summer excursions to cooler climes.

Bailey slipped in among the thin, Botoxed women in gauzy summer cocktail dresses. At Max's direction, Bailey was appropriately attired in her one passable outfit—a short black sheath dress she'd worn to her sister's wedding rehearsal five years ago. When her editor had dropped this story on her, Bailey had made an SOS call to Hannah, needing advice on what to wear, and her sister had convinced her that the little black dress was "sexy" instead of boring and "classic" instead of dated. Bailey tugged at the scooped neckline. The dress was a wee bit tighter than the last time she'd worn it, and her boobs seemed to be overflowing.

She passed a long table, where a waiter stood beside rows of champagne flutes and a silver ice bucket with a bottle of Cristal. She did a double take at the label. Another waiter stopped to fill a tray with flutes, and Bailey wondered how many backpacks of school supplies could have been funded by all that champagne.

"You made it."

She turned to see Mick, the newspaper's veteran features photographer. Mick was in his typical jeans and cowboy boots, along with the khaki vest he always wore, as though he might have just blown in from an African photo safari. He had a Nikon around his neck and a highball glass in his hand.

"I'm jealous," Bailey told him. "I see you missed Max's cocktail-party-attire dictate."

Mick grinned and slurped his drink.

"Do you know who's in charge here?" she asked. "I need to get a quote." Bailey surveyed the crowd, looking for someone who seemed to be a nexus of attention.

"Iva May Boone." Mick lifted his drink and gestured toward the main villa. "She's right over there near the sculpture of the Three Fates."

"White dress?"

"That's her."

"She looks young for that name."

"Think she's in her forties." He stepped closer, and Bailey caught a whiff of gin. "She's married to Grayson Boone, who runs the Rainbow Kids Foundation *and* happens to be on the Board of Regents at UT."

"Think I've heard his name before."

"You have. He's a dick. He won't talk to you, so don't waste your time," Mick added. "But his wife wants publicity, so she should be good for a quote."

"Got it. Thanks."

"No problem." Mick tossed back the rest of his drink and put the glass on a nearby table. He looked Bailey over, and his gaze lingered on her cleavage, letting her know that it wasn't her imagination—she really was busting out of this dress.

"Who else should I know here?" Bailey asked.

"Also, you want to talk to the gal in green over there." He turned and nodded at a mousy-looking woman with a gray braid and a dark green dress that made her blend in with the hedges. She seemed to be hiding behind a palmetto tree as she watched the party with an anxious expression. "Dora Miller. Or maybe it's Millner. She runs Austin Hands."

"She looks a little shy," Bailey said.

"She is. She wouldn't let me take her picture, but get her going about the fund-raiser and she'll talk to you."

"Thanks for the tips. You seem to know everyone."

"I've been to about a million of these things."

"How long do you plan to stay?"

"Until they pass out the first wave of shrimp toast. Then I'm out."

"Good plan."

Mick adjusted his camera. "Well, I'm off to snap some photos. Don't get too crazy."

He walked away, and Bailey scanned the crowd. Iva May was immersed in a conversation with a woman who had big blond hair and a diamond ring the size of an ice cube. Bailey looked back at the palmetto, but Dora had disappeared.

Bailey made her way across the courtyard to the little white building where she had interviewed the art teacher on Tuesday. The green ceramic frog was gone, and now the door was propped open with an easel holding a sign that invited guests to step inside and participate in the silent auction. The grand prize was a five-night stay at a villa in Cabo San Lucas, probably donated by one of the evening's benefactors.

A tuxedo-clad waiter stepped over with a tray. "Care for champagne?"

Bailey eyed the slender flutes, feeling tempted. She was working, but what the hell. Her feet hurt.

"Thank you." She picked up a glass and sipped. It was tart and fizzy and felt wonderfully cool on her throat.

Bailey drifted over to a stone wall, where she had a view of the sunset over the water. The lake looked shimmery and gold, like the champagne, and Bailey tried to imagine living in one of the hillside mansions with this view. She couldn't. And she couldn't imagine a life of parties and shopping and spa appointments, either.

Bailey's phone chimed, and she dug it from her black leather clutch. She suspected it was Jacob canceling, and she felt a stab of disappointment as she pulled out the phone. But it wasn't Jacob. She didn't recognize the number.

"Bailey Rhoads."

"Bailey, it's Seth."

She checked the number again with a frown.

"Seth Cole."

"Hi."

"Am I catching you at a bad time?"

"Not really. What's up?"

"You asked the other day about a tour of our lab. I can get you in, if you're still interested."

Bailey's pulse picked up as she stared out at the lake. "That would be great, yeah. I'm very interested."

"I can meet you at the base of the driveway at eight thirty."

"What, you mean *tonight*?"

"It's the only window."

Something in his voice caught her attention. Nervousness. As though this were some covert operation he was running. She didn't know what he meant by "window" but thought it was better not to ask.

Bailey checked her watch. To make it in time, she'd have to ditch the party and completely wing it with her story.

"Yes or no? I need to leave now," Seth said.

"Yes. Definitely. I'll meet you there."

B AILEY PARKED HER car in the hillside neighborhood beside a giant oak tree. She darted a glance at the two-story house set back on the lot. The front windows were dark, and Bailey hoped no one noticed her parked here.

A pair of headlights winked into her rearview mirror. Bailey watched as a sleek black BMW rolled to a stop beside her, and the black-tinted window went down. Bailey lowered her window as Seth leaned over the seat.

"Get in," he said.

"Why?"

"My car has a tag."

Bailey gathered her purse and phone, then closed her window and got out.

"Leave your cell," Seth said.

Bailey ducked down to look at him through the passenger window. "You can't be serious."

"I am."

Besides being her tape recorder and her camera, Bailey's phone was her primary means of communication. She felt naked without it.

"No electronics," he said. "Deal or no deal?"

"Fine."

She stashed the phone in her console and locked the car, then slid into the little black coupe. It smelled like new leather and had a ridiculously elaborate dashboard.

Seth was watching her, his hand resting on the gearshift. He made no move to put the car in gear.

"Looks like you were out when I called," he said.

"On assignment."

He seemed to accept this explanation and started moving. He turned onto Granite Tech's private driveway and stopped in front of a closed gate that had been open when Bailey visited yesterday. The two sides of the gate slid apart and Seth glided through.

"What did you mean by 'window'?" Bailey asked.

"Our system is down for scheduled maintenance, which only happens about twice a year."

She looked him over. He wore jeans, sneakers, and a faded black T-shirt that seemed at odds with the fifty-thousand-dollar car. And he'd just told her he was basically sneaking her into the building.

They reached the top of the long driveway. Instead of curving left at the fountain, he veered right and drove around the building. Then he hooked a left into a short driveway that sloped down steeply. A black door rose, and they glided into a dim tunnel.

"Feels like we're entering the Batcave."

Seth glanced at her but didn't comment. They moved slowly through a tunnel and turned into a dim parking garage. Bailey counted only three other cars, all luxury SUVs.

"Is this, like, an executive parking area?" she asked.

"Yes."

He cut the engine and reached behind the seat to grab a black sweatshirt off the floor.

"Put this on," he said. "You look a little too . . . noticeable."

Bailey took the hoodie. It was big and soft and felt like it had been through the wash a thousand times. She shrugged into it and zipped up, covering her bodacious cleavage.

"You planning to tell me what we're doing here?" she asked.

"I wanted to continue our conversation." He turned to face her, and she felt a prickle of unease. She was in a dark, subterranean parking garage with a man she didn't know. She rested her hand on the door handle and tried to make it look casual.

"Which conversation?"

"About Lucinda." He glanced down at his key fob, and she noticed the silver medallion there. He stroked his thumb over it anxiously, and Bailey waited for him to talk.

"Lucinda is, without a doubt, one of the smartest people I've ever met. I've known her eight years and"—he shook his head—"she used to be different."

"Different how?"

"More like the rest of us. There was a mentality here when the company got started. Work hard, play hard. Everyone bought into that, even the people with spouses and kids. We had this shared—I don't know—energy, I guess you'd say. Everyone was talking about stock options and vesting schedules and an IPO someday if we were lucky enough."

Bailey just watched him, wishing he'd get to the point. He seemed nervous about this whole thing, and he was making her nervous, too. He'd called her from two different numbers today and had seemed worried about her phoning his office.

He took a deep breath. "When Lucinda lost her daughter Avery, it changed her. What she went through was indescribable. The grief. The weeks and weeks of leads followed by disappointments. The not knowing. I've never seen someone lose a child before, and it was agony to watch. *She* was in agony."

Bailey could only imagine how horrible that would be. If her sister ever lost Drew, she would be shattered.

Seth cleared his throat. "She went through the cycle they talk about—shock, anger, depression. I didn't think she'd come back. But then she did, and it seemed like the depression had morphed into an obsession."

"With finding Avery?"

"With work," Seth said. "We were on shaky ground by that point—in no small part because our CEO had been checked out for nearly six months. But she came back and made it her mission to turn things around, to keep the company afloat. No matter what the cost."

Bailey watched him. The car felt stuffy, and a cloud of anxiety seemed to hang between them. She could practically feel the guilt churning inside him. She wasn't sure precisely what he was talking about, but she sensed he felt deeply conflicted about it.

"You know, Seth . . . there are laws. Whistle-blower laws that offer protection."

The guilty look vanished. He sighed with disgust. "Whistle-blower laws?"

"Yes."

"You know, Bailey, for a reporter, you're pretty fucking naïve."

He got out and slammed the door. She got out and tucked her purse under her arm as he popped the locks with a chirp. Without a word, he crossed the concrete to an elevator bank and jabbed the call button. She joined him by the elevator and glanced at his face, trying to get a read. The flash of anger or hostility or whatever was gone now, and he simply looked blank.

They stepped onto a wood-paneled elevator that seemed cramped and claustrophobic compared to the one she'd ridden in before. Seth pressed his employee badge against a screen and tapped a button, and they whisked up with dizzying speed. Seth stepped off first, and she followed him into a dim, wood-paneled hallway.

"What floor is this?" she asked.

"Nine. We're under the executive suites."

He led her down the hall and used his ID to unlock a plain black door that led to yet another corridor. This one had glass windows along one whole side of it, and Bailey was startled to see row upon row upon row of big black machines.

"Is this a—"

"Data storage," he said, walking briskly down the hall.

"Like a server farm?"

"Oh, no. That's off-site. And it's five acres."

A man's head was sticking up from behind one of the rows of servers. Seth quickened his pace. Was he worried about someone seeing them? They reached a door at the end of the corridor and Seth quickly unlocked it with another swipe of his card. They entered a concrete stairwell, and he led her up a flight. At the top he paused next to the door.

"Walk alongside me, but don't talk."

"Okay."

Another swipe of his card, and he pushed open the door. Together, they stepped into a huge room with high ceilings. Bailey blinked at the brightness as they walked into a maze of cubicles. She looked up to see blue sky and wispy white clouds. It was a digital image projected onto the ceiling.

She hazarded a glance around. There had to be at least fifty cubicles here, but every one of them was empty with the exception of a workstation in the far corner, near the door. A man with a long brown ponytail sat in front of a screen. He wore bulky earphones and acknowledged Seth with a nod as they passed through the room. Seth headed for a smaller computer room, this one behind a panel of glass. Bailey followed him into it, and he closed the door behind them.

This room had only a dozen workstations. Seth walked to the end of a row and pulled over an extra swivel chair before sitting down. Bailey sat beside him.

"This is the inner sanctum," he said. "A lab within a lab, you could say."

"This is the area I saw yesterday? With the iris scans?"

"Correct. We came the back way." He glanced at his watch, reminding her that they were on a clock here. He tapped the mouse, and the screen came to life. His hands flew over the keyboard as he filled in four separate blanks to log in.

A green screen appeared with the Granite Tech logo on it, along with an hourglass.

"He's thinking," Seth said.

"He?"

He smiled. "I call this one Hubert."

Bailey set her purse on the desk, itching for her cell phone. She wanted to record this interview and take a picture of the room they'd just walked through.

"What's with the fake sky?" she asked.

"Studies show working near a window is good for productivity. We can't have windows in here due to security, so this is the next best thing."

"The twenty-four-hour blue sky doesn't get a little . . . grating after a while?"

"We have dusk around eleven. Then it goes into night mode for several hours, complete with constellations."

"Why?"

"Something about the circadian rhythms."

Another green screen appeared, and Seth entered two passcodes this time. "I read your series," he said without looking up from the screen.

"Which one?"

"The exposé about the police officers. The vice squad."

She'd had a feeling that was the one he meant. Last summer she'd written a series uncovering a scheme in which several officers were taking payoffs from drug dealers in order to look the other way. Two officers lost their jobs. Meanwhile, Bailey and her co-author got nominated for a journalism award. The other reporter ended up landing a job at the *Los Angeles Times*, and Bailey was tapped to cover the crime beat full-time.

"It wasn't the entire squad," she told Seth, not sure why she felt the need to defend the police department. "Just two officers, and they were fired after an investigation."

Seth lifted an eyebrow. "You know what they say about bad apples."

The computer screen switched to a water background with various icons on it.

"Okay, here we are." He checked his watch again and

cast a furtive glance over his shoulder. Then he scooted forward in his chair.

"This is it. Granite Tech's crown jewel." He clicked open a file. A cascade of numbers appeared on the screen. "It's called Ruby."

Bailey watched as the numbers scrolled. "Is it a spreadsheet?"

"A database." He looked at her.

"A database of what?"

"Several years ago, we embarked on an effort to amass the largest faceprint database in the world."

"Faceprints."

He nodded. "Each unique record is represented by a numeric code. We have more than a billion records."

Bailey looked at the screen. "I would think the FBI would have the biggest database. Or NSA."

"You'd think, wouldn't you?"

"Are you saying—"

"No, you're right. Of course they do. But ours is *private*. That's key." He leaned back in his chair. "All that stuff Lucinda told you about background checks and document security? That's crap." He nodded at the screen. "This is the engine driving our business."

"Faceprints?"

"Think about it." He sat forward eagerly. "We collect information about where people spend time, who they spend time with, where they spend money. Think of how valuable that information is."

"And this information is being monetized?"

"Absolutely." He tapped into a new screen. "We break it down by age group whenever possible. Look at this. This is our largest tranche of records, and it's eighteen-to-thirty-four-year-olds—a coveted consumer group. We have three hundred fifty million faceprints in that age bracket alone."

"Where did you get them?"

"We started with driver's license databases and built out from there. Not all jurisdictions will share the data, but some have, willingly or unwillingly, and we built on that foundation."

"*Un*willingly? Are you saying some images were stolen?"

He shrugged. "I don't know that for sure, but I can speculate. We somehow managed to amass a shit-ton of records in the last two years, and Lucinda's been vague about specifics."

He leaned forward again and tapped into a new file. Another long list of numbers popped up. "This is our second-largest tranche. We have more than *two hundred sixty million* minor faceprints."

"Minor as in—"

"Individuals under eighteen. These kids can't even vote yet, and their images are being collected and cataloged and sold to marketers."

"Where did you get them all?"

"Some are driver's license photos or passport images. But given the age, a lot more of these come from cams in the wild. Those are surveillance images. Parks, shopping malls, sporting venues. Pictures posted on social media."

"Social media platforms hand over these images?"

"There are ways to get them. And we have." He nodded. "This collection is growing every day as we amass more and more images."

Bailey looked at the computer screen, where numbers scrolled. She felt dizzy. And slightly sick, too. Seth tapped the mouse and made the scrolling stop.

"You're telling me you've collected more than two hundred sixty million images of children. Without their knowledge."

"That's right." He leaned back in his chair and folded his arms over his chest.

"But why would . . ." Bailey looked at the screen. Something niggled at her. Something Seth was trying to tell her, but *not* telling her.

Her skin chilled as realization dawned. "Oh my God." She turned to Seth. "She's looking for her daughter."

H E NODDED.

"So . . . she got her company to undertake this project as part of a personal quest?"

He nodded again.

Bailey shook her head, dazed by the implications.

"At first, I didn't know," Seth said. "About a year into it, I started to have my suspicions. But by then, the company was making money hand over fist, and there was no stopping it. We started to vacuum up more and more images from more and more places, and the whole thing gained momentum."

"I assume what they're doing is illegal?"

He made a pained face. "That's a gray area. I mean, some things definitely would be, such as hacking into state DMV databases and stealing records. But I don't have any proof of that. It's definitely unethical, which is why there's so much secrecy surrounding the project. Very few people working here even know about Ruby, even though the project's success is funding their paychecks."

"No one knows?"

"A few people have to know, but I haven't figured out who they are. Lucinda has the whole thing walled off."

"And you're sure she's the one running this?"

"Absolutely. Bailey, she's obsessed. I'm telling you, she'll do anything—break any law, rationalize any consequence— if there's even the slightest chance that what she's doing will locate her daughter. Lucinda is convinced Avery was kidnapped by a pedophile, and she believes Avery's alive somewhere. She latched on to that idea years ago, and she's never given up hope. But she's desperate. Which means she's the last person who should have control over the bio-metric records of millions of people."

"Why is it called Ruby?" she asked. "Is that someone's name?"

"Not that I know of. Lucinda came up with that. I've always thought it was a reference to *The Wizard of Oz*."

Bailey looked at the screen. "The ruby slippers," she murmured. "'There's no place like home.'"

"Exactly. Like I said, this is deeply personal to her, and she thinks it will bring her daughter back. It's a mission now, and nothing else matters. Not laws or ethics or even the long-term future of the company. She's consumed with this project and has been for years." He glanced over Bailey's shoulder. "Oh, shit. Don't turn around."

Her heart skittered. "What's wrong?"

He turned toward the computer and clicked out of the screen. "*Don't* turn around. Levon's here. I didn't know he was in tonight. If he's here, that means Lucinda might be, too."

Seth clicked into a browser and tapped some words into a search engine. The Granite Tech website popped up and he clicked into a generic press release.

Bailey's pulse thrummed as she stared at the screen.

Would Levon notice them in here? And if he did, would he recognize her? Her hair was down tonight, as it had been when she met him yesterday afternoon.

Seth glanced over his shoulder and let out a sigh. "He's gone." He dug his phone from his pocket and started texting.

"What are you doing?"

"Asking Garrett what he wanted with him. He's the guy with the ponytail we passed coming in here."

Bailey took a deep breath. Her palms felt clammy, and she rubbed them on her dress.

"*Shit.* She's here. She's going over her presentation for the board meeting on Monday. And Levon noticed me." He looked at Bailey. "When Lucinda hears I'm in, she'll probably ping me to come talk to her. Or come looking for me." He unclipped his badge from his belt. "You have to leave. Go back the way we came. My badge will get you through the doors. I'll meet you in the parking garage."

"But—"

"Crap, here's a message now." He looked at a text on his phone and stood up. "I have to go. I'll give her some excuse and then come find you. It shouldn't take long."

He moved away, and Bailey grabbed his arm. "You can't just leave me in a restricted area," she said. "What if I get caught?"

"Use my badge. You'll be fine. We've got twenty more minutes until the security system is back up again, so you should be good."

He rushed out the door, leaving her alone in the dim computer room. She watched him cut through the maze of cubicles and exit a different door than the one they'd come through. The ponytail guy—Garrett—didn't look up from his screen.

Cursing, she got up and shoved her purse under her arm. Even with the hoodie, she felt conspicuous in her short black dress and strappy heels. Her heart hammered and her palms felt sweaty, but she squared her shoulders and tried to look confident as she crossed through the computer lab to the door she'd come through with Seth. She spotted the little panel by the door and realized she needed his ID to get out, too. She swiped the badge, and her nerves did a little dance as a tiny light turned green.

She stepped into the stairwell, which seemed dark and foreboding now that she was here alone. She went down a flight. This door didn't have a panel, so she tried the knob and found it unlocked.

"That's right. Tomorrow."

Lucinda. Bailey's heart lurched as she recognized the voice on the other side of the door. She was talking to someone in the hall or talking on the phone. Either way, Bailey had to get out of there. She glanced up at the door she'd just come through.

Up or down?

Bailey hurried down. As she reached the landing, a door opened above her. Bailey's stomach flip-flopped. Someone was in the stairwell now. Bailey grabbed the railing and raced down another flight, praying her shoes wouldn't make noise.

"I don't want to hear it." Lucinda's voice echoed off the walls as she walked up the stairs. "Just make sure it gets done."

Bailey went down, down, down, flight after flight, keeping her footsteps as quiet as possible. A door above her opened and closed, and she hoped it meant Lucinda had gone.

The stairwell went silent, and Bailey rushed down another flight and another, round and round until she felt dizzy and wobbly on her damn high heels. Finally, she reached the bottom.

She halted.

Would this be the parking garage? She and Seth had gone through a long corridor to reach the stairwell, so she wasn't in the same part of the building where she'd entered originally.

Somewhere above her, a door opened again. Bailey's pulse jumped. She fled through the door in front of her and found herself in a dim corridor with cinder-block walls. Where was the parking garage? The only light came from the red glow of a distant *EXIT* sign. Bailey turned around and tried the door behind her but it was locked now.

"Shit."

She glanced up and down the corridor and hurried for the exit. Her heart pounded as she reached a corner where the corridor opened up into what looked like a maintenance room filled with HVAC equipment. A maze of pipes and ducts crisscrossed the ceiling. A door slammed, and Bailey jumped back. She waited, heart thudding, her back pressed against the wall. What if she was trapped down here? Slowly, she peered around the corner in time to see a man in gray coveralls slip through a doorway.

Bailey made a dash for the *EXIT* sign. No keypad on this door, thankfully. She reached for the handle, then hesitated. What if an alarm sounded? Hopefully, an interior door wouldn't have one. Holding her breath, she pushed through the door.

Relief rushed through her as she found herself in a parking garage.

None of the cars looked familiar, though. She saw a white Mercedes, a yellow Fiat. She spied a concrete ramp on the far end of the space. Maybe there was another level? She hadn't counted the flights of stairs on her way down here.

Bailey cast a nervous look around as she race-walked

across the garage. The warm air smelled of dust and diesel fuel. Glancing around, she spied an eyeball-shaped camera mounted at the top of one of the concrete pillars. Her stomach knotted. She hoped the system was still down, as Seth had said.

She race-walked past the Mercedes and the Fiat and hurried up the ramp. She passed a concrete pillar, and on the far end of the next level were the three SUVs she recognized, and now a silver pickup truck, too.

Where was Seth's car?

She spied another eyeball-shaped camera. It *moved*.

Panic shot through her. Bailey quickened her steps. Had Seth *left* her? She had no phone or way to communicate. No one even knew she was here right now—not her editor, not Nico, not Jacob. She hadn't told anyone she was coming here, and she realized now how careless that was. She passed another concrete pillar, and the back of Seth's car came into view beyond the pickup. Bailey's breath whooshed out with relief.

Behind her, a noise.

She lurched behind a pillar. She held her breath and strained to listen, but the garage was silent.

A rumble started in the distance—an air conditioner maybe, or some other heavy equipment. She listened to the mechanical sound and tried to make out any other noise. Nothing.

Bailey rushed toward Seth's car. Where the hell was he? Her skin chilled at the thought of waiting down here all alone, for who knew how long.

Footsteps.

She darted behind another pillar, panting this time because she *knew* she hadn't been mistaken. Someone was down here.

She cast a frantic look around, searching for movement

or shadows. She didn't see anyone, just rows of concrete pillars. Someone could be hiding behind any one of them.

Why hiding?

If it was just someone down here walking to their car, why hide?

Bailey's heart hammered. She tried to think. Slowly, silently, she unzipped her purse and pulled out her key chain. She fisted her hand around the car key, letting it protrude through her fingers. Not much of a weapon, but it was better than nothing.

She listened. Nothing. Her pulse pounded. Where the hell was Seth? Was that *him* lurking behind her? But why would he sneak up on her?

Bailey eyed his black car, wishing it were closer. Slowly, she reached down to slip off her slingback heels, first one, then the other. She tucked one of the shoes under her arm and then held the other heel out, like a weapon.

Now she was armed with a Toyota key and a Jessica Simpson sandal. She moved to the edge of the pillar and peeked out.

Nothing.

No movement, no sound, no shadow.

Ding.

She whipped her head around as Seth stepped off the elevator. He strode toward his car, and she ran to join him.

Behind her, a metallic *click*. Bailey's heart lurched.

Seth spotted her and stopped beside the BMW. "What's wrong?"

"Go, go, go!"

He popped the locks. She raced for the car. Fire blazed up her foot as she stepped on something sharp. She didn't stop to see what it was—she jerked open the door and jumped inside the car, throwing her shoes and purse on the floor.

"What happened?" he asked.

"Drive! There's someone following me."

Seth started the engine and shoved the car into gear. The BMW lunged forward, and Bailey ducked low in the seat, skimming her gaze over the shadows and pillars as Seth zoomed toward the tunnel.

"*Who's* following you?" he demanded. "Where?"

"I don't know. Just go!"

He raced through the tunnel and slammed on the brakes as they reached the end. Bailey held her breath as the black door slowly lifted.

He gunned it through the opening, and Bailey felt a wave of relief to be out in the open beneath a clear night sky. She looked at the side mirror and saw the building looming behind them. An icy chill raced down her spine.

"You were supposed to take the elevator," Seth said.

Bailey looked at her foot. It was bleeding, damn it. She unzipped her purse and searched for a tissue.

"Shit, are you okay?" he asked.

"I stepped on something."

No tissue, so she tore a piece of paper from her notepad and used it to blot the blood. She plucked a chunk of glass from the cut.

"I heard Lucinda in the hallway," she told him, "so I took the stairs."

"Are you sure it was her?"

"Yes."

"Did she *see* you?"

"No. I don't know. I don't think so. I cut through a maintenance room and found the parking garage, and then I heard someone following me."

"Who was it?"

"I didn't see." Her stomach clenched as she thought of the metallic *click*. "Do you guys have security guards? I heard a noise, a *click*. Like a magazine being loaded."

Seth cut a glance at her. "You mean like—"

"I don't know *who* the hell it was, but I think they had a gun."

CHAPTER

TWENTY-THREE

JACOB MADE ONE more pass by Bailey's building. This time her light was on. He circled the block and spotted her white Toyota parked along the street. He'd been by half an hour ago, so she must have just come home.

Jacob wedged his truck into a too-small space. He took the stairs to her apartment and knocked, struggling to tamp down his impatience as he waited for her to answer.

Finally, the door swung open and Bailey stood there in a short black dress.

"Sorry about Eli's," she said.

His gaze went from her cleavage to her legs to her bare feet and that silver toe ring.

"You're bleeding."

"I stepped on some glass in a parking garage." She turned and limped into the kitchen, glancing back at him over her shoulder. "You want a drink?"

"No."

Jacob shut the door and followed her. A shoebox

crammed with first-aid supplies sat on her breakfast table alongside a bottle of rubbing alcohol. She sank into a chair and bent over her injured foot. She dabbed at the cut with a cotton ball, and he noticed the tremor in her hands.

"I left you a message," she said, not looking up.

"I got it."

"I would have called earlier, but I didn't have my phone."

Jacob pulled out the other chair and sat down, watching her. "Where were you?"

"I left the gala to go to meet a source at a local tech company."

"Granite Tech."

She glanced up, startled. "How did—"

"You mentioned them the other day." And the fact that she didn't remember told him just how rattled she was. He looked her over. Several curls clung to her sweaty neck. No other injuries that he could see besides the cut on the arch of her foot.

"Hold that, will you?" She rested her heel on his thigh. Jacob held the cotton ball in place as she rummaged through the shoebox. She unwrapped a big Band-Aid and sealed it over the cut, then she pulled her foot away and stood up.

"How about a bourbon?" she asked.

"I'm good."

She crouched beside a cabinet and fished a bottle of Jack Daniel's from behind a row of margarita glasses. She plunked it on the counter and blew a layer of dust off it. Looked like she hadn't dragged it out since her last party.

"What did you learn at Granite Tech?" he asked.

"A lot." She took a glass down from an upper cabinet and opened the fridge to get a can of Coke. "I can't talk about it yet. I'm still nailing things down."

Jacob gritted his teeth as she poured bourbon into the

glass and followed it with a splash of Coke. She took a sip. Then she set the drink on the counter and watched him.

"You're pissed that I stood you up," she said.

"No."

She rolled her eyes. "Oh, come on."

"That's not why I'm pissed."

"At least you admit it." She lifted her arms to twist her wild curls into a knot, and her dress rode up a few more inches, revealing those strong thighs she used for rowing.

He walked over to the counter and leaned against it, watching her.

She secured her hair and rested her hands on her hips, regarding him with a suspicious look. "Why *are* you pissed?" she asked.

"You didn't listen to a word I said last night. You're still nosing around a murder case that we both know has an organized-crime connection. And you snuck into some company after hours to dig up dirt they don't want you to have—"

"I didn't *sneak* anywhere. I was escorted by a source. It was perfectly fine."

"Uh-huh." He crossed his arms. "Who'd you say that source was again?"

"I didn't."

"If everything was fine, how come you're still shaking? And how did you end up in a parking garage barefoot?"

She blew out a breath. "It's a long story."

"Let's hear it."

"I'll tell you later. I can't yet."

Jacob's chest tightened. He gazed down at her gray eyes and her flushed skin, and he hated that she was hiding shit from him. He hated even more that she was stubborn as hell, and he couldn't make her tell him a damn thing.

"I will, Jacob. Trust me."

* * *

BAILEY FULLY INTENDED to tell him. Soon. As soon as she had the rest of the info she needed from Seth, and she could present the facts to Jacob in a cohesive way that didn't make her sound like some wacky conspiracy theorist. Hopefully, it would only be a few more hours.

Jacob glared down at her, and she could feel that pent-up emotion he was trying not to show. He was trying to be low key, like getting stood up didn't matter and he hadn't been worried about where she was.

How long had he waited at Eli's? She didn't know, but it pained her to think of him sitting there wondering what had happened. She could see he'd gone home at some point because instead of his detective clothes, he now wore jeans and a black T-shirt, along with scarred leather work boots with tiny flecks of paint that matched the color of his house.

He shook his head and looked away.

"What?" she asked.

"You're frustrating, you know that?"

She lifted a shoulder. "I get that a lot."

He stepped closer, and her nerves fluttered at the dangerous gleam in those dark brown eyes.

He dipped his head down and kissed her. It was hot and intense, and she went up on tiptoes and kissed him back the same way. He was angry. She got that. But somehow that made the kiss even better, and she combed her fingers into his hair and dug her nails into his scalp.

He tasted sharp and musky, and she realized she'd missed him, which didn't make any sense, really, but there it was. She kissed him harder, nipping his lip and eliciting a low groan. She didn't know what was wrong with her. She felt edgy and anxious, and she was spoiling for a fight. Or some good sex.

He clutched her hips, and she felt the warmth of his hands through the thin fabric of the dress. She pressed her breasts against him, and next thing she knew he'd lifted her off her feet and was walking her backward toward the living room. The backs of her thighs bumped against the sofa arm.

She pulled back and rested her palm on his chest. "Where's your gun?"

"Ankle holster."

"Take it off."

He gazed down at her for a moment and then crouched down, hitching up the cuff of his jeans to pull a compact black pistol from his boot. He crossed the room to lock her front door and set the pistol on the counter. He pulled his wallet from his back pocket and tossed it beside the gun, then dug out his phone and keys and added them to the pile. Bailey sat on the sofa arm, watching him with a warm tingle in the pit of her stomach.

He came to stand in front of her. She was eye-level with his chest, and he brushed a curl out of her face and tucked it behind her ear.

"Better?" he asked.

"Yes."

He bent down and kissed her again. Her fingers traced over the stubble along his jaw, then slid around his neck and pulled him close. He lowered her back onto the sofa and hovered over her, and the intent look in his eyes made her heart skitter. She scooted back on the cushions to make room for him.

He rested his knee between her legs and gazed down at her. "You said you wanted to put the brakes on."

God, had she said that? She had. Yesterday. Or the day before. When she'd been leaving his house feeling snubbed after that phone call.

Jacob looked at her with those solemn brown eyes. He was asking her what she wanted, giving her one more chance to change her mind.

"Come here." She dragged his head down and kissed him, and soon his weight was on her, and she felt a flood of relief because this was finally happening after way too many false starts.

His hand slid up her thigh and under her dress, and he made a low noise in his throat. She tipped her head back, and he kissed his way down her neck and lingered over the swell of her breasts.

"Damn, you smell good," he murmured.

"I smell like sweat."

"No." He trailed his lips over her neckline, and she arched into him. She slipped her hands under his T-shirt, loving all that smooth, hard skin. She felt good with him. Safe. And the anxious, acidy feeling in her stomach was giving way to something much, much better.

She loved the feel of his body. She loved the taste of his mouth and the warmth of his hands sliding over her, gently squeezing her curves as though he wanted to learn them. He pulled the strap off her shoulder, and heat flared in his eyes when he discovered she wasn't wearing a bra. His mouth closed over her nipple and he gave a hard pull. She propped on her elbows and tipped her head back, arching against him as he teased her with his tongue.

He slid his hand behind her. "Where's the zipper?"

"Side."

He stopped what he was doing to examine the dress. She turned onto her side, and his gaze met hers as he gave the zipper a slow tug. Then his hand slid inside to cup her breast as he kissed her shoulder.

She closed her eyes and savored the warm feel of his hands moving over her. They were strong and callused, but the brush of his fingers was just light enough to set off hot little ripples throughout her body. He rolled her onto her back and she felt the straps easing off her shoulders as he slid the dress down her body and over her hips. And then she was lying there in only a sheer black thong, and her bare skin tingled as he dropped her dress to the floor.

He gazed down at her with a look so intense it made her stomach tighten. He pulled his T-shirt over his head and tossed it away and leaned over her, resting his palm on the arm of the sofa. He looked like he wanted to say something, but instead he dipped his head down and kissed her again. She stroked her fingers over his muscular shoulders, down the valley of his spine, then rested them on his hips.

She absolutely loved his body, but she didn't want to tell him so. Instead, she stroked her hands over his shoulders, squeezing the muscles as she kissed him. She dipped her hands into his back pockets, pulling him tight against her as she wrapped her legs around him. They moved against each other, creating a rhythm as the heat built and the tension coiled so tightly inside her that she didn't want to wait. He seemed to know what she was thinking because he pulled back and gazed down at her, breathing hard.

"Bedroom," she whispered.

He pushed off the sofa and scooped her up, and she let out a yelp.

"I can *walk*."

"I know."

He carried her down the dim hallway and pushed open the door with his shoulder. The bedroom was dark except for the closet light, and she scanned the room, relieved to see Boba Fett curled up on the armchair instead of the bed.

Jacob set her down amid a pile of pillows. "Are you hurt anywhere else I don't know about?"

"No."

She got to her knees and started unbuckling his belt. He combed his fingers into her hair and kissed her, and she felt his sharp intake of breath as she closed her hand around him. He took her wrist.

"Wait."

She released him reluctantly, and he disappeared down the hallway before coming back and tossing a condom packet on the nightstand. She sat back on her heels and watched as he stripped off the rest of his clothes and came to stand beside the bed. She stroked her hands over him, tracing his wide shoulders and running her fingers over his sculpted chest, brushing her fingertips over the coarse hair. She still didn't know what he did to stay in shape, but he invested some serious time into it.

She tilted her head back to see him, and the simmering look in his eyes set off a flurry of nerves. He seemed so intense. Not just now, but always, and she shivered with anticipation of how they'd be together. She lay back on the bed, pulling him with her, and the delicious weight of him between her thighs made her moan as she hooked her leg around him and kissed him.

He moved down her, lingering over her neck and then her breasts and then her navel before sliding the last scrap of clothing from her body, and by the time it whispered to the floor, she could hardly breathe because her heart was racing. She reached for the condom and handed it to him, and he tore it open with his teeth and got it on quickly. He shifted her legs apart and rested his palm behind her head.

Holding her gaze, he pushed inside her, making her gasp. She closed her eyes and wrapped her legs around him as he pushed again. And again. They fit together perfectly, and she clutched his hips as he surged into her over and over, until every cell in her body burned and glowed. She wanted more. Him. She moved against him, straining to keep up with the pace as he moved faster and faster, until she felt mindless with need.

"Bailey, hold on."

She closed her eyes and dug her nails into him, and he drove into her so hard, the bed jumped.

"Jesus, sorry."

"Don't stop."

He kept going until she felt so hot, she could hardly breathe.

"Bailey . . ."

She heard the edge in his voice, and she pulled him closer, as close as she could until they were fused together.

"Now," she gasped. *"Please."*

Another mind-blowing thrust, and she came apart. He held her through the tremors, and then collapsed on top of her.

She couldn't breathe or move with his weight on her. But she didn't care. She was too blissed out to care about anything.

He pushed up on his arms and stared down at her, breathing hard. Then he got out of bed and disappeared into the bathroom.

She closed her eyes. *Oh. My. God.* All this time she'd suspected. And now she knew.

The bed creaked as he stretched out beside her. She rolled toward him but didn't open her eyes. Her heart hammered inside her chest. She rested her fingers against his sternum and felt his hammering, too. His skin was warm and slick, and she loved that they'd worked up a sweat together.

She had so many questions. Was it always this intense for him? Or was there something special with her? She looked up at him, and his eyes were closed, but his thudding heart told her he was wide awake.

She wondered if he had to leave soon. Or if he was on call tonight. If he was, she didn't want to know about it. She didn't want to think about work or crime or violence. She didn't want to talk or argue or analyze anything. She just wanted to float along on a cloud of perfect, soul-searing sex.

He slung his arm over her waist and pulled her closer, and Bailey's heart melted at the possessiveness of the gesture. Nestling her head against him, she sighed deeply and let herself drift.

TABITHA CUT THROUGH the kitchen and stopped at Theo's office. Empty again, damn it.

A bitter lump of frustration clogged her throat. He'd blown her off Thursday after the wake, and tonight he hadn't been into work at all yet. She needed her money, and she couldn't wait around anymore.

Someone had followed her home yesterday—she could have sworn to it. She'd ducked into a grocery store and sneaked out the back, walking right through the refrigerated stockroom before slipping into an alley. She'd taken a back route home, glancing over her shoulder the whole time, and when she finally reached her door her clothes had reeked of sweat and panic.

Was she being paranoid? Maybe.

But Robin hadn't been paranoid enough. Instead she'd been trusting and look where that had gotten her. She'd trusted the government, not just once but twice, and it had cost her everything.

Tabitha stared at Theo's cluttered desk, and tears burned her eyes. She needed that money, and it was *hers*. She'd earned it. She spied the little brass key beside his computer. It probably opened the top desk drawer where he kept a black zipper pouch, which held a thick stack of cash. She eyed the key, and her fingers itched to grab it.

Four hundred dollars. That was what stood between her and her escape. That amount used to mean nothing. It was a big weekend out. A pair of nice boots. And four hundred dollars paled in comparison to the checks that used to cross her desk when she worked at McKinney Steel. That kind of money was staggering, which made it even more surreal that she was nearly losing her mind now over four hundred bucks.

"Red!"

She jumped and turned around. Layla walked toward her.

"Table ten needs a check. What are you doing back here?"

"Nothing. Have you seen Theo?"

"He's right there." Layla nodded, and Tabitha turned to see Theo walking through the kitchen and reading his cell phone.

Relief flooded her. Thank God she hadn't gone for that key.

Theo glanced up as he stepped into the corridor. His face instantly turned wary.

"I'm busy, Red."

"I know, me too."

He brushed past her into his office.

"I need to talk to you again about—"

"Where's your car?" he demanded.

Her car. Her car. The made-up car she'd told him about earlier.

"Still in the shop," she said.

"*Which* shop?" He sank into his desk chair.

"Riley's Automotive." It was the first thing that popped into her head. She'd seen the sign somewhere.

Theo dropped his phone on the desk. "Buncha crooks

over there. They're probably bilking you." He leaned back in his chair and looked at her. "How much do I owe you?"

She cleared her throat. "Four hundred and ten."

He sighed, and Tabitha's pulse picked up. Her palms started to sweat. He watched her eyes closely, as though gauging her truthfulness.

"I can give you two hundred now and the rest next Friday."

Her stomach clenched. She bit her tongue and nodded. "Thank you."

He dug a key chain from his pocket and flipped out a bronze key like the one on his desk. He opened the drawer and pulled out the black zipper pouch, and she held her breath as he took out four crisp fifties and handed them over.

"Thanks," she said again, and this time she meant it. She folded the bills and tucked them into her apron.

His eyes narrowed with suspicion. "You're closing tonight, right?"

"Actually, Layla and Rita are."

He turned to his computer and jiggled the mouse to wake it. "I need you to stay, too. We're slammed out there. They're three deep at the bar."

"Sure. No problem. Thanks again."

Tabitha headed out the door. With a quick glance over her shoulder, she ducked into the restroom. Her heart was racing, and she was sweating through her clothes. She was a terrible liar. She splashed water on her face and looked at herself in the mirror. She dabbed her cheeks with a towel and reviewed her plan.

Two hundred was only half of what she'd hoped for, but obviously better than nothing. It would cover her bus fare, at least, for the long trip ahead of her.

Tabitha pulled out the bills and tucked them into the

slim wallet she kept in the front pocket of her jeans, where it was safe from pickpockets. Then she opened the door and did a quick check of the hallway before walking straight out the back door.

The alley behind the pub reeked of garbage. The air was heavy and muggy, but it felt good to be outside, and a weight seemed to lift off her shoulders as she walked toward the street. A bluesy guitar riff drifted from the bar around the corner, and pedestrians streamed back and forth. People were out tonight.

I need you to stay, too.

Theo had known something was up. He probably suspected she was about to ditch her job. But he'd done her a favor anyway and look how she'd repaid him. She used to be loyal.

Guilt needled at her, but she pushed it out of her mind. She couldn't think about it now. Blind loyalty was what had gotten her into this mess in the first place. Blind loyalty— loyalty at all—could easily get her killed.

She stopped by a dumpster at the end of the alley and pulled the three leather folios from her apron. She checked each one, making sure she hadn't missed any cash, but she hadn't. She untied her apron and wrapped everything into a ball and tossed it in the dumpster.

Never look back. It had been her mantra for months now, and she needed to get the words locked in her head again.

She rounded the corner and slipped into the stream of people. A group of guys huddled on the sidewalk laughing and hanging on to each other. Probably a bachelor party. Or maybe some stupid college kids looking to get wasted. She'd been that stupid once, too. Never again.

Tabitha strode down the sidewalk, skimming faces as she went. Some people were drunk. Some were sober. Some were homeless or pretending to be. She registered familiar faces of panhandlers and street artists as she hurried down the block, but it was the unfamiliar faces that concerned her. She watched them without eye contact, taking note of anyone whose gaze lingered on her too long.

Across the street, a parked SUV switched its lights on. She kept her eyes straight ahead and walked right past it. When she reached the square, Tabitha paused beside a restaurant and pretended to read the menu posted on the window.

She studied the SUV in the reflection. It didn't move. The driver behind the wheel looked to be on his phone.

She resumed her pace and checked her watch. She'd grab her stuff and hop a quick cab to the station. There were still some buses leaving tonight, and she planned to jump on anything heading west.

She glanced over her shoulder.

The SUV was gone now.

Tabitha's pulse picked up. Maybe something, maybe nothing, but she quickened her steps anyway. Was she being followed? Her chest tightened, and she picked up her pace until her breath was coming in short gasps. The air around her felt charged with energy. She darted her gaze around.

Someone was behind her, watching her. She could feel it.

Up ahead was a crosswalk, and she headed toward the cluster of tourists waiting for the light. It turned green, and they stepped off the sidewalk en masse. She jogged to catch up with them.

A man stepped into her path, bumping into her.

"Sorry." He grabbed her by the arm, and her heart lurched.

Panicked, she twisted and wrenched her arm loose, then turned and ran into the street. Horns blared, brakes shrieked.

Tabitha whirled around and saw a blinding flash of headlights.

BAILEY FELT THE bed shift as Jacob got up. She listened to him pull on his jeans and heard the faint rasp of the zipper.

He left the room, and she waited to hear the front door open and close. It didn't.

She slipped out of bed and grabbed her short silk robe from the back of the chair. Wrapping it around herself, she padded into the kitchen, where Jacob stood beside the counter, shirtless and checking his phone.

"Anything happening?" she asked.

"Not really."

He set the phone down as she walked over to stand in front of him. She couldn't read the look in his eyes, but his hands slid around her waist and came to rest on her butt. His stubble was thicker now, and his hair was mussed from sleep. They'd been out for two solid hours.

"How's your foot?" he asked.

"Okay."

He touched her cheek and softly kissed her mouth, and the serious look on his face put a flutter in her stomach.

She slipped out of his embrace and turned to the fridge. "Are you hungry?"

"No."

"Thirsty?"

She opened the fridge, and he stepped over to reach inside for a bottle of water. He leaned back against the counter and watched her as he twisted the top off and took a long gulp, and the sight of his Adam's apple moving looked ridiculously hot. The sex must be muddling her brain.

He set the bottle down and looked at her.

"If I ask you a question, will you tell me the truth?" she asked.

He lifted an eyebrow. "Yes."

"Why were you so mad earlier?"

He held her gaze for a long moment. "I don't like your job. It's dangerous."

She opened the freezer and took out a pint of ice cream. She set it on the counter beside him and pulled a spoon from a drawer.

"I'm good at my job," she said.

"I know. That's part of why it's dangerous. You take risks to get what you want."

She laughed. "*I* take risks? You're the one who goes to work every day with a gun on your hip." She hitched herself onto the counter and peeled off the lid. "Maybe I don't like *your* job. Ever think of that?"

She was trying to sound playful, but they were talking about their professions, as though there was more happening here than a single night together.

She hoped there was more, even though hoping that was probably setting herself up for disappointment. She couldn't help it. The hope was just *there*, in a secret corner of her mind—a little ember glowing in the darkness—whether she wanted to acknowledge it or not. They had a connection, and it wasn't only physical. The part of her that indulged in dreamy fantasies wanted this to turn into something.

He came to stand in front of her, resting his hands on either side of her on the counter. He gave her his stern cop look. It was probably meant to intimidate her, but instead she felt turned on.

"Double fudge chip?" She held up a spoonful.

"No. Are you ever going to tell me what happened at Granite Tech?"

"I can't yet." She took a bite of ice cream. It was rich and decadent.

"When?"

"Soon."

"When?"

She took another bite. Heat flared in his eyes as she slowly pulled out the spoon. She licked her lip and set the carton aside.

Jacob eased her knees apart with his body. Keeping those dark eyes on hers, he loosened the knot of her robe and his hand slid inside, and the sight of those long fingers curving around her pale breast made her insides tighten.

She wrapped her legs around him, pulling him closer. She pressed a kiss against his neck, inhaling the amazing scent of his warm skin, which was more decadent than any food.

"Later," she whispered. "I promise."

TWENTY-FOUR

THE PARKING GARAGE was dark. Someone was behind her.

Bailey's heart hammered as she peered around the concrete pillar. She couldn't see him, but she knew he was there, watching her, stalking her through the concrete forest. She gripped her keys like a weapon and sprinted for the next pillar, ducking behind it to catch her breath.

There were no cars here now. Not the black BMW or the white Mercedes or the yellow Fiat. Everything was gone except her and the concrete pillars.

And him.

Footsteps thudded behind her, sure and confident, getting closer and louder. He didn't even care about stealth now.

Bailey looked around frantically. She spotted the dark tunnel. An escape. How would she get the door up? She didn't know, but she had to try. It was her only out.

Bailey ran. Her feet slapped against the concrete and she

raced for that tunnel. The footsteps followed her, and she ran harder, faster. She didn't dare look back.

Go, go, go. She sprinted for the tunnel, a big black maw. Her only out.

Something glowed there. An orange ember. It moved, and she realized it was a cigarette.

She halted. Someone stood in the shadows watching her, blocking her way. Panic shot through her.

Behind her, a metallic *click*.

Bailey jolted awake.

She sat up. The room was dark. The space beside her was empty. Her foot throbbed, and she remembered the cut. Then she remembered the sour taste of fear in her throat as she'd run across the concrete.

Keys jangled in the kitchen. *Jacob.*

He was leaving.

Disappointment stabbed at her. He was sneaking out without saying good-bye.

She lay back against the pillow and waited for the *click* of her lock and the sound of her front door opening and closing. Instead, she heard the floor creak. She snapped her eyes shut and immediately felt childish.

The mattress sank with his weight. His warm hand closed around hers, and the relief was so strong it made her breath catch.

"Bailey." His voice was low. "I have to go."

He'd somehow known she was awake, and she felt even sillier.

"What time is it?" she asked.

"Almost five." He kissed her forehead and stood up. "I'll call you." He paused beside the bed and looked at her. Then he walked out.

She lay there listening to all the sounds she'd expected before: the click of the latch, the door opening and closing.

A few seconds of silence and then she heard the barely-there thud of his boots on the stairwell outside her window. If she hadn't been listening closely, the sounds would have been lost in the vague white noise of her apartment building.

She lay stock-still, gazing at the ceiling and thinking of Jacob's deep brown eyes and his skilled hands and the manly scent of his skin. She rolled onto her side and pulled the pillow against her, inhaling deeply.

Why had he left so early? Darts of insecurity pricked at her, and she knew she was in trouble here. She'd ignored caution. She'd ignored all her reservations and his, too, and now here she was. She shouldn't see him again, but the thought of *not* seeing him again put an ache in the pit of her stomach.

She'd thought she could do this once and get him out of her system. But she'd been very wrong, and if anything, her yearning had only ramped up now that she knew how good they were together. The experience was seared into her brain, and there was no going back to *not* knowing what it was like to be with him. Jacob was everything she'd suspected he'd be and more, and she could feel herself getting attached. She rolled over with a groan. What had she done to herself?

Her gaze settled on the glowing red digits of the alarm clock: 4:44.

He'd exaggerated the time. Why?

It was like someone snapped their fingers in front of her. *Bailey, wake up!*

He'd had a callout. And he didn't want her to know. He didn't want her pelting him with questions like the annoying reporter that she was.

Cursing, she kicked off the covers and got up. She grabbed a T-shirt off the chair where Boba Fett slept peacefully on top of her jeans. She yanked the shirt on and padded into her kitchen, and the dull throbbing in her foot reminded her she needed to change the bandage. She found her phone on the table beside her first-aid supplies.

Her ringer was off, and she'd missed a call from Hannah. But nothing from Max. So what had Jacob been called out for? Anything big would have gone out on the scanner.

She had a text message from Seth: Call me ASAP. He'd texted her at 1:23 a.m.

And at 12:55, Call me.

And 12:40, I found something! Call me.

CHAPTER

TWENTY-FIVE

JACOB PARKED BESIDE the CSI van on the edge of the parking lot. As he slid from his truck, he looked around but didn't see Kendra. A blue tent had been erected near a fence surrounding a pair of brown dumpsters. He glanced behind him at the three-story apartment complex nearby. People were milling around near the stairs in bathrobes and warm-up suits, gawking at all the action, and the sun wasn't even up yet.

"Tell me you brought coffee."

He turned to see Kendra striding across the lot toward him. She wore her typical pantsuit—gray today—and the white face mask around her neck told him just what kind of morning he was in for.

"No coffee," he said.

"Shit."

"What have you got?" he asked.

"Caucasian male in a garbage bag with a slit throat. Body's a mess."

"His throat was slit?"

"Yep." Kendra lifted an eyebrow. That was two knife deaths in one week, which was two more than usual. "Not your typical MO, so Crawford thought we'd be interested. He's the lead."

"You two on decent terms?"

"Decent enough."

Kendra had dated the detective years ago, when they'd both been in uniform. Maybe the connection would work to their advantage. The fact that he'd given Kendra a call this morning was a good sign.

Jacob looked at the dumpster. "Age?"

"Based on the body, no clue. I'm telling you, he's a mess. He's been in there a while, and some kind of critter tore into that garbage bag. But a helpful building resident gave a tentative ID based on an Atlanta Braves cap. She thinks it's her neighbor."

"A cap? That's it?"

"I know, I know. But no one's seen this guy around in days, and his brother's been by here twice looking for him." Kendra took a notebook from her jacket and flipped it open. "Missing guy's name is Scott Rydell. Age twenty-nine. He didn't show up for work Saturday. By Sunday, people were worried."

"Where's Rydell work?"

"A kennel on Airport Parkway. Evidently, he loves animals, and people knew something was up when he didn't come in to cover his weekend shifts, because the animals didn't get fed. This is all from the neighbor, who talked to the brother."

He looked at the dumpsters again, frowning.

"Trash day is Monday," Kendra said, reading his mind. "But recycling comes every *two* weeks."

"Any sign of Rydell's car?"

"He takes the bus, evidently. But listen." Kendra stepped closer. "The kennel job isn't his only source of income. He also rents out a studio apartment here in the building."

"Airbnb?" Jacob asked.

"One of those, yeah. Someone was staying there all last week, but no one new has been in since then. A couple came knocking on Rydell's door Thursday, looking to pick up a key, but no one answered, and they left pissed off."

"We need to find out who that last guest was."

"I'm working on it. I don't have a name yet, but I talked to the neighbor down the hall. This man says he saw the last guest pull in here on Friday evening of *last* week."

"He get a look at the person?"

"Not much of one, but he knows it was a man. Says the car was a black Ford Expedition with Illinois plates."

Jacob gave her a long look, and he could tell they were thinking the same thing. This was why she'd called him out here at the butt crack of dawn when it wasn't even their case.

"What about Crime Scene? Who's here?" Jacob glanced at the dumpster, where a guy in a white Tyvek suit was shining a flashlight on something.

"There's a team with the body and another in the apartment building. Landlord let them into Rydell's unit. Crawford is in there now."

"I'm more interested in the rental unit."

They crossed the lot, ignoring the curious glances from building residents who were watching the action unfold.

"Rydell is in 132, and the studio he rents is right across the hall," Kendra said. "Landlord claims he didn't know anything about Rydell renting out the studio—said he thought he was using it as an art space—but I could tell he was lying. He's probably getting a kickback to keep quiet so Rydell can duck the lodging tax."

They stepped onto a sidewalk where a glass door stood

open. The apartments were situated along a long hall that smelled moldy. The teal-and-purple carpeting looked a few decades old, and brown water stains dotted the popcorn ceiling.

"What tourist would want a room here?" Kendra said. "This place is a dump."

"It's five minutes from the airport," Jacob pointed out.

"Still."

She ducked under the yellow crime scene tape blocking off the end of the hallway. Jacob followed, and they stopped to pull paper booties on over their shoes. Both apartment doors stood open.

"His is on the left," she said, nodding at the unit where a pair of CSIs in white coveralls moved around a living room. "Hey, anything in there yet?" Kendra called.

"Nothing so far." The CSI stepped out and passed them a box of gloves.

After pulling a glove on, Jacob stepped into the studio apartment and caught a whiff of bleach. It was faint, but it was one of those things he noticed instantly since becoming a cop.

The studio was sparsely furnished with a gray futon with red throw pillows, a gray armchair, and a light wood coffee table. A tiny kitchen that consisted of about four square feet of checkered linoleum lined the far wall.

"Not much of a kitchen," Kendra observed.

"More than I've got." Jacob stepped over to the stove, which was spotlessly clean. He took a mini-Maglite from his pocket and shined it over the sink. It looked clean, too. There was a pedal-operated trash can. Jacob stepped on the pedal and found the can empty—not even a bag.

Kendra opened the fridge. "No food. No drinks. Whoever was staying here didn't leave much. Or else Rydell cleaned the room right after he left."

"Rydell could have been dead by then. Maybe the guest cleaned up after himself. And how do we know when he left?" Jacob asked.

"We don't."

Jacob walked down a short hallway and opened a door to find a closet with a set of gray sheets and gray towels, along with an unopened three-pack of soap. He stepped into a tiny bathroom, where the bleach smell was stronger. The bathroom had a prefab shower stall and a Formica vanity with a small sink. Jacob shined his flashlight around the rim.

"What are you thinking?"

He glanced at Kendra behind him in the mirror. "I don't like coincidences," he said.

"You're talking about the timing?"

"The timing. The knife wound. The Illinois plates."

She crossed her arms. "So, you're thinking what? McKinney's hit man came down here, checked into this room, murdered Dana Smith, aka Robin Nally, and then decided to kill the man who rented him the room before leaving town? Why do that?"

"Could be Rydell saw something or heard something he wasn't supposed to," Jacob said. "I mean, look around. The place is immaculate and it reeks of bleach." He took out his flashlight and shined it over the vanity. Crouching down, he studied the lip of the sink. "Check this out."

"What?" Kendra knelt beside him, and he pointed his flashlight at a tiny brown speck on the underside of the faucet.

"Blood," she said. "Maybe he cut himself shaving."

"Or cleaned up a murder weapon." Jacob stood. "We need a CSI in here with some luminol. Ten-to-one odds, this place lights up like a Christmas tree."

* * *

Pain pounded through Tabitha's head. Her eyes seemed to be glued shut.

She managed to lift her lids, but closed her eyes again, wincing at the light.

The pain intensified. It had a sound. A rhythm. It echoed through her head and traveled down her body to her toes, making everything in between throb, too.

She wanted water. Her tongue felt dry and thick. The thought of a tall glass of water made her open her eyes again.

She was in a dim room with wavy, flower-printed walls. She closed her eyes and tried to breathe through the pain. Where was she?

She tried again, opening her eyes a slit. The room was small. There was a faint beeping noise coming from somewhere close by. She looked around. The wavy, flower-printed walls weren't walls at all. She was surrounded by a curtain.

The memories crashed over her all at once—the headlights, the impact, the rush of voices and sirens. There had been a man with dark hair looming over her with something blue over his mouth and nose. A mask.

You're in the hospital. Can you tell me your name?

Tabitha sat up. Pain blasted through her skull, taking her breath away. She fell back against the pillow.

She was in a hospital. She wasn't alone. She sensed people on the other side of the curtain.

Looking around now, she noticed the IV bag. The tube attached to her hand. The plastic bracelet. She lifted her hand and looked at it, struggling to bring the blurry words into focus.

WALKER, TABITHA

An electric jolt went through her. She sat forward. As she stared at the bracelet, her breath came in shallow gasps and her head seemed to expand like a balloon.

They knew her name.

How did they know it? She was supposed to be Rachel Moore, known as "Red" to her co-workers.

She glanced around frantically. Tucked around her was a blue blanket. Beside the bed was a table covered with equipment. There was a chair, too, and on it was a folded pair of jeans and a black T-shirt.

Her clothes.

She glanced down and realized she was wearing a thin cotton hospital gown. How long had she been here? Had she been asleep? In surgery?

Tabitha's heart thudded as she looked herself over. Aside from the IV in her hand, everything seemed okay. No casts or bandages. The pain seemed to be centered in her head, radiating down from the back of her skull.

A memory flashed through her brain: headlights coming at her. A screech of brakes. She must have conked her head on the pavement when she bounced off the hood of that car. She remembered a crowd of legs around her and wailing sirens.

Tabitha glanced at her wrist again, and the sight of her name sent a burst of adrenaline through her. She pulled off the covers and swung her legs out of bed. She tugged the IV from her hand. A drop of blood oozed out, and she dabbed it with the edge of the gown.

She stood up, but her knees buckled and she sat down. Shaking off the dizziness, she tried again and took a wobbly step toward the chair. Pain ricocheted through her head as she pulled off the hospital gown and reached for her jeans. It took her two tries to step into them. She shoved her fingers into the front pocket.

No wallet! Panic seized her again. The hospital must have confiscated it. Or someone had stolen it. The result was the same. Half of the money she so desperately needed to leave town was gone.

Her bra and underwear were in tatters. It looked like someone had cut them off her with scissors. Same for her T-shirt. She pulled the shirt on anyway and saw that it had been sliced right up the front. She tied the ends together at her navel and blinked down at herself. Her gaze landed on the wristband again, spurring her into action.

She moved toward the curtain and opened it a few inches to see another hospital bed. On it was a long mound covered with a blue blanket. The person was turned away, and she couldn't tell whether it was a man or a woman. Beside the bed was a pair of plastic slippers. After a quick glance around, Tabitha stepped through the curtain. Her legs felt like wet noodles, but she managed to slide her feet into the shoes, which turned out to be man-sized.

She crept to the edge of the man's curtain and peered out.

The room was long and rectangular with lots of beds and curtains. The space was dimly lit except for a counter at one end where two women in scrubs sat in front of computers. One wore a headset and seemed to be talking on the phone. The other woman was hunched over the desk reading something. Beyond the desk was a glowing red *EXIT* sign.

Tabitha took a deep breath to steady herself. She studied the curtains. Four stalls between her and that exit. She eased past the bed, and the body there shifted. Tabitha froze. She held her breath as she watched him. He shifted again, grunting, but his eyes stayed shut. He was out cold.

Carefully, quietly, Tabitha crept past him.

TWENTY-SIX

T HE POLICE STATION was humming with activity. Bailey watched from the bench as a steady flow of people streamed in and out. Today's visitors looked to be a mix of patrol officers, defense attorneys, and off-duty cops.

Bailey's cell phone vibrated, and she glanced down to check it.

SBUX 10 min.

The response put a knot in her stomach even though she'd expected it. Jacob didn't want to talk to her at the police station. And she didn't blame him.

Bailey gathered her messenger bag and hiked down the street to the coffee shop. She needed to suck it up and not let her feelings get in the way of her work. She had a job to do, and she couldn't get distracted by a budding—or fizzling—romance with the lead detective. Right now she needed his help, and she figured she had a decent chance of getting it if she kept things professional. Jacob was a good cop. He wouldn't turn his back on a victim in need.

She was counting on it.

She cast a glance over her shoulder as she reached the coffee shop. All morning she'd been jumpy and she couldn't shake the feeling she was being watched.

Bailey didn't need any more caffeine, so she stood in line for a juice and snagged a stool at the long wooden table facing the window. The guy next to her finished off a scone and got up, leaving behind a pile of crumbs. As she sipped her drink and waited, Bailey noted the security camera mounted above the coffee shop door. She was hyper-aware of every camera she spotted now, and they seemed to be everywhere.

Jacob walked in right on time and peeled off his shades. He scanned the room, probably looking for any cops he knew.

"Hi," he said, taking the stool beside her.

"Busy morning?"

He nodded. "You heard about the homicide by the airport."

"Yep."

He glanced at his watch. "The press conference is at noon. Don't you need to—"

"It's not mine. They gave it to the weekend reporter. I'm off today, finally. First weekend this month."

His eyes turned wary. She hadn't invited him here to talk about a fresh homicide.

"You wanted to know about last night," she said. "I told you I'd explain."

His look of surprise confirmed what she'd thought yesterday—that he hadn't actually believed she'd tell him. He definitely still had trust issues.

Jacob leaned his elbow on the table. "Okay, I'm listening."

She took a deep breath. "So. I've been looking into the federal witness protection program."

He didn't look happy with the segue. "That's not really your beat, is it?"

"This goes way beyond any *beat*." Bailey leaned closer. "If someone managed to penetrate the witness protection program, that's huge. Just think of the law enforcement implications. Think of all the lives in jeopardy, the cases in jeopardy. Without cooperating witnesses, federal prosecutions would grind to a halt."

"What's this got to do with where you were last night?" he asked. He seemed impatient now. Or maybe he wasn't thrilled about her pursuing such a high-stakes story.

"Since Wednesday, I've been trying to figure out how someone uncovered the new identity of a protected witness," she said. "Is there a hole in the government's program? I thought maybe someone at the Bureau or the Marshals Office messed up. Or maybe someone paid off a federal agent to leak Robin Nally's alias and then passed it along to some hit man. But what I discovered was worse."

"*Worse* than someone selling her out to a hit man?"

"Turns out, a hit man didn't need her alias. He only needed her face."

Jacob's brow furrowed.

"When Robin went into the program, they gave her a new name, a new social security number, a new location. She built a whole new life for herself here, but none of that mattered because her face had already been added to a vast privately controlled database of faceprints. All someone had to do was query the program, and they got a hit."

"Privately controlled as in Granite Tech," he stated.

"Right."

"I thought they did background checks and document security?"

Clearly, he'd been checking up on the company ever

since Bailey hinted they might be linked to his murder case.

"That's not all they do."

"And is this a theory or do you know it for a fact?" he asked.

"It's confirmed. My source—"

"Who is that again?"

"Stop asking me that. My source confirmed that Robin is in the database. Anyone looking for her could have found recent images of her." She swiped at her phone and brought up a photo Seth had sent her this morning. It showed a woman with long dark hair walking across a busy intersection. In the background was the UT clock tower.

Jacob frowned at the image. "This is on campus."

"Right. They've got a number of surveillance cams there. This was captured last month. I'm guessing she was going to meet Celeste Camden and her daughter, Jillian."

Bailey had probably been captured by the same camera walking through the very same intersection just a few days ago.

"You think someone found her based on this surveillance photo?" Jacob sounded skeptical. "With the dark hair, it doesn't even really look like Robin Nally."

"That's not the only photo. Look at this one." She opened the second image Seth had sent. "The angle is straight on, and the facial features are clearer. This is her employee badge from Villa Paloma. Once someone had this, they could figure out where she worked. And once they knew where she worked, they could go there and wait for her to show up and then follow her around and learn her routines."

Jacob looked tense, but he didn't talk. He waited for her to fill the silence. It was one of those conversational tricks he used to get information from people while giving up as little as possible. Bailey knew his tactics because she used them, too.

But Jacob's silence didn't matter. She didn't need him to confirm all this.

"I'm thinking maybe he learned that she ran at the lake every morning," she said. "And he figured that would be a good time to catch her alone, with the added benefit that the crime might look like a random mugging or sexual assault gone wrong instead of what it actually was—a carefully planned hit."

Jacob slid the phone back. "I need your source. And I'm not fucking around, Bailey. Whoever it is, I have to talk to him."

"About Tabitha Walker, right? I already did."

"And?"

"And it's a freaking mess. The worst-case scenario. I submitted a photo of Tabitha to the system through my contact. He got multiple hits."

Jacob rubbed his hand over his chin. "Where'd you get a picture of her? I've been looking, and I've come up with nothing for Tabitha Walker, not even a driver's license photo from when she lived in Illinois."

"Maybe she never had one. Or maybe the feds pulled her records from the database at some point. I tracked down a picture of her from the student newspaper at DePaul University. They ran a story about some service organization, and she was the treasurer. Look."

She brought up the screen shot on her phone—the same screen shot she'd given Seth to use. It showed a smiling young Tabitha standing in front of the student center collecting cans for a holiday food drive.

"Damn, she looks young," Jacob muttered.

"She is. That was taken her junior year, so she was probably twenty." Bailey looked at the picture, and anger swelled in her chest. "I'm sure she never thought her charity work might someday put her in a killer's crosshairs."

"You think McKinney's people found this?" Jacob asked.

"I don't know. *I* did. It took a lot of looking, but it's out there."

"And your source ran this through the program?"

"Yes. He used it as a probe photo and got several hits, not just one. All within the last two months, and all in the same city."

"You're saying—"

"I know where Tabitha is, Jacob."

"Let me guess. New Orleans."

She drew back, startled. "How did you know?"

TWENTY-SEVEN

JACOB DIDN'T ANSWER. He just watched her.

"Oh my God. Is she—"

"As far as I know, she's alive," he said.

Bailey waited, as though she wanted him to reveal more. But he wasn't going to talk about the cell phone he'd recovered near the murder scene or the call they'd traced to a cell tower in New Orleans.

She tapped at her phone and brought up another photo. "Here's one of the images."

"This is in the database you're talking about?" He took the phone from her.

"Yes. They've got more than a billion images."

He blinked at her. "A *billion*?"

"Yes, and they're gaining more every day."

"Where are they getting them?"

"That's what I'm trying to figure out. From what I know so far, there's some hacking involved."

"And this company is local?"

"Headquartered right on Lake Austin."

He was starting to understand the scope of this story and why she'd been so motivated to pursue it. A billion face-print images from across the country. A privately controlled database just waiting to be queried. He tried to imagine the national security implications if a database like that were to fall into the wrong hands.

He looked at the photo on her phone again.

"There are two images of Tabitha similar to that one. Keep swiping. See?" She eased closer, and he tried not to get distracted by the scent of her hair. "Each of these images was taken from a police camera in the French Quarter."

Jacob studied the pictures, then swiped back through and studied them again. Each image showed a woman with short hair and glasses crossing a busy street with lots of people around her. "You're sure this is her?"

"The computer is sure. At least, sure enough to identify her. The haircut and the glasses are probably part of her new look."

"This is Jackson Square. I recognize the cathedral in the background."

"That's right. And each of these images is time stamped between three forty and three forty-eight. So, wherever she's going, she goes there at the same time of day. If I had to bet, she's going to a job near the square."

Jacob looked at Bailey. She had that hyper-alert glint in her eyes. She was amped up about this, and he suspected he knew why.

"Why are you telling me this now?" he asked.

"Why do you think? We have every reason to believe Tabitha is on a hit list. Someone needs to tell her." She leaned back and looked at him. "That's why I'm going to New Orleans."

Jacob bit back a curse. "That's a bad idea."

"I'm going. I want to find her and warn her."

"And interview her for your story."

"That too." She didn't deny it at all, which made him think she'd gotten her editor on board with this crazy idea.

"How do you plan to find her in a city with half a million people? You don't have a name—not even a fake one. You don't have an address."

"So, I'll scope out this location. And ask around. I'm good at getting people to talk to me."

"Do you know how crowded the French Quarter is? You're talking about a big waste of time."

"No, I'm not." She tapped on her phone. "The time stamps show that she frequents that square at the same time of day, and she's dressed the same, too, which means she's probably in her work clothes."

Jacob hadn't noticed the clothes, but he did now that she mentioned it.

"Is your paper on board with this?"

She shrugged. "They want the story."

"Yes, but do they realize what they're asking you to do? This isn't a game, Bailey. You're putting yourself in the middle of something dangerous." He watched her, sensing she was holding back. "They don't know, do they?"

"They know I'm working on this story, and that's enough for now. If I get a chance to interview one of the principals, all the better. This is a huge story. It's a major privacy breach, but people may not grasp the implications. A woman was *murdered* because of this. And another woman's life is in danger. I can't just sit here and not do anything. I have to find her."

He handed the phone back, shaking his head.

"I'd like you to come with me."

The request hit him out of nowhere. But he should have

expected it. Maybe she wasn't quite as oblivious to her safety as he'd thought.

"You want me for protection," he said.

"Yes and no. I mean, you carry a gun, so that's helpful and all, but I was thinking more about your badge. I think it might work better than a press pass in terms of getting information." She paused. "I'll pick up your expenses."

He scoffed. "You think I'm worried about expenses?"

"Well, don't be, because I'll cover it. Will you come?"

Jacob gritted his teeth. Tabitha Walker was in grave danger, yes. But it wasn't Bailey's job to tell her that. It should have been the feds' job, but they'd basically washed their hands of Tabitha after she testified for them and then refused their protection.

"She might have skipped town already," he said. "Maybe Robin got an inkling she was being followed and gave her friend a heads-up."

"Is that what happened?"

Jacob didn't answer.

"Well, she was there seventy-two hours ago, so if she *did* hear something from Robin, it wasn't dire enough to make her pull up stakes and leave." She crossed her arms. "Anyway, there're no guarantees, but I have to at least try. Imagine if this woman got murdered and we could have prevented it."

The frustration was back. Jacob felt pulled in two directions. Part of him wanted to go with her to New Orleans, so he could stay glued to her side and make sure she didn't get into any trouble. Another part of him wanted to shut this whole thing down.

The second option was definitely better, but he doubted it would work. Bailey had that spark in her eyes and that firm set to her chin. If he turned her down, she'd go without him. And who knew what kind of shit she might get into?

She gazed up at him with those defiant gray eyes, and he knew exactly what she was thinking. She was determined to do this, whether he helped her or not.

She checked her watch. "It's 11:20. There's a 1:35 flight to New Orleans, and I plan to be on it. Will you come with me or not?"

TWENTY-EIGHT

THE MAN WAS painted silver, head to toe, and Bailey watched his stilted movements as he entertained a crowd of tourists. Bailey had seen the show twice now, and he was coming up on the moment when he would pull a handful of lollipops from his top hat and offer them to the kids.

Bailey shifted her attention to the oyster bar across the street. She'd rolled the windows down when she parked, and saxophone music drifted into the car, along with the smell of fried shrimp. Her stomach grumbled, reminding her that she hadn't eaten anything besides airplane pretzels since last night's ice cream. And the ice cream didn't really count because Jacob had carried her off to bed, leaving the pint of double fudge chip to melt on the counter.

Bailey thought of the way he'd looked at her last night. His eyes had been dark and intense and . . . frustrated. There was no getting around it. He wasn't happy with how all this had played out. He wanted to control what she was doing, or get her to stop, and the fact that he couldn't bothered him. He was worried about her. And she'd played on that worry by asking him to come with her.

Jacob was used to being in control. But he couldn't control her, and that made him edgy. She knew he saw getting involved with her as a risk, and she didn't know whether he believed she was worth it.

Jacob stepped out of the police station and glanced both ways before jogging across the street to Bailey's rented Kia. That had been another source of friction—*my story, my rental car*, she'd told him. And she'd insisted on driving while he navigated on his phone.

Jacob had won the next battle, though, and dictated that their first order of business would be a stop at the NOPD's substation on Royal Street.

He opened the passenger door and slid in.

"Anything?" she asked.

"No."

Bailey started the car. It was almost five, and she was eager to get moving. She looked over her shoulder before pulling into traffic. "What happened?"

"I showed her picture to a couple patrol cops, in case she's been working the streets or doing something illegal for money."

"And?"

"No one's seen her around."

"I'm not surprised," Bailey said. "I mean, she's an accountant, right? She's probably a stickler for rules. And she testified for the government, so that indicates she has a sense of civic duty. I figure she's living in the shadows here but doing it more or less legally."

Jacob lifted an eyebrow. "Desperate people do desperate things." He looked at her. "Where are we going?"

"St. Ann Street and Chartres. You said that's where the surveillance camera is that caught her, right?"

Jacob studied the printout. "According to my expert, yes."

And his expert was good. The woman—Gabby somebody-or-other from Austin PD—had taken Bailey's black-and-white photo of Tabitha Walker and improved it immensely. She'd zoomed in on the face, sharpened the features, and colorized everything, and the result was a picture of Tabitha that provided much more information than they'd had previously. They knew, for example, that she'd not only chopped her hair but dyed it a dark red. And they knew that she typically passed through Jackson Square wearing a black T-shirt and jeans, with a blue backpack slung over her shoulder. In the monochromatic photo, the backpack had appeared gray.

"It's five fifteen," Bailey said now. "Maybe we'll get lucky and catch her." She stopped at a light and waited for a herd of tourists to cross. "I figure she lives north of the square, maybe on Dumaine or somewhere near there, and she has an evening job on Bourbon Street or St. Peter—one of those streets with all the bars."

"Maybe we've got it backward. She could live on the other side of the square and have a daytime job in a residential area. Maybe she found a nanny gig like Robin did."

"Could be."

"Take a right up here at the light."

Bailey followed his instructions until they reached the intersection they were looking for. She circled the block twice and spotted a car pulling out of a space. She hit the gas and put her blinker on to claim it.

"You realize what a long shot this is, right?"

She checked her mirrors before zipping backward into the space. "What's your point?"

"I don't want you to get your hopes up."

She shoved the car into park and glanced at him. He seemed genuinely concerned about her, and that faint spark of hope was back again.

"It can't be a *total* long shot, or you wouldn't have come," she said.

"You need to be realistic, Bailey. We're looking for a needle in a haystack."

"Why don't you just say what you're really worried about? That she might already be dead."

"There's a definite possibility."

Bailey studied his face, and his dark eyes looked grim.

"You asked about un-IDed victims, too, didn't you? Just now at the police station?"

He nodded.

"And?"

"They've got a middle-aged female on Burgundy Street who died with a needle in her arm."

"When?"

"Two days ago."

"Is it possible—"

"Full sleeve of tattoos and a C-section scar. Don't think it's a fit."

Bailey looked through the windshield, skimming her gaze over the people milling at the edge of Jackson Square. There were food vendors, street musicians, and tourists having their portraits drawn. A bride and her flush-cheeked groom stood beside a park bench, talking to a photographer as they looked around the square, probably searching for a backdrop they could use before the bride's makeup melted off. It was *hot* here. And humid. Bailey figured that if Tabitha was still living in New Orleans, she'd have sense enough to be inside somewhere, not walking around in the scorching heat.

"You know, there's a bus stop at St. Ann and Decatur."

She looked at Jacob.

"It stops at 3:35," he added.

"You checked the schedule?"

"Yeah."

The timing fit with the surveillance images. It was unlikely Tabitha had a car, but Bailey hadn't considered public transportation.

"I hadn't thought of that," she admitted.

"You're tired." Jacob studied the map on his phone. "Not to mention hungry. I can hear your stomach growling." He tucked his phone in the pocket of his leather jacket and looked at her. "Why's this story so important to you?"

The question surprised her.

She took out a packet of cherry Life Savers and pried one off. She offered it to Jacob, but he shook his head, and she popped it into her mouth.

"Why's it so important to *you*?" she countered.

"To me it's a case, not a story. And it's directly related to a murder that happened in my jurisdiction."

"So you can't just toss it to the feds and forget about it."

"No, I can't."

Bailey gazed out the window and sighed. People milled around the square, and she scanned their faces with a growing sense of hopelessness. If Tabitha Walker *was* here, she wouldn't be milling. She'd be walking briskly, with purpose, and probably with a lot more situational awareness than the tourists bumping about like cattle.

Bailey swallowed the candy, but it only made her stomach feel emptier.

"You haven't answered my question."

She looked at Jacob. "Because I'm angry."

"Why?"

"This woman tried to do the right thing and she got killed for it. What does that say about our justice system?"

"Whatever McKinney was doing, she was probably mixed up in it somehow," Jacob said. "Otherwise, the feds wouldn't have had much leverage to get her to testify."

"Still, whatever it was, McKinney's the mastermind. She was working as a *temp*, for God's sake, and she got involved with the wrong man, and she ended up dead. And not only that—" She turned to face him, getting steamed up now in the hot little car. "He didn't just kill her. No. He killed her to send a message."

"You really think he had her murdered from behind bars?" Jacob asked.

"Either him or his family. Same thing. And it's the same message, too. *Don't fuck with us. You fuck with the McKinneys, you'll be looking over your shoulder for the rest of your life, until you end up dead.* This whole thing is a deterrent, Jacob. A protective maneuver. It's a freaking *business* strategy, and it makes me furious."

"How are they sending a message if the victim's name hasn't been in the press?"

"Oh, it will be. Trust me. It's only a matter of time before someone passes along a carefully placed call to the *Tribune* or some other media outlet. Then it'll be splashed everywhere."

He gave her a long look. "Why haven't *you* splashed it everywhere?"

"I told you, I'm focused on something else now."

"Granite Tech," he said.

"One of our city's most successful CEOs may have directed the hacking of multiple government databases. That's computer fraud. Millions and millions of people's biometric records were potentially stolen and sold to the highest bidder. And the technology they're using isn't regulated enough, so it could happen again. It *will* happen again, and it affects masses of people—you, me, everyone. People don't realize how vulnerable they are and how easily this technology can be exploited."

Jacob smiled. "You're an idealist."

"No, I'm not."

But his smile told her he didn't buy that at all. And maybe she *was* an idealist. Well, so what? Too many people had traded their ideals for cynicism.

"Anyway, what's wrong with being an idealist?" she asked.

"Nothing."

There was something wistful in his tone, and she knew he used to be the same. Maybe he still was. Maybe underneath the jaded-cop exterior, he still had some faith in people and institutions. It might explain why he was such a dedicated cop.

He looked away, and Bailey studied his profile. She admired him. She admired his integrity and his work ethic and his unwavering sense of duty. She wanted to tell him, but she doubted he'd be comfortable with the compliment. Maybe she'd tell him when all this was over.

He eyed the side mirror and the last trace of his smile disappeared. An SUV glided past them on the street, and Jacob tensed.

"What?" she asked.

"That black SUV has been by here twice now."

"Maybe it's looking for a parking space," she said.

"Could be."

"What kind was it?"

"A Ford Expedition. He just turned into that alley there. Pull out. Go around the block." He looked at her. "Think you can pick up their tail without being seen?"

"I can try."

"You should have let me drive."

He was probably right, but she didn't comment as she pulled into traffic.

"Hang a left here up here," he said. "Next light."

She turned, but the black SUV wasn't anywhere.

"There. Up ahead," he said excitedly. "*Don't* stop or brake, just drive right by."

Bailey spotted a black Expedition. It was parallel parked in a loading zone, no driver.

"Are you sure that's the same one?" she asked.

"It is. Hang a right up here and go about a block. Then pull over."

"Why?" she asked as she made the turn. "What's the big deal with that SUV?"

"I'm going to check it out."

"But—"

"Roll up the window." He pushed open the door. "I'll meet you back at the square. And if you see anything, text me."

He got out and slammed the door, and Bailey watched him, fuming.

The driver behind her tapped his horn, and she got moving, watching Jacob in her rearview mirror as he sauntered down the street. There was something cool and casual about his gait, and at a glance he probably looked like someone who lived in the neighborhood. You'd have to look closer to notice the sharp cop eyes and the bulge under that jacket he wore to conceal his gun. Bailey had expected him to bring a backup pistol in an ankle holster, but instead he'd brought his police-issue sidearm. He'd notified the flight crew about it when he boarded the plane and ended up getting a meeting with the pilot and a seat near the cockpit as an honorary air marshal.

Jacob disappeared from view now, and Bailey buzzed

up the window and headed back toward her stakeout location.

Why was he hung up on the black Expedition? Annoyance simmered inside her. He was holding back on her. She knew that. He was keeping things to himself, including the reason behind the texts he'd been exchanging with Kendra all afternoon. Something was going on in Austin, and his partner kept pinging him with updates.

Did it have to do with the Robin Nally murder case? Or the case from this morning? Whichever case it was, something was going on, and Jacob was being tight-lipped about it.

Bailey found another parking space—not as good as the last one, but it had a better view of the church. She parked and turned her attention to the square again, where the wedding couple was now mugging for the camera in front of a fountain. Just looking at that poofy white dress made Bailey itchy. It was way too hot for a photo shoot, but maybe with some creative editing the sheen on their skin would look like something besides sweat.

A woman on the sidewalk caught Bailey's eye.

Slender, sunglasses, black Saints cap with tufts of dark red hair peeking out. Bailey's pulse sped up. The woman wore a green peacoat and had a blue backpack slung over her shoulder.

"No way," Bailey muttered, reaching for her phone. Where the hell was Jacob?

The woman passed the wedding party but didn't give them a charmed smile like everyone else. She walked swiftly, darting her gaze around.

It was her.

Underneath the hat and the shades and the peacoat— who wore a coat in this weather?—it was Tabitha Walker.

Bailey jerked the keys from the ignition and stuffed

them in her pocket. She grabbed her phone and got out of the car.

I think I see her! she texted Jacob. Black Saints cap NE corner of the square.

SOMEONE WAS WATCHING her. Tabitha could feel it.

She cast a glance over her shoulder but couldn't pinpoint where the feeling was coming from. Everyone seemed suspicious, from the man at the bus stop smoking a cigarette to the guy loitering near the pub, who seemed to be talking on his phone. Even the couple in front of her strolling hand-in-hand down the street seemed to be moving at an unnaturally slow pace.

Tabitha quickened her steps, darting around the lovebirds and slicing her way through a gaggle of tourists with ice cream cones. Two blocks ahead was a red-brick hotel with wrought-iron balconies and a trio of French flags hanging above the entrance. She trained her gaze on the line of taxis waiting outside. She'd jump in one of those cabs and be at the bus station in ten minutes.

She adjusted her backpack on her shoulder. It felt heavy, and her back was sweating beneath her thick coat. She'd divided her money into two stashes—one in her front pocket and one in the coat lining—and crammed every scrap of clothing she could fit into the backpack. If she got hard up for cash, she could sell off some of her clothes.

Tabitha crossed a street and scanned the hotel. Beside the valet stand, a businessman stood next to a black roll-on suitcase. A uniformed valet stepped into the street and whistled, and the taxi at the front of the line rolled forward.

The taxis were for guests. Tabitha's chest tightened as she realized her mistake. Could she pretend to be one of them? She glanced at the valet again. Maybe if she tipped him, he wouldn't care.

The businessman was looking at her now. Something flickered across his face. Recognition? Then he looked away.

Tabitha's blood turned cold. She turned and ducked into a store.

B AILEY CROSSED THE intersection just as the light turned red. She hopped onto the sidewalk, bumping into someone.

"Sorry," she said.

He shot a glare over his shoulder.

Bailey looked up, and the black Saints cap had vanished.

Damn it, she'd just had her. Now where had she gone? Bailey broke into a jog, scanning all the heads in front of her on the sidewalk. No black Saints cap. Had she removed it? Bailey didn't see anyone with short red hair, either.

A text landed on her phone from Jacob: Where r u?

T ABITHA STOOD BEHIND the rack of T-shirts, ducking low as she peered out the store window at the hotel down the street. The businessman was still standing on the sidewalk. Had he seen her step in here? Was he even *watching* her?

Tabitha's heart hammered. Her chest tightened until she felt like she was sucking air through a straw. She looked out the window and tried to figure out whether the businessman had noticed her ducking in here. Was she being paranoid? No. The look he'd given her had made her skin crawl.

A taxi stopped in front of the businessman. The cab's

trunk popped open, and the valet rolled the black suitcase to the back as the businessman slid inside the car.

"May I help you?"

Tabitha jumped.

A saleswoman stood behind her. She looked down pointedly, and Tabitha realized she was holding one of the T-shirt sleeves in a death grip. She must look like a lunatic.

She released the shirt and forced a smile. "Sorry, just . . . browsing."

The saleswoman watched suspiciously as Tabitha left the store.

J ACOB EYED THE black Expedition, and he approached it. No one inside, from the looks of it. He was almost certain it was the same SUV he'd seen earlier, and he wanted to check the plates.

His phone vibrated with a text from Bailey.

On St. Ann walking toward hotel.

Jacob glanced around for the nearest street sign. Half a block up was St. Ann Street.

He jogged across the street to the Expedition. With one glance, he confirmed his suspicion: Illinois plates.

"*Fuck.*"

He broke into a run.

S HE WAS ALMOST there. One more block. Tabitha skimmed the faces of the waiting cabbies, trying to decide who might be willing to move out of line to pick her up. The cabbie at the end of the line caught her eye. She waved, and he nodded.

A man stepped from a doorway in front of her. Tall,

bulky, thick dark eyebrows. He wore a heavy jacket and walked toward her with a hand in his pocket.

Tabitha dove behind a car.

Pop!

B AILEY'S HEART LURCHED at the gunshot. She dove between two cars and landed heavily on her knees. *Gun gun gun!* The words reverberated through her brain, along with the echo of the sound. Chest heaving, she crawled around the side of the car and peeked out.

The sidewalk was empty.

Then she heard yelling, car horns, a squeal of tires. A taxicab zoomed past in a blur.

Bailey peeked at the sidewalk again just in time to see Tabitha with her black Saints cap as she scrambled across the sidewalk and dashed into a bar.

A FTER WATCHING FROM a distance as the gunman fled into the crowd, Jacob had jumped into a cab to go after him. Now he spotted the man racing down the sidewalk.

"Pull over up here!" he yelled. "Stop!"

The cabbie screeched to a halt, and Jacob jumped out.

The gunman darted around a horse-drawn carriage and took off across the square. Jacob sprinted after him, hurdling a flower bed and dodging a bride and groom posing by a fountain. The gunman was fast, and he seemed to be racing straight for the cathedral.

Jacob's heart clenched as he thought of the potential hostage situation if the shooter grabbed a tourist. This whole place was crawling with kids and families. Jacob hurdled another flower bed and cut through a group of people.

The gunman darted up the steps and into the cathedral, realizing Jacob's worst fears.

Cursing, Jacob charged after him. He took the church steps three at a time, yanked open the heavy door, and rushed inside.

Jacob stopped to get his bearings, and his heart pounded wildly as his eyes adjusted. The church was dim and quiet and smelled of incense. They were between services. A few women sat in pews and other visitors milled along the side aisles lighting votive candles.

A shrill yelp shattered the quiet, followed by a loud clatter near the altar. Jacob rushed toward the noise, pulling his weapon. Reaching the sacristy, he found a robe-clad altar boy sprawled on the floor beside a toppled candelabra.

A door slammed. Jacob raced down a hallway toward the sound. He yanked a door open and ran outside, tripping over a clay flower pot that had been hurled into the path.

"Hey!" An elderly black man lifted his cane and pointed toward the square. "He ran that way!"

Jacob spotted the gunman and took off. The shooter sprinted left, then right again, seeming to change his destination on the fly. Jacob ran harder and harder until it felt like his lungs would burst. As he raced around a big bronze statue, the gunman changed directions *again*, darting around a park bench and running straight for a stoplight.

Jacob looked ahead with dread. He saw the move the instant before it happened. The shooter raced up to a motorcyclist, pointing his gun at the man's chest. He yanked the man off the bike, flinging him onto the street just as the light turned green.

Horns blared. People stopped and pointed at the spectacle. The man threw his leg over the motorcycle and took off.

Jacob rushed into the intersection. Brakes squealed.

Horns blasted. Jacob planted his feet and took aim at the back tire. But he was well out of range.

"Fuck!"

The motorcycle got smaller and smaller as it cut between lanes and disappeared in the sea of traffic.

B AILEY JOGGED DOWN the alley behind the sports bar. The woman in the black Saints cap had run out the back door. A witness had seen her. But where the hell *was* she?

The alley was hot and smelled of rotting garbage. Bailey checked doorways and looked behind dumpsters. Music drifted from a gate up ahead, and Bailey jogged over.

She tried the gate. Locked. Peering between the iron bars, she saw a cobblestone courtyard and a cat lounging lazily on a table beside a fern. Could Tabitha have climbed the gate? Or maybe run through here and locked it behind her?

Sirens sounded faintly on a nearby street. They grew closer. Frustration filled her as she looked up and down the empty alley.

A dull *clink* made her turn around.

Her pulse quickened.

Cautiously, she approached the nearest dumpster. Shards of glass crunched under her shoes and she held her breath against the stench.

"Tabitha?"

Nothing.

Bailey's heart thudded. Sweat streamed down her temples. The rusty brown container was about five feet tall. Discarded wooden platforms were piled beside it, almost like a stepladder.

Bailey moved closer. "Tabitha?"

Nothing.

"I'm unarmed. I'm here to help you."

She stepped closer again, resting her hand on the hot metal lid. She took a deep breath and lifted it several inches.

No sound.

The lid squeaked as she lifted it all the way and rested it against the brick wall behind the dumpster. She tested the wooden platform with her shoe, then stepped on it and looked inside.

Tabitha blinked up at her. Her eyes were wide, her pupils dilated. The black Saints cap was gone, and her red hair was plastered to her head with sweat.

"I'm not here to hurt you. My name's Bailey Rhoads. I'm a journalist."

Tabitha's mouth fell open.

"You're . . ." She swallowed. "You wrote the news story. In Austin."

"Yes."

Bailey's pulse pounded. She couldn't believe they were face to face after all this time.

"How . . . how did you find me?"

"I'll explain later. Right now, I'd like to help you out of here."

"I won't go to the police." Her voice trembled. "You can't force me."

"I understand," Bailey said. "I won't force you to do anything. I can give you a ride, okay? My car is nearby. Just a block away."

A second siren joined the first one, and Tabitha's eyes widened.

"If you don't want to talk to police, we need to go now." Bailey held her hand out. *Trust me,* she tried to tell her with her eyes. *I promise, you can trust me.*

She waited a heartbeat. Two. Three.

Tabitha's hand closed around hers.

THE NEON SIGN flickered, casting an irregular red glow over the rain-slicked parking lot.

"Okay, I'm sending it now," Kendra said over the phone.

Jacob stared through the windshield at room 112. He'd been staring at it for fifteen minutes now as the rain drummed on the little Kia.

Jacob's phone vibrated, and he checked the text.

"You get it?" she asked.

"Yeah." The man in the photo was lean. Tan. Close-cropped hair and hazel eyes with thick dark eyebrows. "That's him."

Kendra let out a *whoop*.

"I knew it! His name is David Langham, thirty-six. Last known address is Algonquin, Illinois, which is north of Chicago."

"He looks military," Jacob said.

"He is. You were right about that, too. Former Navy. Some kind of special crew."

"A SEAL?"

"No, something else. Anyway, he was dishonorably discharged eight years ago."

"Why?"

"I'm still looking. Mullins knows, but he's hoarding information again, big surprise. You're *sure* he's the shooter?"

"I'm sure."

"Okay, good." She sounded genuinely relieved. "Now that that's out of the way, I've got good news and bad news. Which do you want first?"

"Good."

"The crime scene was just like you thought. That bathroom lit up like a Christmas tree. Blood trails everywhere, and someone had cleaned up with bleach. We're still running the droplet on the faucet, but I bet it comes back to either the perp or one of the two victims. He'd wiped down his prints, too. The whole place was clean *except* for one spot. The CSIs recovered a fingerprint from the toilet seat, and we got a match."

"Damn."

"I know, right? Screwed himself taking a leak. You gotta love it."

Jacob stared through the rain-soaked windshield at room 112. He checked his watch, then adjusted the vent and tried to defog the windshield.

"What's with the silence?" Kendra asked. "I thought you'd be happy we got an ID."

"An ID's not the same as an arrest."

"Don't be a pessimist," she said. "We'll get there. Soon. The feds have a warrant out, and it's only a matter of time before he turns up at some airport or border checkpoint."

"He's too smart for that."

Bitterness welled up in Jacob's throat as he looked at the photo. He'd been so fucking close today. He should have had him in cuffs.

"He'll mess up," Kendra said. "Trust me. He already has."

The motel door opened, and Bailey stepped out. She held a folded newspaper over her head to shield it from the rain and ran to the room next door. The door to 112 slammed shut as Bailey slid her keycard into 114. She didn't notice Jacob parked here in the Kia.

"What's the bad news?" he asked.

"I just got off the phone with my FBI contact in New Orleans. He said there's still no sign of Tabitha Walker. She's in the wind again."

"No, she's not."

"She's not?"

"She's with Bailey."

Silence.

"Tabitha Walker. Is with Bailey Rhoads." It was a statement, not a question. "*Why* is she with Bailey?"

"She trusts her."

Silence again.

"Kendra?"

"How the hell did—wait, don't tell me. I don't think I want to know. You're involved in this, aren't you? Are you freaking *with* the two of them? Wait. Don't tell me that, either. Shit, shit, *shit*, Jacob. I knew this would happen."

"What?"

"You're letting her cloud your judgment. And *why* would Tabitha Walker trust a reporter over a team of federal agents who want to help her? I don't get it."

Jacob didn't, either. He could see what Bailey was getting out of it—a crucial source for her story. But what was Tabitha getting from Bailey?

"When are you coming back from New Orleans?" Kendra asked.

He wasn't in New Orleans anymore, but there was no reason to tell Kendra that. The less she knew about what he was up to, the better. His job was already at risk if things went sideways and they were looking for someone to blame. Kendra's job didn't need to be in jeopardy, too.

"I'll be back tomorrow," he said.

"Okay, I don't know what you're doing, but . . . be careful."

"I will."

"And don't get in any more shootouts on public streets, all right?"

"It wasn't—"

"I'm *kidding*! Geez. The story's all over the squad room, so you better get used to it."

She hung up, and Jacob looked down at his phone again.

David Langham. He clenched his teeth as he studied the picture. One minute sooner. *One* minute and he probably would have had the guy down and cuffed before he got that shot off. Instead, Jacob had watched the whole thing go down from fifty yards away and then jumped in a cab to go after him.

Tabitha could have been killed.

Bailey could have been killed. She was even closer to the shooter than he was, although he didn't know it at the time. Jacob's gut churned every time he thought about it.

He grabbed the bag of carryout off the floor and got out. He jogged through the rain to Bailey's door and popped the car locks with a *chirp*. The curtains parted and Bailey yanked open the door before he had a chance to knock.

"Find something?" she asked.

He stepped into the dim little motel room, dripping water all over the carpet. Not that it mattered. The place was a dump. It smelled of mildew and had the same sad brown carpeting that had been in Jacob's first apartment back when he'd been a boot.

"Hope you like po'boys." He set the bag on the fake wood dresser.

"Love 'em. They come with fries?"

"And hush puppies."

"Even better."

He unloaded the food and turned to face her.

She was soaking wet from the short sprint from Tabitha's room. Her skin was damp, her makeup was smudged, and her wild curls were everywhere. She looked like she had the day he'd first met her, and he felt a jolt of lust, same as he had then.

She smiled up at him. "What?"

"How'd it go over there?"

She tipped her head to the side. "Okay. Not great, but okay."

"Sure she doesn't want a sandwich?"

"I asked her twice. She's stocked up on junk from the vending machine."

Jacob leaned against the dresser. "How is she?"

"Freaked out. Like you would expect. But she calmed down some as we talked." She stepped to the end of the dresser, where she had two Cokes chilling in a plastic ice bucket. Jacob wished he'd stopped for some Jack Daniel's when he'd gone out for food. He looked at the rip in the knee of Bailey's jeans. She'd torn them on the pavement when she dived out of the way of that bullet. The palms of her hands were torn up, too.

"Coke?" she asked.

"I'm fine. Did you convince her to talk to the FBI?"

"Maybe."

"What's that mean?"

"It means maybe. She isn't sure she wants to. She cooperated once already, and it didn't work out too well."

"She needs to talk to them," he said. "Her statement is critical for making the charges stick when we get an arrest."

"That's law enforcement's objective. *Her* objective is to stay alive. She's worried about her safety."

He bristled. "Don't you think law enforcement is, too?"

"If they were, they would have gotten to her before a hit man did." She twisted the top off her drink and took a swig. "From what I can see, the government has one main priority, and it's to sweep this case under the rug before they get any bad publicity over it. She doesn't trust them, Jacob. She doesn't trust anyone right now."

"She trusts you."

Bailey's brow furrowed. "Actually, that worries me, too."

"I thought you wanted her to trust you? Aren't you hoping to interview her for your story?"

"I already did. We established a good rapport and had a long talk. She gave me a boatload of information about what she's been doing the last twenty-two months since she testified in that trial. It's been a nightmare. Imagine trying to start your whole life over on six hundred dollars and no identification."

"I thought she cleaned out her bank account on the way out of Chicago?"

"Only the checking account. She left everything else in the bank because she didn't want to tip off the agents that she was leaving town. She's been moving from place to place, job to job, with no car, no ID, no support. It's been rough. I offered to do what I can to help her."

"Which is what?"

She shrugged. "You know. Put her in touch with the Marshals Office."

Jacob studied Bailey's face. He had the distinct impression he wasn't getting the full story.

"I thought she didn't want to involve the feds," he said.

"She doesn't. That's why I said it's a 'maybe.' But what option does she have? She agreed to go to the FBI office at nine tomorrow morning."

"Which one?"

"Here. Baton Rouge. I said I'd set up the meeting for her." Bailey took a deep breath and blew it out. "But something tells me she's going to change her mind. The idea that that hit man's still out there is freaking her out."

Jacob felt a stab of guilt.

"It's not your fault," she said. "Don't get that look on your face."

"I don't have a look."

"Yeah, you do. There was nothing you could have done."

He didn't argue. No point in it.

"We got a name," he told her.

"You *did*? How?"

"A fingerprint from a homicide scene in Austin."

"That thing near the airport?" She stepped closer. "I knew there was something up with that! Kendra's been texting you all day, hasn't she?"

He nodded.

"So, the two murders are related?"

He nodded again. He wasn't telling her anything that wouldn't come out soon anyway.

She tipped her head to the side. "You're not going to tell me the name, are you?"

"Sorry. Not my case."

"Is it Kendra's?"

"Nope. Special Agent Richard Mullins in Austin has taken it over. Hit him up if you want info."

She watched him, and he could tell she didn't like him holding out on her. That shit worked both ways. He knew for a fact she was holding out on him, too. It was becoming a pattern, and now they were well on their way to a dysfunctional relationship.

Relationship.

He hadn't been in one—or even thought about being in one—since Morgan. The difference now was that Jacob had seen all the red flags, clear as day, from the very beginning. Even his partner had seen them and warned him. But he didn't care.

Bailey stepped closer and gazed up at him. "Come on, Jacob. You can tell me."

"Save the puppy-dog eyes. It's the feds' investigation now. Talk to Mullins."

"Fine, I will. But how come you're not happier? You've solved your case."

He scoffed. "No, I haven't. The killer is still at large."

"But you've IDed him, at least. And you've got the FBI looking for him now, too, so it's only a matter of time."

"An ID isn't the same as an arrest," he said. "I'll be happy when we get an arrest."

She moved closer, and he could smell the rain on her skin, her hair. Her soaking-wet clothes got to him. To hell with the food he'd just bought. He wanted to drag her onto that bed with him and do all the things he'd been thinking about doing since that first afternoon.

What he needed to do was avoid getting more deeply involved with her. It was a bad idea, and anyone could see it. They couldn't even have a normal conversation about work without getting tangled in a web of half-truths. Their professions put them on a collision course with each other.

She wanted inside information, and he couldn't give it to her. If he did, he'd be putting his job on the line. Even the mere perception that he was leaking info to a reporter would mess with his reputation among cops.

But the simple fact was he *liked* her. She was evasive, and determined, and stubborn to the point of recklessness when she got her mind set on something, and Jacob still didn't care because all the things that ticked him off about her were the same things that had attracted him in the first place. Bailey had his number, and she knew it.

She slid her hand into his, and Jacob's heart gave a kick. She gazed up at him with those gray-blue eyes, and a little line appeared between her brows.

"You're thinking," she said. "What is it?"

Instead of answering, he turned her hand over. Her palm was scraped raw, and his stomach clenched as he thought of how close she'd come to taking a bullet today.

"I need to get back to my room and clean up," he said.

"Don't go." She rested his hand on her hip. "Clean up here, with me. Or don't." She smiled up at him, and he felt his resolve slipping.

She reached up and traced her finger over his stubble.

"Don't go. Please?"

It was the *please* that did it. Again. When she looked at him that way, he couldn't say no.

He pulled her close and kissed her.

BAILEY LAY CURLED against Jacob's back, breathing in the scent of his warm skin as she drifted in and out of sleep. A band of gray seeped through the gap in the curtains. Traffic gradually began to pick up on the highway outside.

Jacob's phone buzzed on the dresser. The mattress

shifted, and she pretended to be asleep as he crossed the room.

"Hey," he said quietly.

His tone told her it was his partner.

"Yeah." Pause. "Roger that."

She lay still, waiting for more. He rested the phone on the dresser, and she realized the call was over. She opened her eyes as Jacob stepped into the bathroom and shut the door.

The shower went on, and Bailey smiled. He'd showered last night, too, but they'd gotten distracted a few minutes in.

She pulled Jacob's pillow against her and sighed. She needed to get up. She needed to get dressed. She had things to check on and messages to send, and she couldn't afford to let the morning get away from her. And then there was the problem of Jacob and what to tell him.

Her stomach knotted, and she hugged the pillow closer. She'd promised Tabitha that she could trust her. But Jacob trusted her, too. Bailey was caught in the middle.

A low grumble in the parking lot caught her attention. The engine noise neared the door of the motel room. Then it cut off.

Bailey bolted upright. She glanced at the clock and grabbed a T-shirt off the floor as she rushed to the window. Parting the curtains, she spotted a charcoal-gray pickup with black-tinted windows. Bugs and dirt on the windshield hinted at a long road trip.

"Crap," she murmured, pulling the shirt over her head. It was Jacob's, and it hit her midthigh. She rushed to the door, quietly undid the security latch, and stepped out, keeping the door ajar with the heel of her foot. It wasn't even light out yet, and the motel's red neon sign looked blurry in the predawn mist.

John Colt stepped onto the sidewalk. Gray shirt, black

jeans, shit-kicker boots. He hadn't shaved, but he looked alert, despite the drive from Austin. Bailey had called the skip tracer last night to enlist his help. Colt had a unique set of skills, and Bailey was in over her head.

"You're early," she said.

"That a problem?"

"Just . . . give me a minute."

She slipped back into the room and cast a glance at the bathroom, where the shower was still running. She took off Jacob's shirt and yanked on her own clothes, then shoved her feet into flip-flops. She cast another look at the bathroom as she grabbed her phone and slipped out again.

Colt leaned against the hood of his truck, surveying the motel.

"This way," she said, leading him down the sidewalk.

"Nice place."

"It's inconspicuous."

He lifted an eyebrow at her as they stopped in front of 112.

"She might be still asleep." Bailey knocked quietly on the door.

It swung open. Tabitha was fully dressed, right down to her worn sneakers. Her newly blond hair was damp. Evidently, she'd been up a while. Or maybe she'd never gone to sleep.

Tabitha's gaze darted past Bailey, and the fear in her eyes was unmistakable. Colt had that effect on people.

Bailey cleared her throat. "Tabby, this is the friend I was telling you about."

THE SIZE, SHE'D expected.

John Colt was tall and bulky, and clearly spent a lot of time in a weight room. But the swagger was missing. So was the confident, know-it-all tone that had grated on Tabitha's nerves throughout the trial.

Of course, he'd only been here five minutes. He could turn out to be an arrogant prick.

Bailey shot another look at the door, and Tabitha could tell she was antsy to leave. Maybe she wanted to get back to her cop.

"So, unless you need me for anything . . . ?" Bailey looked at Colt.

"We don't."

She looked at Tabitha. "Text me before you leave. Use his phone."

"I will."

Bailey surprised her then by stepping over and giving her a hug. Tabitha froze. She hadn't been hugged in ages, and it felt oddly comforting. Then Bailey's arms loosened and she gave her a smile. Tears flooded Tabitha's eyes as she watched Bailey slip out the door.

And then she felt ridiculous. Why was she getting weepy over a hug from a woman she barely knew?

John Colt was watching her silently from across the room. He leaned against the ugly dresser, palms resting beside him, the heel of his boot propped against the bottom drawer. The stance appeared casual but wasn't. Tabitha had become an expert at body language over the past two years.

"You have a gun on you?"

Surprise flickered across his face. He nodded.

"Put it on the nightstand. Then sit in the chair by the window."

He looked amused, but he did as she asked, slowly sinking into a crouch and hiking up the cuff of his jeans. He pulled a black pistol from an ankle holster and stepped over to place it on the nightstand. Then he pulled out the chair and sat.

Facing the door, she noticed. He didn't like his back to the door any more than he liked being unarmed, even for a short period of time. Two points in his favor.

He rested his ankle on his knee and leaned back. Again, it was a posture designed to look casual. He was trying to put her at ease. It wasn't going to work, but she appreciated the effort.

"You want coffee?" she asked. "I made some."

"No, thanks."

She picked up her paper coffee cup and took it to the side of the bed near the nightstand and sat down. She didn't know how to use his gun or if it was even loaded, and he could probably get it out of her hands in a heartbeat if he wanted to, but it was the principle of the thing.

She smiled nervously. "I couldn't sleep last night." Or

any night since she'd listened to Robin's message. "I feel like a walking zombie." She took a sip. The coffee was weak and lukewarm, and just the taste made her stomach twist, but she forced herself to swallow.

"How much did Bailey tell you?" she asked.

"Some. Not a lot. You can tell me more."

"Is that really necessary?"

He nodded.

She took a deep breath and blew out a sigh. "Okay."

"I need to know everything from your childhood on. Names, dates, schools, cities, all of it."

"Why?"

"So we don't make stupid mistakes."

"Such as . . . what? I've been very careful."

"Not saying you haven't."

She sounded defensive, but she couldn't help it. Her whole life had become one long defensive maneuver.

"How's this going to work, exactly?" she asked.

"How do you mean?"

"To start with, who's paying you?"

"Someone you don't know."

She drew back. She'd thought maybe Bailey was paying him since she'd arranged this meeting. The thought of someone she didn't know paying him put her instantly on guard.

"Who is it?" she asked.

"Someone who works for the tech company that outed you and Robin. He wants to make things right."

"He's too late," she said bitterly.

"He wants to try." Colt looked at her for a long moment. "If you're worried about confidentiality, don't. I'm like a black box."

Tabitha studied his expression, trying to figure him out. She didn't know if she should trust him. Would someone she'd never met really pay to help her simply because he felt guilty over what his company had done? And would helping her now, after Robin had already lost her life, really clear his conscience? How could it? Tabitha didn't know, and she couldn't afford to care. She didn't have a lot of options at this point.

It was John Colt or the feds. Or strike out on her own again, and given what she knew now, the last two options were definitely out.

"And you're comfortable with this arrangement, this third-party payment?" she asked. "Because I don't know if Bailey told you but I'm practically broke. I have, like, three hundred dollars to my name."

"I know."

She took a deep breath. "I guess we have a deal then."

"Good." He leaned forward and rested his elbows on his knees. "First things first. You listening?"

She nodded.

"No more coffee."

She blinked at him. She'd expected something serious, like she was going to have to shave her head. Or move to Mexico.

She smiled, but he didn't look amused.

"Are you joking?"

"No."

"What does—"

"Caffeine messes with your sleep," he said. "If you can't sleep, you can't think. You can't think, you make careless mistakes. You make careless mistakes, you die."

She bit her lip.

He was right. She'd been bumbling around all week, out of her mind with stress, dropping things, bumping into things.

Stumbling in front of cars.

Staggering in front of that car had landed her in the hospital, which had somehow led to her identity being discovered, and soon there had been people coming out of the woodwork looking for her.

She didn't know if it was the hospital, or the faceprints Bailey Rhoads kept talking about, or a corrupt federal agent that had blown her cover. Bailey said that the hospital might have fingerprinted her and retrieved her ID through an old DMV record. Evidently, hospitals were using biometric technology now, too.

However it had happened, Tabitha's luck had run out. Permanently. McKinney's hit man was still out there, and even if they arrested him, there would be a line of others willing to take his place. She had to be vigilant going forward, zero mistakes.

"All right," she told Colt, setting the coffee on the nightstand beside his pistol.

"You ever used a handgun?" he asked.

"No."

"I can teach you."

"Okay." The idea would have once been repugnant to her. She was an accountant, for heaven's sake. The tools of her trade were spreadsheets and Post-it notes. But a gun sounded tempting. Up to now, she'd only had a tube of pepper spray, and that was back at the hospital with her tattered underwear and the cash they'd confiscated. Learning to use a gun would be good for her.

"What else?" she asked.

"There's a lot."

"I figured that, but—" She sighed. She didn't know what this man could do for her that she hadn't already tried to do for herself. She'd abandoned her life, her name, her city. She'd changed her appearance and moved around and stayed completely offline for more than twenty-two months. And still she hadn't managed to remain off the grid.

She was at the end of her rope. Tears burned her eyes.

"But what?" he asked.

"I don't see how this is going to work. I thought of everything. I mean, *everything*. And I thought I was doing okay, and then the whole bottom fell out of it all. I mean, what am I supposed to do? I can't change my *face*. There's no way I can run forever."

He just looked at her.

"Do you think that's how they found me?" she asked.

"Yes."

No hesitation. Tears spilled over again at the futility of it all.

"Sorry." She brushed her cheek with the back of her hand. "I'm just . . . rattled."

"I understand. There's a lot to think about. We've got a lot to cover." He looked at his watch. "And I'd prefer to do it from another location because this one's blown."

"How is it 'blown'?"

"Bailey's next door with a cop. She trusts him. You don't."

"Do *you* trust him?"

He shrugged. "I don't know him. But if he reaches out to the FBI or the Marshals, you've got a problem. So we need to move." He nodded at her backpack perched on the table by the door. "You ready?"

"Yes."

The word popped out without her thinking about it. She was ready. She'd done everything she could by herself, and John Colt was her last good option. Her only option.

She stood up. He stood, too.

"Can I have my gun back?"

She appreciated that he'd asked. She picked up the black pistol. It was heavier than it looked. The grip felt good in her hand, and she pointed the tip at the floor as she handed it over.

He tucked it back into his boot without comment and stood again.

"Check the bathroom," he said.

"It's clear. I even wiped it down."

"Good." He grabbed her backpack and hooked it over his shoulder. "Let's roll."

KENDRA CAUGHT JACOB in the lobby of the police station just as he was leaving.

"Hey, there you are," she said. "I was about to call you."

"What's up?"

She looked him over, no doubt noticing he hadn't been home yet and it was almost ten p.m.

"I went by the ME's office." She held up a file. "Managed to get my hands on a copy of the preliminary report from the Scott Rydell case. Want to hear about it?"

"Yeah."

"I'll walk with you. Where are you parked?"

"Right out front."

He held the door for her, and they stepped outside into the humid August night. It was dark now, as it had been when he'd come in here this morning. He'd put in a marathon workday, only breaking once for food.

"Anything new on the manhunt?" Kendra asked.

"No."

"They've got every agency in the country looking for him. I'm surprised something hasn't popped by now."

Jacob wasn't surprised. He'd spent the better part of the day building a dossier on David Langham. He'd pulled every string he could think of for information, even tracking down the man's former CO and some of his Navy buddies. Jacob had interviewed dozens of people and their feedback was the same. Langham was smart, confident, and highly trained. He'd been part of an elite combat unit before getting discharged for reasons no one was willing to talk about. Whatever the reasons, he'd been in the private sector now for almost eight years.

Jacob looked at Kendra as they walked toward his truck. She was in her workout clothes—yet here she was coming to the office at night. She had even less of a personal life than he did.

"So, what's in the ME's report?" he asked.

"Everything we expected. Plus some interesting stuff about the murder weapon."

"What about it?"

"The blade is about one point two inches wide and has a serrated edge."

"It's a match," he said.

"Yup. He keeps using the same weapon. Makes me think he's attached to it, for some reason, and that's a mistake."

Jacob stopped beside his pickup.

"Wouldn't you agree?" she asked.

"Probably."

"He'll make some other mistake, and we'll bag him up. It's only a matter of time."

A pair of scooters buzzed by, probably on their way to the bars on Sixth Street. Jacob watched as they passed

Paco's taco truck and the picnic table where he'd sat with Bailey that first night.

"You think he's still on the job?" Kendra asked.

"What, you mean hunting for Tabitha Walker?"

"Yeah."

"Highly unlikely. The operation's blown, and he knows that. It's every man for himself now."

Kendra followed his gaze to the end of the block. "Yeah, I heard the McKinneys are refusing to talk, except through their lawyers."

"Not surprising."

She looked at Jacob. "What's Bailey think?"

"Of what?"

"Of everything. Tabitha's disappeared. Langham's on the run. The McKinneys aren't talking. The FBI is looking really bad here. Not to mention the Marshals. Isn't she still covering the story for her paper?"

"I don't know."

Kendra's brow furrowed. "Why don't you know?"

"I haven't talked to her."

"Why not?"

He popped the locks on his truck and opened the door. "Because."

Bailey had called him three times since yesterday afternoon when they'd parted ways at the Austin airport. Jacob hadn't called her back. He couldn't talk to her right now. He was still too pissed off.

"Because why?"

"Kendra. Drop it."

"No. You went all the way to New Orleans with her and put your ass on the line to help her run down a story and—"

"I've been working. So has she." He slid into his truck. "And I really don't want to talk about this now."

She sighed heavily. "You're doing it again."

"What's that?" He shoved the key into the ignition.

"Avoiding relationships."

He raked his hand through his hair. "Jesus. Can we skip this? I don't need a lecture right now. I need a beer and a shower."

"All right, all right." She held up her hands. "I'll lay off."

"Thanks." He started to close the door, but she caught it.

"But let me just say this. Whatever it is, you should work it out with her."

He tipped his head back against the seat.

"I know you care about her, or you wouldn't have gone all the way to New Orleans to help her," Kendra said. "You should give it a chance. I think she'd be good for you."

He stared at her, incredulous. "I thought you didn't like her."

"Of course I like her. She's tough. And you need someone who isn't intimidated by you." She stepped back to let him close the door. "I just wanted you to think it through before you got involved with a reporter. Now you're involved, so . . ." She shrugged. "You should try to make it work."

Jacob shook his head.

"Call me if you get any updates from Mullins," Kendra said.

"I won't."

She closed the door, and he watched her walk back to the station, probably to spend another late night catching up on paperwork. Kendra was a good detective. She was sharp and experienced and hardworking as hell. But he couldn't take her relationship advice.

Jacob checked his phone one more time before pulling into traffic. He wended his way through downtown, thinking about the case and the autopsy report and everything he'd learned about David Langham.

A tight wire.

That was how one of Langham's buddies described him. He and Langham had been through training together and done two consecutive tours in Afghanistan. They'd had a falling-out after that, but the man wouldn't say why. He hadn't seemed surprised to get a call from a homicide cop, though. In fact, not a single person Jacob had talked to was surprised to learn Langham was wanted by the FBI. That told Jacob a lot.

He crossed the bridge and caught a glimpse of the *Austin Herald* building. Would Bailey be there now? He figured she would. She was probably pounding away on her story, a story that was sure to be explosive. Which meant it would likely be picked up by news outlets across the country. Bailey was about to expose some powerful people, but in doing so, she was exposing herself, too.

I know you care about her. Jacob's gut clenched. The thing of it was, Kendra was right. He could admit it to himself, but he was too pissed off to figure out what to do about it.

His phone buzzed in the cup holder, and he checked the number before answering. *US GOV.* Given the last few days he'd had, it could be anybody from the Marshals Office to the New Orleans FBI. He braced himself for bad news.

"Merritt," he said.

"Hey, it's Morgan."

"What's up?"

"Did you hear about Langham?" she asked.

Something in her voice made Jacob's shoulders tense. "What about him?"

"He hijacked a car in Beaumont this evening. We think he's in Texas."

*   *   *

DON'T KNOW HOW you work in a pub."

Bailey glanced up with a start. "God, you scared me," she told Nico.

He smiled. "*I* scared you?"

"I didn't hear you walk up." She'd been nervous all day, glancing over her shoulder and jumping at shadows, but she didn't want to tell Nico that.

She moved her computer over, and he set his bag on the table. "Thanks for meeting me," she said. "How'd it go with your source?"

"Awesome," he said, sliding into the booth across from her.

"Who was this again?"

"A former Granite Tech employee who used to be on their red team. Now he works for a software start-up."

Bailey took a sip of her wine. "And a red team—they do what, exactly?"

"It's a group of white-hat hackers. As opposed to black. They run penetration tests." Nico leaned his elbows on the table. "Basically, they get assigned to try to hack into systems and find holes in security. Companies hire them to sniff out vulnerabilities that can be exploited. Anyway, this guy worked for Granite Tech, and he told me how about two years ago he was given a special assignment by none other than Lucinda Oberhoff. She asked him to hack into three state DMV databases and collect records, supposedly to demonstrate flaws in their security systems."

"Whoa."

Nico smiled. "It gets better. He said he always thought the project was suspicious because he never dealt with anyone on the client side. Just Lucinda. Everything went straight to her."

"That's especially interesting because Lucinda told me

that Granite Tech doesn't have any government clients," Bailey said.

He unzipped his backpack and pulled out a notepad. He flipped through the pages. "Get this. My guy said, quote, 'I don't know where all those records ended up. But it was frighteningly easy getting them.'"

"He said that?"

"Yep."

"On the record?"

"Yep."

"We need that in the story."

Bailey clicked open the article on her computer. She and Nico were collaborating on a three-part series that would run on A-1, above the fold, for three consecutive days. Max and the business editor and even the publisher were involved.

"What are *you* working on?" Nico asked.

"The story for day three."

"Mind if I look?"

"Go ahead."

Nico scooted around to Bailey's side of the booth and she pivoted the screen so he could read what she had so far. The other two articles were almost finished. The first laid out Granite Tech's secret effort to compile the largest privately controlled faceprint database in existence, through legal and illegal means. The second story focused on Lucinda and the personal motive behind her obsession. The third story detailed the dangerous consequences of Granite Tech's massive information raid.

Bailey rubbed her eyes. She'd been working nonstop for two days, corralling sources and nailing down details, and she was running on fumes.

"I keep tinkering with the lede," she said.

"Is this your working headline? *Witness Protection Program Compromised with Help of Local Company*?"

"It's just a placeholder."

"It's too passive. How about, say . . . *Woman in the Crosshairs after Data Breach*?"

"That's better, but Max will still change it." Bailey quickly made the change as Nico read over her shoulder.

"This is looking good," he said. "You need more about the murder here in Austin, though. You should add a quote from one of the investigators."

"I'm working on it." Bailey rubbed a kink in her shoulder. "No one wants to go on the record."

"Don't you have a friend over at APD? That detective? Merritt?"

"I don't know. Maybe."

Her stomach knotted as she thought of Jacob. They'd parted on chilly terms yesterday. She'd left him three messages since then, and he hadn't returned her calls.

"Here." She closed out of her article and opened the day-one story, which was in the final stages. "Work in your quote. Put it somewhere near the top."

Nico checked his notepad and added the quote. Together, they read through the first few grafs and saved it.

"Think it's ready?" he asked.

"Yeah. Max wants it tonight so he can run it by the legal department first thing tomorrow." Bailey wrote him a quick note and attached the article. "Okay, here we go." She took a deep breath and hit send.

"Wow." Nico looked at her. "That's the biggest story I've ever worked on."

"Me too."

He gave her a fist bump. "It feels good, doesn't it?"

"Yeah." She checked her watch and blew out a sigh. "I didn't realize how late it was, though. I need to get home."

And she had to swing by Stop-N-Save before it closed for the night.

Bailey left money on the table to cover her bill and followed Nico out of the pub. It was hot and muggy outside, and her legs felt stiff from sitting in the booth for three hours. The street in front of the bar was dark and deserted.

Nico turned to look at her, and the troubled frown on his face made her pause.

"What?" she asked.

"I'm sorry I doubted you," he said. "Earlier. When I accused you of poaching."

"Forget it."

He shook his head. "That was a dick thing to say. I've been stressed out lately with all the layoffs and everything. I always feel like I'm about to get axed."

"I understand. Forget about it."

He nodded, looking relieved. "Well. Thanks for sharing a byline. I think this series is going to make an impact."

"We can only hope."

He looked up and down the street. "You need a ride?"

"I'll walk."

"You sure?"

"Yeah, I've got to stop at the store, anyway."

"Okay, see you in the office, then."

He crossed the street to his dinged black hatchback, and it took him two tries to get it started. Bailey watched him pull away.

She set off down the street. Up ahead, the glow of a Lone Star beer sign told her the corner store was still open. She'd come home from her trip to an empty fridge and a cranky cat that held a grudge. This morning she'd fed him tuna for breakfast.

She checked her watch again and clutched her computer bag close as she hurried down the sidewalk.

Jacob still hadn't called. An ache spread through her chest as she thought back to yesterday. The drive to the airport had been tense and quiet. And when they'd parted ways in Austin, he'd been agonizingly polite.

Drive safely. Best of luck with your article.

She wished he'd yelled at her and gotten it out of his system so they could move on.

Bailey glanced up at the moon. It peeked out from behind wispy gray clouds. She remembered how peaceful it had looked at Jacob's house the other night.

Was he there right now, maybe watching a ball game or sanding out his frustration on his bookshelves? She understood that he was angry. But it wasn't for the reason that she'd expected. He hadn't been upset that she had helped Tabitha skip town. In fact, he'd agreed that John Colt, and not the U.S. Marshals, was Tabitha's best chance of making a new start. If anyone could help her drop off the radar and stay there, it was Colt.

What had upset Jacob was that she'd acted without telling him. He'd stood in that motel room with his hair still damp from the shower and looked at her with disbelief. She couldn't get his look or his words out of her mind.

All this time you've been telling me to trust you, Bailey. That works both ways.

Bailey's stomach knotted. They'd had something good. Something unique. When they'd been wrapped up in each other, Bailey had felt it. And she'd blown everything by not being honest with him. She hadn't outright *lied* to him. Not unless you considered it a lie by omission—which she suspected he did. She didn't know for sure, though, because he'd refused to discuss it.

Bailey neared the corner store. Across the street was a shiny white Mercedes with its headlights on. Bailey watched it for a moment as she reached for the door. A bell jangled as she entered the store, and she nodded at the shopkeeper on her way to the back. She picked up a bag of cat food and paused in front of the beer section.

She owed Jacob an apology. Maybe she should swing by his house. Or invite him over. She grabbed a chilled six-pack of Shiner Bock, then checked her phone as she set the groceries on the counter.

Still no messages.

"No Powerball tonight?" the clerk asked her.

"Nope."

"Eight million."

"Maybe next time."

He clucked his disapproval as he rang her up, and she balanced her groceries in one arm as she opened the door with another jangle. The Mercedes was still there, no lights now, and something about it seemed familiar. She tried to place where she'd seen it.

Bailey's phone vibrated. Her heart lurched, and she balanced the cat food on her hip as she pulled the phone from her jeans.

Jacob.

Pain seared up her arm as someone twisted it and slammed her against a wall, smacking her face against the brick.

A hand slapped over her mouth as she tried to scream. Her knees buckled, but something sharp pinned her in place as all her groceries fell. Her body jerked backward and then forward as someone shoved her into the alley and slammed her against another wall.

Bailey's face burned. Her cheek was pressed against the hard brick as she struggled to breathe. Pain shot up her arm, and a hard knee jabbed into her lower back.

"You lying little bitch." The voice was low and raspy.

Bailey's arm twisted again, and the zing of pain nearly

blinded her. She couldn't scream, couldn't breathe. She felt like her arm was being wrenched from its socket and she tried to crane her head around.

Fingernails dug into her face as the hand squeezed her mouth shut.

"You sneaky, lying *bitch*!"

Spittle misted her face, and Bailey tried to see the person behind her. It was a woman. She was strong and had fingers like talons. Her sharp knee dug into Bailey's tailbone.

Lucinda.

Bailey's heart jackhammered. She tried to get a breath. Her shoulder was on fire, and those fingernails cut into her cheek. Bailey reared her head back, desperate to breathe.

"Don't make a sound."

The grip on her mouth loosened a fraction, and Bailey sucked in air. Relief flooded through her, but then something cold and hard pressed against the back of her neck.

"I could blow your head off right now. You realize that?" The voice was low and scratchy. It sounded like Lucinda, but different somehow. Disconnected.

The muzzle of the gun pressed harder against her neck.

"I need to know one thing. Just one." She eased closer, and Bailey smelled her sweat. A memory flashed into her brain: the white Mercedes in the parking garage at Granite Tech. It was Lucinda's. So, she'd driven over here, but she was sweaty and amped up as though she'd just run a sprint.

"Who else knows?"

Bailey's mind reeled. She tried to process the question. *"Who?"*

The hand over her mouth loosened.

"I . . . don't understand," Bailey croaked.

Pain seared her shoulder joint as Lucinda twisted her arm tighter.

"Who besides you?"

Bailey didn't answer. She couldn't. The question made no sense. Lucinda was unhinged. Bailey managed to turn her head a fraction.

Lucinda's hair was a wild mane around her head. Her blue eyes were bloodshot and frantic.

"Who knows what?" Bailey asked.

The eyes bulged. "Don't play *dumb* with me, you little bitch. You think I don't *know*? You think I don't have *eyes* and *ears* everywhere? My security chief followed you out the other night!"

Pain shot up her arm as she twisted it again.

"You and Seth think you're so smart together, don't you? But I've been doing this *five years*. I'm *committed*! You think you can just come along with your fucking press pass and ruin everything? My daughter is alive. Do you hear me? And you *won't* stop me from finding her."

The muzzle of the gun dug harder into Bailey's neck and she stifled a yelp. Maybe she should scream. Or kick. But Lucinda seemed just desperate enough, just crazy enough, to pull the trigger.

Bailey turned slightly, trying to make eye contact, hoping eye contact might snap her back to reality.

"I . . . It's just Seth and me. That's it."

The blue eyes narrowed. Bailey took in Lucinda's frizzy hair and her flushed skin. She wore a black T-shirt, and the neck was torn as though she'd been in a fight. Tiny red flecks dotted her cheek.

She smiled slowly. "I'm not worried about Seth now. Who else?"

Bailey's stomach filled with dread as she looked at the red flecks. *Blood*. Had she shot someone at close range?

Adrenaline zinged through her like an electric current. Bailey stomped as hard as she could and flung her elbow

back, then ducked and spun away. Lucinda tripped backward, but then she was on her again like a lamprey, and
Bailey saw a flash of black as the gun came up.

Screaming, Bailey batted her arm away.

Pop!

Grit stung her eyes as the bullet ricocheted off the wall.
Shrieking, Bailey spun toward Lucinda and batted her arm
again, and the pistol flew from her hand and skittered
across the pavement. Bailey lunged away, bumping into a
trash can, and it went over like cymbals clanging. Bailey
tripped over the bag of cat food and fell to her knees. She
spied the six-pack of beer on its side. She grabbed a bottle,
then turned and hurled it at Lucinda's head just as she
snatched up the gun. The bottle shattered as Bailey turned
and sprinted for the street.

Pop!

Lightning-hot pain knocked her feet out from under her.
She crashed to her hands and knees.

"Police! Stop!"

Bailey crawled toward the street as footsteps slapped
against the pavement behind her.

"Nooo!"

Lucinda's keening wail reached her, but all Bailey could
think about was getting away. Fire burned her leg, and Bailey clutched it. She tried to stand, but her legs didn't work,
and she landed on her palms again. Her hands were red
with blood. The pavement, too.

"Bailey!"

Jacob dropped to his knees beside her.

"Call 911!" he shouted at someone.

"Lucinda—" she gasped.

"We got her."

Bailey looked over her shoulder to see a uniformed cop
hunched over Lucinda. She was facedown on the pavement

with her arms cuffed behind her back as the cop roughly patted her down.

"She shot you, babe."

Bailey looked at Jacob as he stripped off his T-shirt. Sweat streamed down his face. He wrapped the shirt around her leg just below the knee, and Bailey slumped against the wall. She felt dizzy. Disoriented.

Jacob tied the shirt and pulled it tight.

"Ahh!"

"Sorry." He looked at her. "We've got an ambulance coming."

Bailey's mind reeled from the burning pain. Her vision went gray around the edges. She leaned her head against the wall and felt her heart hammering, *tha-thump tha-thump tha-thump*, as she tried to catch her breath.

"What . . . how . . . ?"

Jacob picked up her hand and squeezed it. His fingers were red and slippery, like hers.

She looked up at him, and his deep brown eyes were intent on hers.

"Hold on." He kissed her forehead. "Okay?"

"Don't leave."

"I'm not going anywhere."

"I'm scared." She squeezed harder. "Don't leave."

"I won't."

THIRTY-TWO

S HE DRIFTED IN and out. The room was dim. Each time she opened her eyes, Jacob was a dark silhouette in the chair. Then she'd let her eyes close again.

And then she was sailing. It was sunset, and she was with her dad cutting across the shimmery waters of Laguna Madre on the *Mary Alice*. The sail caught a gust and the boat tipped. Bailey grabbed a cleat to keep from sliding. She tried to hang on, but the boat kept tipping and her grip wouldn't hold. She called for her dad, but he wasn't there.

Bailey shifted in the bed. The room was brighter now. Colder. She heard voices in the hallway.

Jacob sat forward.

"Hey," he said.

She tried to speak, but her throat felt raw.

Jacob took her hand. "How do you feel?"

"Weird."

"You're still doped up."

"I'm thirsty."

He reached for a pink plastic pitcher with a lid. It had a big plastic straw poking out of it, and he lifted it to her mouth and positioned the straw so she could sip.

Grape juice. And crushed ice. Memories flooded her of hot summer days playing in the sprinkler with her sisters. Their mom would leave a pitcher of purple juice on the porch. Bailey guzzled down the liquid until her throat felt numb.

"Careful or you'll get a head freeze," Jacob said.

"It's so good." She pulled back. "Where did you get it?"

"Your sister brought it." He set the drink on the table by the bed. "There's a kitchen at the end of the hallway."

Bailey looked him over now, more alert from the cold juice. Dark stubble covered his jaw, and his hair looked like he'd run his hand through way too many times. His deep brown eyes rested on hers as he took her hand again.

Everything came back.

He'd ridden in the ambulance even after the paramedic said he couldn't. He'd stayed with her in the ER and talked to her, only letting go of her hand when they'd wheeled her back for surgery.

Bailey looked at her leg. It was in a blue cast on top of the blanket.

She had a broken tibia. And it had been a through-and-through bullet. That was the good part, supposedly. When she'd first heard *GSW* flying back and forth, she had wanted to throw up.

Jacob lifted her hand and kissed it. "I'm glad you're awake."

She looked down at her thin hospital gown and knew she must look horrible. She could only imagine her hair.

"Thanks for staying with me." She cleared her throat. "What happened last night?"

He sighed.

"Tell me all of it."

He reached over and brushed the hair from her forehead. "We arrested Lucinda Oberhoff."

"How did you know she'd be there? Right near my house?"

"We came looking for you."

Something tugged at Bailey's mind as she stared at him. Something vague and elusive that wouldn't snap into focus. She remembered blood droplets. She remembered spittle hitting her face. She remembered Lucinda's crazed eyes.

"Seth."

He nodded. "Some people at his condominium reported a gunshot. Officers showed up and found him bleeding from a gunshot wound."

"Is he—"

"He didn't make it. Died en route to the hospital."

Bailey's chest clenched. She closed her eyes.

"He told the first responder about Lucinda. He said she was coming after you."

Bailey's chest clenched again, and she squeezed her eyes tighter.

What could she have done differently? She should have told Seth to take his story to the police. Or take precautions. Or something. Anything. She hadn't grasped the danger.

She opened her eyes as Hannah strode into the room.

"You're awake. Finally!" Her sister wore her blue scrubs and had her nurse's badge clipped to her waist. She smiled at Bailey and her gaze dropped to Jacob's hand clasped around hers.

"You thirsty?" she asked. "We have juice."

"I drank it."

She went to the other side of the bed and picked up Bailey's wrist to check her pulse.

"You're not my nurse, are you?"

She gave her a lopsided smile. "No. I'm just checking. This morning you've got Shelby, so you're in excellent hands."

Hannah released her wrist and pulled a clipboard off a hook on the wall. That would be Bailey's chart, and her sister read it with a carefully neutral expression.

"So." Bailey braced herself. "How am I doing?"

She hesitated a split second. "Good."

Bailey shot her a look. "Could you be more specific?"

She rested her hand on her hip. "Dr. Chan is the best orthopedic surgeon in town. He put two pins in your leg."

"I thought they said I needed one?"

"He decided on two once he got in there." She turned and replaced the chart. "The wound looks good so far and shows no sign of infection."

Two pins.

Bailey's chest felt tight again.

"You scared the hell out of us." Tears welled in Hannah's eyes. "You know that, right? I was getting off my shift when they called me." She shook her head. "Mom flipped out when she heard. She wanted to drive up here, but I downplayed everything and talked her off the ledge. I knew you wouldn't want her leaving Dad to come here and fret over you."

"Thanks."

Hannah walked around and picked up the juice. "Want more?"

Jacob stood. "I'll get it." He took the pitcher, looking relieved to have a reason to step out and give them some privacy.

Hannah watched him leave and then sat down on the edge of the bed.

"Did anyone feed Boba Fett?" Bailey asked.

"I went by on my way in."

"Thank you."

Hannah leaned closer. "Bailey, what the *hell*? How did all this happen?"

"I don't really know."

"This was some woman you're covering?"

"Yeah." She closed her eyes and felt a headache coming on. "She's been arrested."

"Jacob told me."

Bailey opened her eyes.

"Thanks for talking to Mom."

"Sure." Hannah's eyes welled with tears again and she glanced at the door. "You know, the overnight nurse said Jacob didn't leave your side once. Not even to eat. He spent the night in that chair."

Bailey looked at the door.

"He seems like a stand-up guy," Hannah said.

"He is."

Hannah patted her hand as another nurse bustled into the room. She wore green scrubs with yellow emojis all over them.

"She's up," Hannah said brightly.

"I see that." The nurse wrote on the whiteboard with a marker and then picked up Bailey's chart.

Bailey's gaze fell on a pair of crutches propped against the wall, and a ball of dread filled her stomach. She took a deep breath and looked at the nurse. "How long will I be on crutches?"

"The doctor said six to eight weeks. And we'll get you started on some physical therapy."

Eight weeks! How would she work? Or row? Or even walk around? Tears stung her eyes and she looked at Hannah.

"I'm going to get fired," she said.

"No, you won't."

"How will I do anything? I won't be able to drive."

"It's not as long as it sounds."

Bailey laughed through her tears. "It sounds like shit." She lifted the neck of her hospital gown and dabbed her eyes. "Sorry. I'm a little overwhelmed."

Hannah smiled with sympathy.

The nurse walked out as Jacob returned with the pink pitcher. He set it on the table, and Bailey heard the ice sloshing.

"Thanks," she told him. Instead of resuming his place in the chair, he leaned back against the wall.

Bailey took a deep breath and looked at Hannah. "So, when can I go home?"

"If Chan clears you, probably tomorrow."

Thank God.

"You can stay with us for a while," Hannah said.

"Why?"

"You're got all those stairs at your place."

Bailey hadn't even thought about the stairs. "My building has an elevator." It even worked sometimes.

Hannah patted her hand. "It'd be easier to stay with us, for at least the first few weeks. I'll set up a room for you. Drew can sleep in ours."

"I really don't want you to go to all that trouble."

"It's not trouble."

"You just got him sleeping on his own. And you work night shifts. I don't want to disrupt your whole house."

"You can stay with me," Jacob said.

Bailey and Hannah both turned to look at him. His attention was locked on Bailey.

"Thanks, but that's totally unnecessary."

He folded his arms. "David Langham hasn't been arrested yet."

Hannah frowned. "Who's that?"

He kept his eyes on Bailey's. "A hit man who killed a woman at the lake."

Her sister's mouth fell open.

"He wouldn't come after *me*," Bailey said.

"You don't know that."

"Jacob, get real."

"It would be wise for you to stay somewhere else for a while," he said. "At least until he's in custody."

Hannah stood up. "I'll let you two talk."

She left the room and Bailey turned to Jacob. "Great. Now she's terrified. You did that on purpose."

He sat in the chair again and scooted close to her.

"There's no reason for David Langham to come looking for me," she told him. "I thought you said the job was over, and his goal now is to evade police?"

Jacob rubbed his hand over his bristly jaw. "It probably is. But we don't know that for sure." He leaned forward on his elbow and looked at her, and she noticed the deep lines around his eyes.

"I want to be straight with you, Bailey. No more word games." He picked up her hand. "You almost died last night, and I need some honesty now."

Bailey just looked at him. His eyes were tired, and there was a vulnerability there she'd never seen before.

She nodded.

"Unless one of us has an ethical obligation not to share something because of our job," he said, "I want us to be straight with each other from now on. Okay?"

She nodded again.

"Here's the situation: David Langham has a federal warrant out for him. He's probably focused on evading capture, and it's unlikely he'll come looking for you. But I don't know that for sure. Okay? There's also a chance he's still trying to finish a job, and he may be looking for Tabitha. He might think you know where she is."

"I don't."

"He might think you do anyway. I won't rest easy until we have him in custody."

Bailey bit her lip.

"Do you understand?"

"Yes." She sighed. "Thank you for the honesty."

He closed his eyes and leaned his forehead against her hand. "Yesterday scared the shit out of me. I was racing over to your place, and all I could think of was . . ." He shook his head.

"What?"

He shook his head again.

"I hear what you're saying, but you aren't obligated to offer me a place to stay."

"I *want* you to stay with me." He looked at her. The tenderness in those deep brown eyes made her heart squeeze. "I want to be near you. You're going to need some help for a while. I know your sister could do it, and she's probably better equipped. But I want to do it."

She watched him, at a loss for words. Emotions swirled inside her, and she felt dizzy. She wanted to stay with him, but the implications felt daunting. More damn tears welled in her eyes, and she blinked them back. She *hated* crying. It had to be the drugs.

"The logical thing is probably for me to go to Hannah's," she said.

He sighed deeply and kissed her knuckles. "It's your decision. I won't pressure you."

She laughed through her tears. "You already did."

"Just think about it."

THIRTY-THREE

Three weeks later

JACOB WATCHED THE narrow storefront through the dusty windshield. People streamed back and forth on the sun-baked sidewalk in front of the building, but no one stopped to go in.

His cell buzzed. Jacob lowered the binoculars and grabbed the phone from the cup holder.

"Merritt."

"Hey, where are you?" Kendra asked. "I came back from my court appearance and you were gone."

"I'm following up on something."

"Well, did you hear about McKinney?"

"No." Jacob put the call on speaker and lifted the binoculars again. "Which one?"

"Senior. The dad. I just got off the phone with my FBI friend in New Orleans. He told me there's been a breakthrough. McKinney senior now admits to *hiring* Langham—as a PI, he's claiming. His story is that he only intended for him to locate Robin and Tabitha and write up a report."

"A report? That's it?"

"That's what he's saying."

"So, Langham threw in the hits for free?"

"I didn't say it was a good story. But at least they've got him on record with it," Kendra said. "Looks like they're looking to cut a deal with prosecutors. I think they must have proof of their communication, or McKinney wouldn't be copping to anything."

"Hmm."

"You don't sound too excited."

"I am," he said. "Did you hear we've got a lead on Langham?"

"Damn, when it rains, it pours. What happened?"

"The feds have been watching several of his contacts. This morning one of his military buddies wired some money to a Western Union office. It's waiting there for him under a fake name."

"And they've got the place staked out?"

"Yep."

"That's awesome," Kendra said. "Did you tell Bailey?"

"No."

"Are you going to?"

"If they take him down, yeah."

Jacob lowered the binoculars and checked out the street from his elevated vantage point. From the second floor of the corner parking garage, he had a 270-degree view of both vehicular traffic and foot traffic.

"How'd the feds get this lead?" she asked.

"The buddy's name is Ryan Penning. I interviewed him three weeks ago when I was researching Langham."

"*You* gave them this?"

"Yeah. I got a weird vibe from this guy. He was tight-lipped about Langham and he lied about something minor, which raised a red flag. So, I passed his name along to Mullins as someone to watch."

"Ha. You know if they *do* arrest him, he'll give you exactly zero credit. Guarantee it. Just watch the press conference. Mullins is a publicity hound."

Jacob didn't care. He just wanted Langham behind bars or dead. He wanted Bailey to be able to get through a night without waking up in a cold sweat. He didn't know if it was Lucinda or David Langham or both that were messing with her head. But Jacob felt like shit every time it happened. There wasn't a damn thing he could do, and he hated it. He'd never felt so helpless.

"So, where's this Western Union located?" Kendra asked.

"Corpus Christi. The theory is he's on his way to Mexico and he needs funds."

"Corpus."

"Yeah."

The phone went silent.

"Don't even tell me you drove down there."

"Yeah."

"What the hell, Jacob? They're not actually going to let you in on the arrest, are they?"

"I'm here to watch."

"You drove three hours just to watch?"

Jacob didn't respond.

"Don't you think that's overkill?"

"No."

"Geez. And I thought I was obsessed with this thing. When's he supposed to show up?"

"The money went through at noon," he said, "so could be any time."

A man turned the corner, and Jacob's pulse kicked up. Tall, bulky. He wore jeans, a baseball cap, and sunglasses. Jacob watched through the binocs as he approached the Western Union office from the opposite side of the street.

"Jacob?"

"I have to go."

"Oh my God, is he *there*?"

It was Langham. Jacob knew it with every cell in his body. Where was the takedown team?

"Call me back," Kendra said.

"I will."

Jacob watched him, clenching his teeth. The man waited for a break in traffic and then jogged across. It was only half a block to the office, and now Jacob could only see his back.

But it was him. He knew it.

Jacob thought about Robin Nally in the mud by the lake. He thought about Scott Rydell with his neck cut open, decomposing in the summer heat. He thought about Bailey bolting upright in bed with the sheets tangled around her. Jacob had been doing this job twelve years, and he'd never wanted an arrest like he wanted this one.

The man glanced over his shoulder as he neared the office. He reached for the door.

Two SWAT teams rounded the corners and were on him like a pack of wolves. The black-clad officers had him on the ground and handcuffed in under three seconds.

Jacob held his breath as they patted him down. The man's face was turned away and pressed flat against the pavement. His baseball cap had come off, revealing a dark buzz cut like the runner on the lake had described to Jacob and Kendra.

Sirens filled the air. Vehicles converged on the scene. Soon the entire block was swarming with SWAT jocks and special agents with flak vests strapped over their clothes.

Jacob set the binoculars aside and watched everything unfold.

The knot of tension in his chest loosened. He tipped his head back against the seat and thought of Bailey at that juice bar, striding up to him with a press pass around her neck and a determined gleam in her eye. She'd had no idea what she was in for.

Neither had Jacob.

He took a deep breath. Then he picked up his phone and texted his partner.

IT'S DONE.

BAILEY LAY ON the lounge chair gazing up at the stars. Loose guitar chords drifted over the trees, and she closed her eyes to relax.

Maybe she'd sleep tonight.

Maybe she wouldn't.

She hated the bouts of panic and the cold sweats. But Jacob's special brand of physical therapy made up for it.

A chorus of cicadas surrounded her, adding to the guitar music. And then she heard the familiar rumble of a truck pulling into the driveway. Bailey's pulse picked up as the engine cut off.

She closed her eyes and waited. The front door opened and closed. Then the back-porch light came on. The back door creaked, and she heard footsteps on the deck.

"Hi, honey, I'm home."

She smiled without opening her eyes. "Hi, honey, you're late."

They'd been doing the honey-I'm-home thing for weeks now. It helped gloss over the uncertainty about their new living arrangement.

"I stopped to get your mail. And while I was in your

neighborhood, I stopped at Eli's for veggie supreme, extra jalapeño."

She opened her eyes. "God, that sounds awesome. Thanks." She lifted her hand to her forehead to block the glare of the porch light.

Jacob gazed down at her with his hands on his hips. His sleeves were rolled up, his shirt was wrinkled, and his thick, dark hair was oddly windblown.

"Everything okay?" she asked.

"Yeah. Why?"

"You look . . . whipped."

He smiled. "I'm completely, utterly whipped."

"What happened?"

"And I'm starving. Come on." He held out a hand and helped her to her feet. Then he picked up her crutches and waited patiently as she snugged them under her arms.

"How was work?" he asked as he opened the door for her.

"Boring as hell." She loped into the kitchen and balanced on one crutch as she took a bottle of wine from the fridge. "They've got me fact-checking football stats now. I swear, all this desk work is driving me batty. If Max doesn't give me back my beat soon, I'm going to lose it."

Jacob got down a pair of glasses and took over the wine pouring.

"They'll give it back as soon as you're walking again." He handed her a glass and poured one for himself.

"I thought you didn't like pinot grigio?"

"I don't." He smiled and clinked his glass against hers. "Cheers."

She eyed him suspiciously. "What's going on?"

He set his glass down on the counter and leaned back against it, watching her.

Bailey's stomach knotted. "What? You're making me nervous."

"Langham's in custody."

She stared at him.

"We arrested him in Corpus Christi this afternoon."

"*We?*"

"The Marshals arrested him. I observed."

"You drove all the way down—"

"Yes." He stepped over and rested his hands on her hips. "I needed to be there."

Bailey's heart was racing. She didn't know why. She felt cold all over.

"Hey." He frowned. "Are you all right?"

"Yeah. I'm just . . . are you *sure* he's in custody?"

"He's in custody."

She blinked up at him, not sure why she felt dizzy all of a sudden.

Jacob held her steady with one hand while he moved her crutches aside. Then he slid his arms around her and eased her against him.

"Take a deep breath."

She did.

"I didn't mean to spring that on you. I should have called you."

"No, it's fine." She pulled back and looked up at him. "I'm just glad it happened. All the waiting and wondering has been making me crazy."

And the anxiety attacks. And the insomnia. She'd been a wreck for three weeks, and it had been getting worse. She knew that it wasn't only her mobility issues that had prompted Max to put her on desk duty for a while. She'd been distracted at work and making careless mistakes.

She leaned back against the counter and looked at Jacob. He cupped his palm against her face and stroked her cheek with his thumb.

"How'd they track him down?" she asked.

He just looked at her, and she knew what that meant. He couldn't talk about the details yet. Or maybe ever. And they'd agreed to respect each other's work boundaries.

"Tell me this," she said. "Do they have enough to keep him?"

"Yes."

She closed her eyes and sighed.

"You okay?"

"I didn't realize how relieved I'd feel. It's like there were these sandbags on my shoulders and you lifted them off."

He smiled down at her, but his eyes looked concerned. She'd been trying not to let him know how stressed she'd been, but she hadn't done a very good job of it. During the day was one thing, but nighttime was harder.

"Why don't you go sit down and I'll make us some plates?" He kissed her. "I'm starved."

"Me too."

She crutched into the living room and lowered herself onto the sofa. Boba Fett rubbed up against her leg. She scratched him behind the ears, and he let out a mew.

"Should I feed him?" Jacob asked from the kitchen.

"I already did. Don't be fooled by his pitiful sound effects."

She rested her crutches by the sofa and stared at her cast. She'd learned to get around pretty well on it. She was taking an Uber to work every day, and her editor had carved out plenty of phone assignments for her until she was able to drive again. The limitations were frustrating, but whenever she felt exasperated, she thought of Seth, and a deep sorrow overtook her self-pity.

The desk work was temporary. Bailey knew that. The series she'd written with Nico had garnered national interest and praise for the *Herald*. Practically overnight, Bailey had established a name for herself as a formidable investigative reporter. For the first time in months, she could go to work in the morning without the nagging fear that she would be summoned into a conference room and handed a cardboard box.

But her feelings of relief alternated with intense guilt over the human cost of what had happened. Tabitha's life had been saved, but Seth's was gone. Would one have happened without the other? Bailey would never know. But Seth had been determined to help Tabitha disappear, determined to give her back the anonymity that his company had stolen.

Would it work? Would Tabitha be able to create a new life for herself? Bailey had no idea where she was, and John Colt would never tell. Maybe she was in Barbados or Baja California or Nova Scotia. Bailey figured he'd helped her slip away to someplace remote where there weren't surveillance cameras on every street corner. The world was running out of places like that.

Jacob set two plates of pizza on the table, along with their drinks. Then he sat down next to her.

"Come here." He pulled her against him, and she rested her head on his chest.

"I thought you were starving."

He sighed. "I need this first."

She slid her arms around him, breathing in his familiar scent. Having his arms around her had become the highlight of her day.

"Thank you," she whispered.

"For what?"

"If it weren't for you—" A hard lump clogged her throat. She swallowed it down. "I keep thinking about Seth."

"Me too."

"And Robin, and Scott Rydell," she said.

"Same."

"I feel so . . . grateful. For everything. You. My health. My job. My *life*. I never realized how good I had it, just day-to-day *good*, you know?" She tipped her head back to look at him. "I feel lucky."

He sifted his fingers through her hair, and the expression in his deep brown eyes made her heart ache. He had a sensitive side that he never showed in public. It was like he took all those detective traits—the observation skills, the intensity, the attention to detail—and focused them on her, anticipating exactly what she needed before she even knew herself. She'd never felt such intimacy with anyone, ever.

He brushed a curl away from her face. "I'm the lucky one." He kissed her forehead.

She tightened her arms around him. "Jacob?"

"Hmm?"

Her heart was beating double-time now. "I love you."

"I love you, too."

She pulled away and looked at him. "Really?"

He smiled. "You look shocked."

"I just . . . I didn't expect you to say that."

"Why not?"

"Because. I don't know. Everything seems fast."

"It is. That's why I've been waiting to bring it up. I didn't want to throw too much at you at once."

"Too much, as in what?"

"Telling you I love you, asking you to move in with me. For real, not just until your cast comes off."

She stared at him, at a loss for words. His tone was light, but his eyes were solemn.

"You want me to—"

"Yes." He reached over and stroked her cheek. "Does that scare you?"

"A little." A lot. Her heart was doing flip-flops now. "Everything with us is happening so fast."

"That doesn't make it wrong."

"No, but it makes it risky."

"So what?" He picked up her hand and laced his fingers through hers. "You take risks to get what you want at work. Why not take a risk with me?"

The tentative look in his eyes made her chest fill with love and joy and nervousness, all at once.

She smiled. "Nice tactic. You phrased it like a dare, so I'd be tempted to say yes."

He kissed her knuckles.

"You really want me to move in here?"

"You. Your books. Your cat. Everything. I want to be with you, Bailey. I know it's happening fast, but I also know we have something good. This feels right to me."

She smiled. "Same."

He leaned forward and kissed her softly.

"You're smiling," he said. "Does that mean—"

She cut him off with a kiss.

"That means yes."

Continue reading for a
special preview of Laura Griffin's

FLIGHT

available in spring 2021!

THE LIGHT WAS perfect, but she didn't have long.

Miranda Rhoads dipped the paddle and glided smoothly through the water as she composed the shot. Cattails in the foreground, the tall lighthouse a distant spire. In between, the bay was a vast mirror that reflected the pinkening sky.

She lowered the blade of her paddle again, this time pushing off the spongy bottom to maneuver around a clump of reeds. This was it. She balanced the paddle on her thighs and adjusted the strap around her neck. Anticipation thrummed through her as she lifted the camera. Conditions were exactly what she'd hoped for when she saw the weather report last night and remembered one of her father's sayings: *Red sky at morning, sailors take warning.*

Miranda took a deep breath and waited. Seconds and minutes slipped by, and she let her mind drift like the kayak. The humid air settled around her. She listened to the hum of insects in the marshes behind her, a trilling chorus that swelled and subsided with the breeze. She took another deep breath, and for a perfect, endless moment she felt truly okay. Her thoughts were clear and crisp. The sunlight-saturated air seemed to vibrate around her. The day was still new, limitless, and she gave in to the notion that she was going to be all right.

Movement in the corner of her eye.

She remained utterly still as a great blue heron stepped from the reeds, tall and elegant on his spindly legs. Another step. Miranda held her breath and brushed her fingertip over the shutter button. If he sensed her watching, he didn't show it.

She waited for the shot. It was instinct now. Like a hunter. Another deep breath and a long respiratory pause as she stayed motionless.

Click.

He stepped closer and dipped his head down. Then he lifted his head and turned toward her, regarding her with a regal look. Posing?

His silhouette was black and perfect against the fiery sky. Miranda's heart hammered.

Click. Click.

This was why she'd come here. This was why she put up with cold showers and rusty water and a bleating alarm clock at four thirty a.m. This was why she schlepped her kayak to the dock all alone, slapping at mosquitoes before her first sip of coffee. Photography was all about light, and mornings offered the best chance of getting something useful. Not a guarantee but a chance, and it paid to play the odds. She couldn't sell what she didn't have.

Click.

Another careful step. *Click click click.*

The heron turned and took wing. She lowered the camera and watched him soar over the marsh, then swoop down into another clump of reeds.

Miranda sighed. Not bad for a day that had barely begun.

She shifted the camera under her arm and picked up the paddle, scanning the marshland for new possibilities. She had thirty minutes left. More, if the distant line of storm clouds lingered off the coast.

Her paddle snagged on something. She spotted a slim yellow cord stretched taut across the reeds. She paddled closer and spied something green tucked among the cattails. A canoe.

An explosion of feathers nearby made her heart lurch as a trio of white ibis flapped away. Behind her, something thrashed in the water. A fish? A cottonmouth?

Her attention snapped back to the boat. Her heart was thudding now as she drifted closer. The air felt charged, and all her senses went on high alert. Habits kicked in. She noted the direction of the wind. She noted the height of the sun. She noted the air, damp and pungent, pressing around her. Her stomach clenched tightly as she took a slow, shallow stroke, careful not to bump the canoe with her kayak as she peered over the side.

They looked peaceful, with their long limbs intertwined. His arm around her was protective. Tender.

Obscene.

Miranda's vision blurred. Her brain recoiled from the sight in front of her, but she couldn't turn away, couldn't stop from registering every detail.

The man's head was nestled on the woman's shoulder just beneath her chin, and their pale skin looked rosy in the morning glow. An inch of water filled the bottom of the canoe. The woman's dark braid drifted there like a snake.

She stared unblinking at the morning sky.

* * *

DETECTIVE JOEL BREDA pulled into the marina parking lot and slid his truck into a space beside a dusty police cruiser. He scanned the boats bobbing in their slips before turning his attention to the caliche lot. He recognized most of the vehicles, including the hulking old Suburban that belonged to the Lost Beach police chief.

Joel surveyed the two-story building as he got out. The marina occupied the first level, and a seafood restaurant with sweeping views of Laguna Madre occupied the top. Neither was open yet, but the weathered wooden bait shop near the boat docks would have been busy since sunrise. The shop owner stood beside his hut now, smoking a cigarette and watching a cluster of boats about a hundred yards offshore.

"Thought you were in Corpus."

Joel turned to see Nicole Lawson trudging toward him. She wore a blue Lost Beach PD golf shirt and black rubber waders that were covered in muck.

"Not anymore," Joel said. "Who's here?"

"McDeere got here first. Then the chief. Still no sign of the ME." Nicole turned toward the water, and Joel followed her gaze to the boats. An LBPD speedboat and several small skiffs blocked his view of the crime scene.

"What do we know?" Joel asked.

"So far, not much. Two victims, both shot in the gut. Randy called it in."

Joel cast a glance at the bait shop owner as he flicked his cigarette to the ground. Randy chain-smoked when he was nervous. He'd probably gone through half a pack by now.

Nicole turned to face him. Her long red hair was tied in a messy bun instead of her usual braid, which made Joel think she'd been called out of bed.

"Male and female?" he asked.

"Yep. And they're young, too. Maybe early twenties."

Something in her tone caught his attention. He eased closer and lowered his voice. "What is it?"

She shook her head. "Nothing, just . . . freaky crime scene."

She'd been out there already, and Joel felt a stab of regret that he'd been off island when he got the call. He lived less than a mile away from here and should have been the first one on scene.

He studied Nicole's tense expression. "Does it look like a murder? A murder-suicide? A suicide pact?"

"Don't know." She wiped her brow with the back of her forearm. "Could be any of those. I didn't see a weapon aboard, though. 'Course, I didn't touch anything."

"Good." Joel stepped around her and reached into the bed of his truck to unlock the chrome toolbox.

"Don't bother with waders," she told him. "With the storm coming, they're bringing everything in."

He glanced at the sky. Given the angry gray clouds rolling in, it wasn't a bad call. He shoved his waders aside and grabbed his binoculars.

"Sure you want in on this?" she asked. "Technically, you're on vacation till Thursday."

"I'm sure." The department had only three full-time detectives—himself, Emmet, and Owen. Nicole was good, but she was still in training.

"I'm just saying," she went on. "You could probably let Emmet take the lead with this one."

Joel slammed the toolbox shut, not bothering to argue about it. "Fill me in as we walk."

She fell into step beside him, and her waders made little squeaking sounds. "So. How was the wedding?"

"Fine."

She cut a look at him. "You sure?"

"Yeah. Anyone call the sheriff's office?" he asked. The last thing he wanted to talk about was the wedding he'd just attended.

"The chief called them. They're sending down one of their CSIs."

"Who?"

"Bollinger, I think."

Joel winced.

"You don't like him?"

"No."

"Well, he should be here soon." She checked her watch. "We called them forty-five minutes ago."

"He'll be late, count on it." Yet another reason the chief had probably decided to tow the canoe in. Joel passed a row of fishing rigs and catamarans, all neatly covered and secured in their slips. Joel reached the end of the dock and lifted the binoculars.

The distant crime scene snapped into focus. Chief Brady stood at the helm of the police boat as Emmet and Owen attached a line to the bow of the canoe. Joel studied the long green boat. It didn't look like a rental from one of the island's rec shops.

The police boat got moving, and the bow of the canoe tipped up. Joel muttered a curse as he imagined the canoe's contents shifting to the stern.

"We don't have much choice with the rain coming," Nicole said, clearly picking up on his concern.

"Tell me they got pictures."

"Emmet had the camera."

"Who found them?"

"Some woman in a kayak. She paddled to the marina to report it."

Joel lowered the binoculars. "Why didn't she call it in herself?"

"I don't know."

"Where is she now?"

"Um . . ." She turned around and scanned the parking lot. "McDeere was getting her statement. I'm sure she didn't leave yet. There she is. Just past the boat trailers."

"Black Jeep, red kayak?"

"That's her. Here, let me use your binocs while you talk to her."

Joel handed them over and returned to the parking lot, watching the woman as he approached. She stood on the running board of the Jeep, struggling with a bungee cord as she secured her kayak to the roll bar.

"Need a hand?" Joel asked.

"I'm good." The woman didn't look up. She had honey-brown hair pulled back in a ponytail. She wore stretchy black pants that clung to her curves and a loose white top over a black sports bra. Her cheeks were flushed from exertion, but the pissed-off look on her face warned Joel not to intervene as she wrestled with the final hook. After getting it attached, she stepped down.

"I'm Joel Breda, Lost Beach PD."

She gazed up at him and dusted her hands on her pants. "Miranda Rhoads." Her gaze dropped to the detective's shield clipped to his belt. When she looked up again, her caramel-colored eyes were wary.

"I already gave a detailed statement to Officer McDeere," she said. "And I talked to someone named Lawson."

"I understand, ma'am. I just have some follow-ups."

She blew out a breath and tucked a curl behind her ear. "All right."

"Care to sit down?" He nodded at a picnic table not far from the bait shop.

"No, thanks. One second." She eased past him and opened the door of her Jeep, then reached across the seat and popped open the glove compartment. She pulled out a small red zipper pouch. "I just need to clean this," she said, propping her foot on the running board.

She wore silver flip-flops, and Joel saw a gash on the side of her little toe. The cut was bleeding. He hadn't noticed, probably because he'd been distracted by the rest of her.

"What'd you do there?" he asked.

She tore open a sterile wipe and dabbed at the cut. "I got out of my kayak to look at the canoe and stepped on a board covered in barnacles."

"You had a tetanus shot recently?"

She laughed. "Uh, yeah."

Joel looked at her. "Why is that funny?"

Her smile disappeared. "It's not."

She reached into the Jeep again to get rid of the wet wipe and tossed the pouch on the seat. Taking a deep breath, she squared her shoulders.

"Sorry. Okay. What were your questions?"

Joel looked her over, puzzled by the brisk attitude. Typically, innocent witnesses were pretty deferential with cops. Then again, she'd had a rough morning and people handled stress in different ways.

"Tell me how you found the boat," he said. "What were you doing out there?"

She rested her hands on her hips and gazed at the bay. Her arms were tanned and toned, as though she spent a lot of time in her kayak.

"I got to the marina about five fifteen," she said.

"That's early."

"I was photographing the sunrise."

"Okay. And you were coming from where?"

"The north end of the island. I'm renting a beach house about half a mile from here."

"All right."

"I put in my kayak. Paddled about a hundred yards out, straight toward the marshes near the nature center. As the sky brightened, I took a series of photographs. Nautical twilight is the best time to get silhouettes. That's between first light and sunrise." She looked at him, probably sensing that he didn't know shit about photography. But fishing, he knew, and he understood the different phases of daylight on this bay.

"Anyway, as I was paddling, I scared up some birds." A lock of hair blew against her face, and she peeled it away. Joel noticed her hand was trembling. "That's when I noticed a yellow line."

"A fishing line?"

"No, like a rope. A thin one. It was attached to a canoe hidden in some cattails." She paused, and a somber look came over her face. "That's when I saw them."

"The couple."

"Yeah."

"And you could tell they were dead?"

"Yes." She broke eye contact and looked at the bay again. The wind had picked up, and the water was getting choppy. "There was no mistaking it. I mean, you'll see when they bring them in."

"You know what time this was?" he asked.

"About six forty."

Joel watched her face as she looked out over the water. The boats were coming in, and he could hear the motors getting closer. But he was more interested in Miranda Rhoads's carefully calm expression.

"Do you recall any noises?" he asked.

She looked at him. "Noises?"

"When you were out on the water taking pictures. Did you hear any gunshots? Or yelling, screaming, anything like that?"

"No."

"Think back. Sometimes seagulls screeching can sound similar to—"

"I didn't hear anything like that." She was adamant. "I didn't hear anyone or see anyone until I got back to the marina and asked the guy at the bait shop for help." She turned to look at Randy, who was smoking another cigarette and talking with McDeere. "That guy there, with the beard."

"So, you didn't have a cell phone out there with you?" Joel asked.

"Not on the kayak, no. I keep it locked in the console of my Jeep."

"All right. And when you arrived here, did you see any other cars in the lot?"

She shook her head. "I was the first one."

"Any other boats? Fishermen?"

"No."

"What about pedestrians? Dog walkers?" He nodded at the marshland between the marina and the nature center. "Some people use the trails in the morning."

"There was no one out when I first got here. At least, not that I saw. Only person I noticed was a cyclist on the highway. He was riding along the shoulder."

That piqued his interest. "Where, exactly?"

She blew out a sigh. "He was on a bike about fifty yards north of the turnoff for the marina. He was heading north. I described him to McDeere. He had on a light-colored T-shirt and a baseball cap. I remember noticing because he should have been wearing a helmet, especially riding in the dark like that."

Joel cast a glance at McDeere, who was watching him now with a look Joel couldn't read. He had no doubt the officer would have taken all this down. A former Marine,

McDeere was thorough and paid attention to details. It was one of the things Joel liked about working with him.

"As I said, I gave all this to the officer already."

Joel looked at the witness. Her cheeks were still pink, and she seemed antsy. Like she was itching to leave. She glanced over Joel's shoulder, and her brow furrowed.

Joel turned to see the ME's van swinging into the lot, followed by a white SUV. Both vehicles pulled into spaces near the bait shop. The door to the SUV opened, and Bollinger hopped out.

Joel checked his watch. Almost an hour since Nicole had called the county for a crime scene investigator. Joel gritted his teeth.

"Detective? Is that all right?"

He shifted his attention back to the witness. Those caramel-colored eyes looked worried now.

"Ma'am?"

"I need to head out. I'm late for something." She nodded toward the bait shop. "If you have any more follow-ups, your officer there has all my contact information. And he gave me his card."

Joel didn't want to let her go, but he didn't have a reason to keep her here, either. The boats were pulling in, and Joel wanted to get a look at everything before the ME's people started.

"Let me see that card," he said.

She hesitated a moment before pulling a card from her bra and handing it over. Joel took out a pen and wrote on the back.

"That's my mobile," he said. "Call me if you remember anything else."

"All right."

"Thank you for your time today."

"No problem."

She stepped around him to open the Jeep, and Joel moved out of the way.

Bollinger was still with his vehicle, zipping into his white Tyvek suit. Meanwhile, the boats had docked, and Emmet was securing the canoe to a cleat.

Thunder rumbled, and Joel glanced at the sky just in time to catch the first fat raindrops. He looked at the canoe that held two dead young people, along with any forensic evidence he hoped to recover. All of it was going to get drenched.

Joel started for the dock.

"Detective?"

He turned around. Miranda wore a rain jacket now with a hood that covered her head. Wherever she was going, she was about to get soaked.

"Make sure they bag her hands," she told him.

"What's that?"

"The female victim," she said. "She's holding a feather. You don't want it getting lost in transport, so tell your CSI to make sure to bag her hands."